More praise for *My Lover's Lover*:

'Absorbing, beautifully written . . . a sensual celebration of language . . . this book warns against the blindness of falling in love' Mavis Cheek, *Daily Express*

'A gripping and passionate double love story . . . supremely well done . . . It is a hard task to capture precisely the elusive, slippery nature of love but [O'Farrell] achieves this with writing of such simplicity and honesty that passion is left unobscured by unnecessary words' *Literary Review*

'Lily is a twenty-first century equivalent of du Maurier's Rebecca and of Jane Eyre too . . . O'Farrell is so good at exploring the most inscrutable aspects of relationships, and those who lure us into them, that it would be almost a crime for her to stop' *Independent on Sunday*

'A mixture of metropolitan satire and ghost story . . . a stylish take on the supernatural' Christina Koning, *The Times*

'Brilliantly evokes the raw pain of breaking up – and the pure relief of moving on' *She*

'Part chiller, part love story, with lurching twists and poetic bravura, this is *Vertigo* for the *What Lies Beneath* generation' *The Face*

'What begins as a ghost story soon becomes scarily real. The book seems to be saying that nothing in our imagination can be quite as unsettling, or destabilising, as the potential chaos we invite into our lives every time we connect with another human being' *Observer*

'Set once again in relationship territory, O'Farrell brings her emotionally acute writing into play with good effect . . . a novel full of spine-tingling intrigue' *Glamour*

'Another remarkable work, part gothic ghost story, partly a story of romantic loss' *Yorkshire Evening Press*

'Mingles the suspense of a ghost story with the impact of a thriller . . . The dark themes of obsession and passion are compellingly gothic; the modern setting only heightens the book's contrasting and compulsive sense of unease' *The Big Issue*

'Maggie O'Farrell explores with great panache the gothic-horror potential of relationships, the haunting severed-limbs of love' *Times Literary Supplement*

'The intensity of O'Farrell's prose style sucks you into this story of obsession . . . spookily sexy, and gripping from the start' *Marie Claire*

'She is undeniably skilful, a good plotter and a confident stylist, and she is brave to write about love and sex with such passionate conviction' *Financial Times*

'O'Farrell is an insightful and passionate chronicler of human emotions. It's compulsive and thrilling stuff' *Amazon.co.uk*

'This is contemporary literary fiction at its best' *Bookseller*

And for *After You'd Gone*:

'Maggie O'Farrell's first novel, *After You'd Gone*, had me so gripped I had to feign illness in order to devote myself to it entirely. It's a beautifully constructed story of family history, religion, separation and death, all held together by an unashamedly passionate love story' Esther Freud, *Guardian* Books of the Year

'Unputdownable, beautifully written . . . with compassion and humour [*After You'd Gone*] brings to new life a traditional story of three generations of women, their silences and betrayals, their domino effect on each other. A sharp, fresh talent to watch' Michèle Roberts, *Independent* Books of the Year

'Such an accomplished performance' Shena Mackay, *Daily Telegraph*

'O'Farrell is a born novelist . . . *After You'd Gone* is gripping, delivered with clarity, care, generosity . . . supremely moving' Ali Smith, *Scotland on Sunday*

'Incredibly affecting . . . a devastating debut' *The Face*

'This tense, involving and disturbing read . . . kept me up half the night, unable to put it down' *Mail on Sunday*

'A writer of rare insight with a feel for language that renders her love story both tender and tragic' *Financial Times*

'Love in many guises – romantic, familial, unwilling, redemptive – powers the novel . . . it's passionate, tender, and portrayed with a refreshing lack of cynicism . . . a compulsively readable and accomplished first novel' Lesley Glaister, *Independent*

'Riveting . . . O'Farrell has a gift for storytelling that makes the reader long for her next effort' Erica Wagner, *The Times*

'O'Farrell is blessed with a tender, solicitous intelligence . . . Honest, moving and wise beyond its author's years' *Time Out*

Also by Maggie O'Farrell

After You'd Gone

Maggie O'Farrell | my lover's lover

review

First published in 2002
by REVIEW

An imprint of Headline Book Publishing

First published in paperback in 2003

10 9 8 7 6 5 4 3 2 1

ISBN 0 7472 6817 7

Set in Perpetua by Palimpsest Book Production Limited,
Polmont, Stirlingshire

Printed and bound in Great Britain by
Clays Ltd, St Ives plc

Headline Book Publishing
A division of Hodder Headline
338 Euston Road
London NW1 3BH

www.reviewbooks.co.uk
www.hodderheadline.com

For Catherine and Bridget,
with all my love

ACKNOWLEDGEMENTS

My thanks to: William Sutcliffe, Ruth Metzstein, Flora
Gathorne-Hardy, Victoria Hobbs, Mary-Anne Harrington
and Geraldine Cooke

now that I'm nearly gone, I'm more here than I ever was

ALI SMITH

good lovers. make great enemies

BEN HARPER

part | one

As I was going up the stair,
I met a man who wasn't there.
He wasn't there again today;
I wish that man would go away.

ANON

She steps from the taxi, pushing at the metal weight of the door,
clutching cigarettes, change and the thorned stems of roses.
Sarah says something to her over the taxi roof and she half
turns. She's aware too late of her foot catching on the granite
curve of the kerb, and the next moment she is airborne,
falling upwards.

Lily sees the world swivel on its axis, her hair, lighter
than her, flowing past her face, her fingers shedding roses
and spinning discs of coins. As she arches through space she
sees, walking along the pavement towards her, a man. It
seems odd somehow that he should be alone because he
strikes her, in that split-second shutter-snap moment, as the
kind of person who is rarely without others. He walks with a
peculiar emphasis, as if trying to leave an imprint of himself
on the air. Then concrete and grit smack against her body,
and the skin is flayed from her hands.

At the touch of fingers, tight as ivy on her sleeve, she
looks up. His eyes are a surprising, unambiguous blue. The
flowers are crushed beneath her, seeping yellow pigment
into her clothes. He is helping her upright, speaking to her,
asking her are you all right, are you hurt. Her hands feel

3

scalded, raw, and when she looks at them she sees beads of blood springing from the skin in neat rows. Then Sarah has made it round from the other side of the taxi and is holding her arm, pressing tissues to her grazes, thanking the man. When Lily looks round, he's vanished.

'My God,' Sarah says, peering at her. 'Are you OK?'

'Yeah,' she says, laughing now, embarrassed, 'I'm fine. Don't know what happened there.' And they walk through the night air, towards the party. A repetitive, thrumming pulse of music is stretching at the walls of the building.

Inside, the rooms and corridors are crushed with people and hung with heavy nimbuses of smoke. It's the exhibition launch of a friend of Sarah's, but no one's looking at the art – photo-realistic paintings of people and animals being consumed by fire. Lily has the sensation of wanting to stretch up to the ceiling where there might be more air. Her injured hands feel sensitised, peeled like eggs.

She leaves Sarah in the main room, talking to a girl in a turquoise dress. The dress is rimmed with silky, frail fur, strands of which cling to the moistness of the girl's skin like seaweed. The people all seem to be of a type, or wearing some kind of uniform. The girls are small and gamine with cropped hair and dark-kohled eyes. The men are brash, filling their clothes complacently, gripping cigarettes between meaty fingers. Maybe it's the fall, or the pain in her hands, but she can't get over how distant everyone seems, as if she's looking at them down the wrong end of a telescope.

At the drinks table, she picks up a fragile-feeling plastic cup filled with acidic pale wine. Next to her, a woman is fanning herself vigorously with the exhibition catalogue, her cup-rim stained with a simulacrum of her violent crimson lips. Holding her drink above her head, Lily starts pushing her way through groups of people and cross-currents of conversation, towards the back and shoulders of a man she knows. She hears the rub of her black corduroy trousers as her legs move under her — a sound of secret, velvet friction. She had a lover who'd been obsessed with these trousers. '*Cor-du-roy*,' he would say as he eased them off her, separating each syllable in a fake French accent, 'cord of kings.'

A hand darts through the crowd and seizes her arm. It's brown-skinned, crooked-fingered, with silver nails. She stares down at it, surprised, then leans around the back of a thickset woman with bristly hair to see Phoebe, Sarah's friend who works at the gallery. 'Hi,' she says. 'How are you?'

'Come and talk to us.' Phoebe tugs at her. The abrasions on her palms and wrists ache, threatening to split apart. 'This is my cousin, Marky Mark.' Phoebe moves to one side and Lily sees the man who'd picked her up off the pavement. Phoebe holds out her hand, flat, palm up. 'This is Lily.'

Lily steps forward. He looks different in the light. His shirt, hectically patterned, is rolled up at the sleeves, one higher than the other so that she can see the line of his tan. The curve of his bicep is a pale, milky white, his forearms a deep brown. His fingers are stained with green ink and he has the heel of his right shoe balanced on the toe of his left.

'Marky Mark?' she repeats, when she is close enough for him to hear her. 'That's a funny name.'

'It's Marcus,' he murmurs, lifting his glittering blue gaze

to hers. He scans her face for a second or two, then smiles. 'How are your hands?'

Lily holds his gaze. She refuses to be intimidated by flirtatious men. 'All right, thanks.'

'What's wrong with your hands?' Phoebe is saying, but neither of them replies.

'Can I see?' he asks.

She holds out her wrist. He transfers his beer can into his other hand and reaches out for her arm, curling his fingers around it. His touch is surprisingly hot. Around the pressure points of his fingertips, her skin empties of blood.

'Hmm,' he says, leaning close, 'nasty. You should get it cleaned up properly.'

Lily retracts her arm. 'I'm sure I'll live.'

Again, he smiles. 'I'm sure you will.'

'What happened? What happened?' Phoebe twitters.

'Lily fell,' Marcus replies, still looking at Lily. 'Outside. Tell me, do you make a habit of falling –'

'Not really,' she cuts across him.

'– at people's feet?'

There is a pause.

'No,' she says again. 'No, I don't.'

'Marcus,' Phoebe begins, in a strident, bossy voice, obviously put out, 'I want to hear about you.'

Lily raises her eyebrows at Marcus, but then becomes aware of a shift between the three of them. Marcus looks at Phoebe quickly, moving his mouth as if about to speak. Phoebe is gazing at him intently and he is staring back at his cousin with a strange, wry, almost pained expression, one hand pressed, oddly, to the centre of his thorax.

'How are you doing?' Phoebe's voice is nearly a whisper. Something private, hidden, is being referred to. Lily looks from one to the other, suddenly wanting to be away from them both. Whatever this is, it has nothing to do with her.

'Well, I—' He stops. Slowly, he rubs his nose with his knuckle, managing to keep his beer can upright at the same time. Someone passes in the corridor beyond the kitchen door, saying, 'And she never knew, never found out.' Marcus sniffs in a deep breath, seems to be examining the lino on the floor. Lily sees in horror that he might cry. But then he grins and says, 'I think I need a new flatmate.'

He and Phoebe collapse into sudden hysterics. Phoebe hoots with laughter, leans on Marcus while the two of them giggle and snort and hiccup and wipe their eyes. Lily smiles at them both and turns towards the wall of people and sound. As she walks away, she hears Phoebe, behind her, ask: 'What on earth happened?'

Last night, the radio he'd thought long broken sputtered into life. Suddenly, a woman's voice, in the cracked vowels of a language he couldn't fathom, was sliding down the spiral staircase of his ear.

Aidan flicks over a page of the magazine, and takes a tentative sip of his tongue-flayingly hot coffee. He'd lain there for a while, listening to the sound of a distant radio station, broadcasting from somewhere, surfacing in his room. He hadn't been able to get back to sleep and half an hour later he'd been sitting on the edge of his mattress, screwdriver in hand, the radio in pieces around him, trying to find the loose connection.

The magazine is one he found in the café. It's about 'lifestyle choices', it tells him, and is full of soap stars he's never heard of in their underwear. He spends a few minutes doing a ridiculous questionnaire entitled 'So you think you're immune to love?', and scores dismally low, putting him at highly infectious. He does it again, fiddling his answers, until he gets cross with himself and turns instead to an article about a testicle festival in Montana.

He's been to see a movie and he knows he won't sleep for a while, so has found this late-night coffee bar. He had to go out, had to leave the flat, had to pretend he'd had other plans all along. He's supposed to be at Phoebe's exhibition launch, but just couldn't face it.

He sits on a high stool with an iron rung for his feet and a mirror in front of him. He avoids his own eye and looks instead at the room behind him. The people under the white strip-lights look pallid and vitamin-less. Cigarettes balance between fingers or in ashtrays, legs are crossed, feet dangling in the air, napkins are concertina-folded against the table surface. No one talks much. The Italian men behind the counter mutter monosyllabically to each other and gaze at the large TV screen where two teams zigzag up and down a lurid green pitch. Outside, late-night crowds drift past the glass door.

Without warning, a huge yawn overtakes him, and his jaw hinge cracks – a startling, inappropriate noise that from inside his head sounds like a gunshot. He suppresses an urge to laugh, and glances about him to see if anyone else has heard it. What would he say? Sorry to have disturbed you, that was just my malfunctioning mandibular joint. A man brushes past him, putting on his coat. The waiter flaps a tablecloth free of crumbs at the door. Someone standing in the corner lets a cup of coffee slip from their fingers and it shatter-smashes, a hot, dark lake of coffee spreading over the neat chess-squares of lino.

Lily slips into the back stairs of the gallery, in search of another bathroom. There's a toilet on the ground floor, but a long queue of people is snaked around its door. The sweat she's broken out in from being crammed in a room with too many people cools on her skin. As she climbs the flight of stairs she imagines she's leaving a swirl of water molecules in her wake.

The gallery is in one of those Victorian terraced houses that stretch in rows all over the city. They are all roughly the same layout, but where the bathroom usually is – at the back of the house on the first floor – Lily finds a small office smelling faintly of wet coffee granules.

She leans on the spiralling banister and looks down. From this distance, the mass of voices sound like frogs, high-pitched and regular. Then she hears something else – heavy footsteps of someone descending the staircase.

The floor judders as Marcus comes down from the upper floor. She straightens up, turning towards him in the half-light. But he moves nearer and, without speaking, slides one arm around her shoulders and the other around her waist. The length of his body rests against hers. He bends his head and presses his lips to the dip just below her cheekbone.

Lily is so shocked she does nothing. She stands in the

cage of his arms, breathing in the scent of his hair, his skin, the wool of his sweater, the wine on his breath. His face feels damp, as if he's just washed it.

Then she feels something else entirely. A movement of air, tiny, imperceptible, a slight disturbance in the atmosphere. Someone else is there. Someone else is with them, watching them. She pulls away from him, twisting her head round. No one there. She cranes her head past him. No one there either.

She looks back at him, slightly thrown. It's in her mind to ask him a question, but she can't quite form what it is. The moment see-saws between them, and it's one of a peculiar, febrile clarity: she can hear the blood-throb of his heart, the static shift of her shoe-soles against the carpet. There are textures everywhere: he scratches his head and hair-shaft crackles against scalp, nails against follicles. Their clothes, moving on their bodies, are bonfires of silk against cotton, wool against denim.

He is rooting for something in his back pocket. 'I've got something to show you.' He makes an elaborate circling movement with his hands, like an illusionist revealing the final apparition of a trick. He opens his palm, flat, and holds it out to her. In its centre is a slip of paper. 'It's a piece of paper,' he says.

Lily reaches up and touches the place where his lips had been. 'I can see that.'

'Do you want it?'

They look at it together, a tiny runway on his outstretched hand. She keeps her face serious. 'Not really.'

'How about if I write my phone number on it?'

Lily laughs.

'Well?' he says.

'No,' she says, an inexplicable belligerence taking hold of her, 'still don't want it.'

'That's very rude,' he says. He stretches the paper between his hands and snaps it against the air. 'Didn't your mother ever teach you any manners?' Leaning on the banister, he scribbles on it with the narrow lead of a propelling pencil. 'Here,' he says, pushing it into her pocket. 'Promise you'll call me.' He keeps his hand in her pocket, pulling her to him. 'Promise?'

And because she doesn't want to give him what he wants, or at least not yet, doesn't want to let him have things his way, she asks, 'Are you really looking for a new flatmate?'

He blinks. The hand in her pocket moves, tenses, then withdraws. 'Maybe. Why?'

'I know someone who's looking.'

'Who?'

'Me. I've been living at my mother's for two months and it's driving me mad.'

He studies her face with such intensity that she knows he's thinking about something else. 'You,' he says, as if weighing the word on his tongue. Then he swallows. 'Yes,' he says, 'yes I am. You have to call me now,' he shouts, as he thunders down the stairs.

Seconds pass. Lily stares up at the shut, opaque windows, waiting. Nothing.

'Marcus!' she calls again, scanning the brickwork, as if expecting it to register some kind of reaction. The narrow-mouthed courtyard, surrounded on three sides by wide-windowed warehouses, swallows the impact of her voice, leaching it of decibels. She sighs and glances at the scrap of notepaper to check the street number he'd given her, before stepping up to the door again. There are four separate bells and beside the top one is written 'Sinead + Marcus'. The bell didn't work, he'd said; she'd have to shout up, he'd said. He'd come straight down.

She steps back, away from the door, shading her eyes against the dull glare of the sky. The top windows look blank, impervious, throwing back reflections of their counterparts opposite. She looks out beyond the mouth of the courtyard and down the street. Two elderly people in beige mackintoshes are crossing the street at a painfully slow pace, followed by an arthritic-looking terrier in a tartan coat. She could just go. She could just walk away, get on the tube, go home, take off her makeup and tights, which are cutting into her middle, and sit under the flickering blue gaze of the television. She could just forget the whole thing and go. She jiggles keys inside her pocket, considering this idea.

But then she inhales deeply, imagining her alveoli filling out, darkening with oxygen. 'MARCUS!' she bellows. It comes out much louder than expected, and she giggles in surprise and a kind of private pleasure at the noise she's capable of making. His name bounces off the wet cobbles, the polished panes, the windscreens of the cars hunched along the pavements. Then, above her, a window swings open and a man appears. It's not Marcus. He's got black hair. He's also frowning. They examine each other for a moment.

'He's not here,' he calls down, leaning with one hand on the sill, the other holding his hair out of his eyes. He looks as if he's been interrupted from a deep sleep.

'Oh,' Lily says. 'Do you know when he'll be back?'

The man shakes his head and shrugs.

'I was meant to meet him here at seven.'

The man looks at his watch. Lily doesn't look at hers. She knows it's about ten past.

'No idea.' He gazes down at her. Lily waits. 'Maybe you'd better come in.'

'Thanks,' she mutters.

Moments later, the heavy grey door opens on to the street. It swings outwards, the man pushing it with his foot. Lily has to duck in under his arm. 'Thanks,' she says.

He is examining her curiously, unsmilingly; she beams back at him. Sulky people always make her want to do this — annoy and irritate them out of their glumness. Then he lets the door slam closed and they are plunged into complete darkness. Lily starts and puts up her hand to feel for a wall, a surface. She would never admit it to anyone, but she's never liked the dark. She is locked into the foyer of a large warehouse in darkness with a man she's never met. She has a dim memory of seeing some stairs climbing up and turning a corner, but are they to her left or to her right?

'Dark, isn't it?' she hears herself say to the grumpy bloke, but her voice sounds high and thin.

There is no response. Lily shuffles her feet towards where she thinks the stairs might be, holding her arm outstretched. The floor surface feels grainy. Something crunches underfoot.

'This way.'

The voice is very close to her ear, and on the other side of her head. He must have moved around her and she didn't even notice.

'Is there a light?' she says, turning her face towards the direction of his voice.

'There's one up here.'

His voice is further away now, higher up. He must have started climbing the stairs. An inexplicable fear infiltrates her like a chemical, her head hot, her breathing fast. She is telling herself off for being stupid, but salted water is prickling at her eyelids when there is a burst of light like a flashbulb going off: the front door opens, and someone – Lily is too blinded to see who – comes in. The door slams shut and a light is snapped on, and in front of her, holding a bicycle helmet under his arm, is Marcus. His hair is wet, velvet-short, holding webs of drizzle.

'I'm so sorry,' he says. 'I'm late, aren't I?' He pushes
back the cuff of his jacket to see his watch. 'I am. I'm really
sorry. I got held up by this idiot person I work with and
I couldn't get away and . . .' He comes close to her, so
close that she can smell the rain off him, seizes her arm, and
pulls her towards the stairs. 'Let's go up. We mustn't waste
another second. Did Aidan let you in? Where did he go to
anyway? How come he left you standing in the dark?'

She follows the backs of his shoes – different from the
ones he'd been wearing at the party – up the stairs. The
stairs are rickety, narrow and steep: thin, bendable boards
and a wooden handrail slippery with cheap paint. They go
up two floors, three, four, and on the fourth is a door left
ajar. Marcus pushes it, and holds it open for her.

'There you go, Lily.'

'Thanks,' she says, and they inadvertently catch each
other's eyes as she passes close by him in the doorway.

But she isn't thinking about that because she's looking
around the room she's been shown into. She would never
have imagined that such a worn, dirty building could contain
something like this vast, echoing space. Scrubbed, polished
floorboards stretch away from where she is standing to a
kitchen in one corner, a big table in another, to huge
windows at the other end. Red lampshades hang from the
double height of the ceiling; the wall from the door where
she is standing to the kitchen is painted a pale green; the
rest is white, with shelves and shelves of books.

Marcus has walked in, and is taking off his coat, slinging
his bag into a chair. Lily advances across the boards, her
shoes clacking on the polished wood.

'Lily's come about the room,' Marcus says.

Aidan, standing at the long kitchen counter, drops something. 'The room?' he snaps, his head jutting out as if Marcus has said something obscene. 'What do you mean?'

His anger pulls her up short like a dog that's reached the end of its leash. She looks at Aidan and then Marcus.

Marcus says nothing, levelly regarding the other man. Then he shrugs. 'Well, you know, we need someone to help pay bills and stuff.'

'Oh.' Aidan picks up an ice tray and cracks it between his hands. It steams as he slams it against the rim of a pint glass of water. Lily hears the ice cubes splinter on contact. 'Do we.'

Marcus seems unconcerned by the venom in Aidan's voice, rubbing his palm over his head. They watch as Aidan snatches up the glass and strides across the centre of the room. He then opens some heavy double doors and disappears like a magician's assistant into a box.

'Don't mind him,' Marcus says, searching for something in a drawer.

'Where's he gone?' she asks.

'Gone?'

'Yes, gone.' She points. 'Through those doors.'

'Oh,' he laughs, 'that's the lift shaft. It's his room.'

'The lift shaft?'

'Yeah. It's quite big. About twelve by fourteen.'

'Oh, right.' She has no idea what size that is.

'Have you never been in a warehouse before?'

'No. Seen pictures of them, but never anything like this.'

'When we found it,' he has moved into the kitchen area now, and is putting the ice tray back into the steel-fronted fridge, 'it was just a shell.'

Lily leans against the other side of the counter. 'A shell? Really? None of this,' she waves her arm, taking in the kitchen, the lights, a small area boxed in by glass bricks that she assumes is a bathroom and, down past Aidan's lift shaft, near the windows, two doors leading off the main space, 'was here. You built all this?'

'Yeah.'

'You and Aidan?'

'No.' His voice drops, diving down to sound low in his body, making her look up. There is a pause. Marcus runs his finger along the side of the counter, his head bowed. 'Me and my girlfriend.'

The words make Lily feel as though she is standing on a floor made of rice paper. He has a girlfriend. He has a girlfriend. The fact turns over and over in her head, and, aware that he is looking at her, she has to smile and nod when she actually feels as if she is missing a skin. 'Sinead?' she asks, and the word feels odd in her mouth. She's never said it before, she realises, her lips and tongue have never conspired together to perform this series of shapes.

Marcus looks at her and the blue of his eyes is like the thickest, coldest block of ice. 'Yes. How did you—'

'It's on the bell.'

'Oh. Oh, yes. So it is,' Marcus says, his voice still unsteady. Lily feels confusion swarm at the back of her head. He stands up straighter, seems to push something off his shoulders. 'Why don't I show you the room?'

She walks after him, deeper into the flat, and as she does so she builds an image in her head. She'd be Irish with a name like that, so Lily gives her flowing skeins of burnished red hair and quick, green eyes. She is small, neat and petite, and her skin is the colour of buttermilk, with a snowstorm of freckles. She has a soft, full, voluptuous body. She says his name with a soft, drawn-out R. Lily is trying to assemble these elements in her head but somehow the image won't meld, won't coalesce.

When he stops at a door right at the other end of the warehouse, Lily sees that a partition has been built, floor to ceiling, across what would have been an alcove. She turns her head and sees that there is another room, built in exactly the same way, directly opposite the one they are about to enter.

'You've done a lot of work, haven't you?' she says.

'Yeah, we did. But it's not too difficult for me,' says Marcus, 'I'm sort of . . . in that line of business.'

'You're a builder?'

He shakes his head. 'An architect.'

She is working up to asking what Sinead does, but she steps into the room and for a moment she can't say anything. It is rectangular and the ceiling seems even higher in this enclosed space. The outer side is dominated by an expanse of glass. The curtains are drawn right back; and across the courtyard, Lily can see into a room where a woman in a lilac dress is leaning on a computer, talking to a man with his back to them.

But it's not the space or the dimension or the aspect or the deep indigo blue of the walls that stuns her, but that this room is obviously still very much lived-in: there's a half-open wardrobe from which a tangle of clothes — female, from what Lily can see of their texture and shape — is strewn on the floor. The desk is covered in a tumble of loose sheets of paper and piles of books; nail-varnish bottles are lined up on the window-sill, their iridescent colours of blue, orange, purple, green, deep red glinting like cats' eyes. The bed looks as if whoever it is has just got up, the sheet whipped up into peaks, the duvet flung back, the pillows with rounded indents, crumpled tissues scattered across the mattress. Up on the walls are black and white prints of Marcus running with his arms outstretched along a beach, of an older woman with a hissing tabby cat tucked under her arm, of Marcus again, this time balancing on one foot on the roof of what could be this building. A glass of water stands by the bed, and a book with a pen stuck in to mark the reader's place. It seems as if someone has just left it for a moment, to fetch something from the kitchen or to answer the telephone. Lily feels uncomfortable, as if this person will at any moment return and find them standing there and ask, 'What are you doing in my room?'

Marcus moves, and Lily sees him take two steps into the room. He stops by the desk and takes a leaf of a succulent plant between his finger and thumb. The tendons in the back of his neck arch up through his skin.

'I don't understand,' Lily bursts out. 'Is this the room? I mean the room you want to rent?'

He nods.

'Then why — Whose is all this stuff? Whose room is this?'

Marcus goes to fold his arms, but he seems rather to wrap them round himself, his hands tucked under his arms, his fingers clutching at his own ribcage. 'It's . . . it was . . .' his voice is barely audible '. . . it was Sinead's.'

'Sinead's?' Lily repeats, before she can stop herself, before she realises the import of his words. 'Oh,' she says, thrown, 'I—'

'I'm sorry . . . all this,' he gestures around him, 'is still here. I intended . . . I thought it would be . . . cleared away by now. But . . .' He trails away, touches the plant again.

'She . . . she . . .' Lily attempts to take hold of the situation, to steer the conversation away, but her throat is blocked. Part of her wants to touch him, and the other part wants to get the hell out of here and never come back. Whatever it was that had made this girl leave in such a hurry could not have been good.

'What?' he says, and his face seems weirdly altered in the bright light from the bulb.

'She . . . er . . . she painted the room a good colour.'

'Yes.' Marcus presses his hand to the vertical, vibrant blue slats. 'She did.'

They shut the door behind them with the pressure of both their weight, and as it clicks into its frame, they move closer to each other.

'So, you like it?' He touches her shoulder, but doesn't draw her near, the space between them the width and length of a third body.

'The room?' She presses her lips together. It disturbs her, unsettles her; she wants to ask what happened, why did she go, when did she go. What on earth could make someone leave in such an evident tempest? What could end a relationship so quickly that you don't even take your clothes with you? The room feels to her like the scene of an accident – perversely compelling to look at, but not something you'd ever want to be a part of. His face, close to hers, is tense, waiting for her answer, and his hands, pressing hot on her arms, confuse her. Something is telling her to leave, leave now, walk away down the stairs, through the mouth of the courtyard and never come back. 'I love it,' she hears herself say.

'Then you'll move in?' he says, a smile breaking across his features. 'You'll come and live here?'

'Yes,' she says, nodding, more for herself than for him, 'I will.'

He leans his forehead to hers. They don't kiss, but their hands move over each other, slow and tentative, like skaters unsure of the ice.

When Aidan was a child, he stopped speaking for a year. Not for any reason – he just wanted to see if he could. One morning he woke up and decided that this was how it was going to be, his lips shut over his teeth, his tongue flat and still, a white, pure silence around him, and the clamour in his head just his, private, shuttered up.

His parents turned like litmus paper from exasperation to anger to concern. He wrote them notes in blue pencil on a notepad held together with a metal spiral. He was sent to a psychiatrist who asked him to write down what personalities he thought colours had. The children in his class at school called him 'spaz' and 'mongol' until his sister Jodie gripped fistfuls of their hair and rattled their heads like maracas. And when the year was up – he remembered the date, but nobody else did – he sat at the breakfast table and felt the words rising up in him like the thin thread of mercury in a thermometer.

Aidan sits in a chair, one leg resting on the other, one hand supporting his temple. He is regretting not taking off his jacket like the man suggested: he always forgets that the

air-conditioning in this country isn't as fierce as it is in
the States. The chair is soft, with hard plastic arms, and
is digging into the space between his shoulder-blades. He
can't find a way to be comfortable in it. Which is ridiculous,
he reflects, because an orthopaedic specialist probably spent
months working on the optimum ergonomic design for this
swivel-based, seat-adjustable, back-supporting contraption.

Wardour Street hums, six floors below. He is sitting
in the personnel office of the company for which he'll be
working. In front of him a man on the other side of a desk
is talking. The human brain is capable of decoding up to
forty-five different speech sound units per second. Maybe,
Aidan thinks, this man is talking at twice the normal speed
because he's not hearing anything he's saying; his voice is
reaching Aidan as a low, incomprehensible drone. The man
is trying to persuade him to sign the contract between them
on the desk. He has got Aidan to drop in here discuss this.
But Aidan isn't going to sign it. Don't you have anything
better to do? he wants to ask him: take off your suit, go
out, meet some people, have some fun.

Instead he makes an elaborate looking-at-my-watch gesture, and is surprised. He's meeting his sister in fifteen
minutes for lunch. The movement has caused a clink of
metal against metal in his pocket. The keys. He'd almost
forgotten.

'I really must be going,' Aidan says gently, edging
forward in the uncomfortable chair.

The man looks alarmed. 'Well,' he says. 'Thank you for
coming in at . . . at such short notice.' He picks up a pen
and proffers it hopefully.

Aidan smiles and shakes his head. 'When you've made the changes,' he gestures at the pages filled with tightly spaced type, 'I've marked them in pencil, we'll talk again.'

'Oh.' The man looks crushed, fingering the silky nap of his tie. 'Oh. OK. I'll let them know.'

Aidan nods. 'Thanks.' And he walks away, out through the sprung-hinged metal door, taking the stairs down to the street.

Lily is processing photographer payments at the agency where she works. A pile of unfolded papers sits next to her left wrist. She picks them up, one by one, types a number in a column, hits the return key and waits as the sluggish hard drive turns over. In one hand she fiddles with a paperclip, unwinding it from its tightly set form. Across the office, a woman wrenches open and slams shut the photocopier doors, swearing.

Lily doesn't believe in careers. She had a 'proper job', as her mother referred to it, or the beginnings of one a few years ago, working as an interpreter, translating the strange desires, beliefs and objections of diplomats and politicians. But – and she hadn't admitted this to anyone – she'd found that after a few weeks she'd become unable to switch off the translating synapse in her brain. Like a tap left running somewhere, it became the constant background noise to her life. Having conversations with her friends, watching TV, listening to the radio, some small, inaccessible, ungovernable part of her mind would persist in translating whatever she heard into French. And when the translating devil within her began to give a running commentary on each and every tiny act in her life (*Ouvres ton porte-monnaie, prends les pièces – tu as la monnaie? oui – et mets les l'une après l'autre dans la machine, appuies sur le bouton, et maintenant ou vas-tu encore?* it would crow at her as she stood in front of the ticket machine in the Underground station) she decided she had to take some drastic action. These days, she has it largely under control; only occasionally does her inner interpreter start whispering to her about herself in French.

So she has three jobs – none of which she cares about and none of which invades and colonises her mind when she's away from it – which she does from nine until six, six days a week. Monday to Thursday she performs various administrative and organisational tasks for a group of actors' agents; Friday she has charge of a mostly silent toddler, Laurence, from Stoke Newington so that his mother can attend her yogacise and pottery classes. Lily is supposed to be teaching him French, but there is a limited amount of conversation to be had with an eighteen-month-old, French or otherwise. On Saturdays she works as a bra fitter in the lingerie section of a big department store with Sarah, who is supplementing her weekday incarnation as an art student.

Lily tells her mother that she's saving to do an MA. Sometimes, she tells herself she is saving to go travelling. Or for her own place. Or for a computer. Or for some course that will train her to do something brilliant and interesting. She's saving for something, she knows that, some indistinct future as yet unformed in her mind. When whatever it is presents itself to her, she tells herself, she'll have the resources to do it. And, besides, the jobs have a way of soaking up time, giving life a structure, a momentum.

Lily's phone rings, making her jump.

'Hi, it's Reception. There's a man here to see you. He says he's got a key for you.'

Marcus. It's Marcus. Lily sits still for a moment, her pulse thudding past her ears. Then she saves her work and gets up. In the smoked glass of the office wall she is bleached black, walking in the opposite direction to herself, moving towards a head-on collision with a darkened doppelganger.

At the front desk, under the candid stare of the receptionist, stands Aidan, a large bag on the floor next to him. Lily stops where she is. 'Hi,' she says. Aidan seems taller, broader than she remembered him. He's not skinny, as the image she held of him in her head, but well-built, with shoulders that obscure a large section of the room behind him.

'All right,' he says, raising his chin in a kind of nod.

The receptionist taps a biro against her nails, grins at Lily and winks. Lily ignores her.

Aidan holds out his hand, palm up. 'I brought these for you.' Hooked around his middle finger is a ring of keys.

Lily moves towards him and slides them off. 'Thanks.'

'The big one's for the outside door. The silver one's for the top lock. And the other's for the . . . well, the other.'

'OK. Great. Thanks a lot.'

He shrugs, reaching for the bag.

'So . . . where are you off to?' she asks, hoping to stall him. It seems odd for him to leave just like that. They are going to be living together, after all.

'Japan.'

'Oh.'

'For work.'

'Right.' She is gripped suddenly by an urge to laugh and has to pretend to cough, putting her hand over her mouth so that he doesn't see her smile. She is aware that for some reason, this man has taken a dislike to her, and she wants him to know she knows. And that she doesn't care. She decides to keep asking him questions, to prolong his agony. 'What do you do?'

'I'm an animator.'

'What do you animate?'

'Er . . . adverts.'

'Yes?'

'Music videos.'

'Oh?'

'And some films.'

'That must be great.'

'It's . . . well, yeah . . . it's all right.'

Lily smiles at him effusively. He looks away, at his feet, at the pavement outside, at the veneer of the reception desk. She decides to let him off the hook. He's suffered enough. 'Well,' she passes the keys from one hand to the other, 'I suppose I'll be seeing you when you get back.'

'Uh, yeah. See you then.' He backs away and out of the door, his bag held awkwardly over his shoulder.

''Bye!' She waves at him until he disappears from view.

As she returns to her desk, she is accosted by Sonia, the woman who had been swearing at the malfunctioning photocopier. 'Who's the GLM?' she demands, hands on hips, blocking Lily's path.

Lily suppresses a sigh. Sonia has an irritating habit of

giving everything an acronym. GLM meant Good Looking Man.

'Who *was* that?' another woman shouts from her desk. 'He is *gorgeous*.'

Lily laughs and sits down in her chair. She glances to where she and Aidan had been standing, as if she might see some after-image of him there. 'He's my new flatmate.'

'Nice,' Sonia says, shuffling pages around, dropping some to the floor, 'very nice. Can I come round for dinner?'

'Sure,' Lily says, picking up her next payment form. 'But he's not a GLM. He's an RPITA.'

Sonia looks up. 'A what?'

'A right pain in the arse.'

She must have moved, jerked her arm or shifted in her seat or something, because the keys suddenly fall from the desk to the carpet. Lily bends to pick them up and for the first time she wonders if they were once Sinead's.

Aidan walks away, the white level light of the low winter sun obscuring his view of the street ahead. The air is still today, unmoving, cold, amplifying the sound of his footsteps, the crack of a car engine further down the street, the staccato shout from a window above. He shivers inside his clothes.

Outside a shop, he thinks he might go up to the men's department to buy a shirt. He stands in front of a display of identical shirts in twelve different colours and finds he is unable to make a decision. A wordless version of a pop song trickles from speakers hidden in the suspended ceiling. He circles a stand of ties and touches a pair of socks. Then he takes the escalator down, surrounded by tourists and rich, jobless women with expressionless faces.

The warehouse is empty when Lily arrives. She struggles up the narrow stairs, a rucksack on her back, heaving at the handrail, the suitcase banging against her leg. Her mother, Diane, had offered to drive her there and help her 'settle in' but Lily couldn't think of anything worse. After the flat she'd been renting had flooded, she'd been forced to move back into her mother's, shrinking herself down to fit the life she'd had as a teenager, living in the house in which she'd been born – 'Right there in that bed,' Diane was fond of saying to almost anyone who would listen. Her father had left them, in what Lily always considered a flagrant disregard for male cliché, for his secretary, years ago.

She's forgotten, or failed to pay any attention to, Aidan's lesson on the keys, so spends ages at the door, fiddling with locks and latches.

Inside, it seems unnaturally quiet and still. The fridge trembles, notes pinned to its outer skin. A mercuried bead of water collects on the kitchen tap. The red lanterns overhead cast the room in a hellish, kiln-like glow. Her footsteps on the boards make a crashing, echoing sound as she walks towards the room that is now hers. She pulls at the handle, but nothing happens; she tugs harder. The wood seems to have swollen into the frame. She puts the keys in her pocket and pulls with both hands. Then she is falling back on to the floor, landing hard on the base of her back. Lily sits for a moment in agony, rubbing her back, cursing.

Then she stops, because she can see through into the room. Slowly, without taking her eyes from what she sees beyond the doorframe, she slides her rucksack off her shoulders and staggers forward into the doorway, clutching with one hand at her injured back.

Everything is stripped bare. It could be a different room. The blue walls are empty, the desk is gone, the nail varnish and books from the shelf, even the bed has gone. In the place of the big, rumpled-sheeted mattress is a new bed, still in its clear plastic wrapping. Just beside it, near the corner, is a small hole in the wall – a dent, as if something has been pulled out of the plaster, a distracting flaw in the wall's perfect block of colour. Lily sits down on the bed, the polythene crinkling beneath her. The bareness makes her jumpy, wary, as if in all the emptiness there is space for something else, something other than her.

Sinead must have met someone else, she decides. Maybe it had been going on for a while, Marcus had found out and kicked her out. Why else would she leave so suddenly? She wonders who came and packed everything into boxes to take away and whether Marcus was there, whether he and Sinead did the packing together, whether they argued or silently avoided each other, and whether the other man was there. Lily pictures him outside on the pavement, jiggling his keys impatiently, looking up at the windows, his car boot open, ready and empty, waiting to receive the boxes and take them to another room, another flat, another life. How could Sinead have done that to Marcus, when it was obvious to anyone that he'd loved her? What kind of a woman could she be?

Lily gets up and drags in her bags from outside. She unfastens the catches of the suitcase and up-ends it. Clothes tumble out: socks, knickers, jumpers, trousers, shirts. She steps over them all and pulls open the door of the wardrobe. Empty hangers clatter against each other, but in the middle of the rail is something that makes her flinch in a kind of fear: a dress, strung by narrow straps, swaying slightly from the movement of the doors. She watches it until it is once more still. Then she puts out a hand and runs her fingers down its length. The material is cool and moves like liquid. It is dark blue, darker than the walls, and if it is pulled one way, the colour bleeds into black.

Lily curls her hand around the hanger, lifts it over the rail and draws it towards her. In the mirror inside the wardrobe door, she holds the dress against herself. Sinead is slim, Lily can see, thin even. Lily morphs the image she has of her in her head. Why, out of everything, has it been left? Did she want Marcus to see it? Was it some kind of message, a private sign?

She presses the material with the flat of her hand to her body, and moves closer to the mirror. A floorboard behind her creaks as her weight shifts and she gets that crawling feeling where her hair meets her neck that someone is watching her. Her head jerks round, as if she is expecting to find Marcus standing there, looking at her with Sinead's dress. But there's nothing there.

As if it might burn her, Lily places the dress on the rail so quickly that it slips off the hanger to the floor. She leaves it there, slumped in a puddle of material like a discarded skin, and walks out of the room, fast. It's another hour or so before she can bring herself to go into it again.

Marcus returns just as she is putting sheets on the bed. The swathe of polythene lies crushed into the corner, rustling and uncurling. The acoustics of the place distort and deaden sound, and she doesn't hear him until he's knocking on her open door.

'Hello?' he says, leaning into the room.

'Hi!' Lily leaps across to slam the wardrobe door shut. She has shoved the dress to one side and crammed her clothes in alongside it. 'Hi.'

They stand a few feet apart.

'So how's it going?' he says, looking about. 'All un-packed?'

'Almost. I'm sure I've forgotten everything.' She is going to mention the dress to him, she really is, but she sees that his face looks exhausted and white, and it somehow doesn't seem the right time. 'But I can always go back and get stuff I need.'

He nods. She finds she wants to look at him for a long time, memorise the set of his jaw, the way his shirt sits on his chest, how he grips his thumb in his opposite hand, as if she's going to have to sit a test on him. She had forgotten the way his hair parts just to the left of his crown and how he presses his teeth into his bottom lip. She is surprised at how pleased she is to see him, at how strong the pull of her attraction for him is. And she is surprised at herself. She always thinks of herself — prides herself almost — as having no illusions about men or the reasons for her need of them. She has them sometimes, and other times she doesn't. But this one seems to have got round her cynicism somehow, circumnavigated it, short-circuited it. She feels self-conscious suddenly, gripped by an irrational fear that she may, in that second, have become transparent, as if he can look at her and see her veins, spread out like webs, and her heart, pulsing, caught in the branches of her ribs.

He smiles at her. Has he read her thoughts? He suddenly seems a lot closer than he did, as if the room has shrunk around them. She has to bend down, pick up a book from the floor and place it on the bed so that he doesn't see the rather inane grin that has spread over her face. 'So,' she says assertively, then realises she has no idea what she is about to say. 'Um . . . thanks very much for having me,' she improvises.

'It's a pleasure,' he says quickly, and touches her arm. 'It's really good to have you here.'

'Oh,' she says, her hand moving involuntarily to meet his, 'well, thanks.' Their fingertips bump, his thumbnail touching the healing grazes on her palm.

Marcus breathes in deeply, passes his hand through his hair. 'Do you want a cup of tea?'

'That would be great.'

He disappears out of the door. Lily slumps to the bed. This is ridiculous. How long is it going to be until they sleep together? About two hours, by the way things are going. Sarah had been dubious about her moving in with Blond Man, as she called him. Sex with flatmates was never a good idea, she'd said on the phone yesterday, don't shit where you eat, Lily.

Not yet, Lily is saying to herself, as she walks towards the kitchen. At least, not tonight.

'I'm working on site this week,' he says, as he fills a kettle at the sink. 'The builders are really messing things up, and I've got to be there to sort it out. I've been away working on this building in New York, you see, so I'm getting all the shitty, tying-up-ends jobs until they put me on to something big again.'

He takes two mugs down from a shelf and shoves a tea-bag into each. She watches the way he does this – his thumbs flicking open the lid of the chrome tea caddy, his hands gripping the tea-bag like tweezers before he drops it, the two cups next to each other on the counter.

'I don't even know what you do, Lily.'

'I . . . er . . .' She laces her hands into each other. 'I do a few different things.'

'Really?'

'Yeah. I'm . . . I don't really know what I want to do yet.'

He hands her a mug of tea. It is too brown and steeped for her liking. She chases the bloated tea-bag around with her spoon, trying to hook it out.

He crosses the room and sits on the sofa. 'Do you have any ideas?' he asks.

'Well,' she says, 'you know, it's a bit of a thing with me—'

'What?' he interrupts. 'Jobs?'

'Yeah. People are always saying "What are you going to do with your life?" and I hate that. It doesn't mean anything to me. What about what life is going to do with you?' She takes a sip of her scalding tea. 'Have you ever—'

She stops. Across the room, Marcus has pulled out from under a cushion a single black leather glove. A woman's. It has taken on the shape of its owner's hand, its fingers curled slightly, its thumb almost touching the middle finger. He holds it up in front of him by its narrow wrist. His face is strained, set, but somehow unreadable. As she watches, he places the glove on the arm of the sofa beside him, smoothing the leather flat.

Lily puts down her mug on the counter, walks through the room and sits down next to him.

'What happened?' The words have slid out of her before she can check them or stop herself or decide if indeed she should really ask. 'Something happened, I know. Did she meet someone else? Is that it?'

Marcus shakes his head, then inhales and holds his breath, rubbing his fingers over and over his forehead. 'She . . .' His face is stiff, pulled, as if he's trying to prevent any expression making its mark. 'She's no longer . . . here.' He speaks the words with great effort and attention, as if there are many, many more inside him that he's holding back. 'She . . .' he hesitates, as if unable to decide how to put it '. . . she's no longer with us,' he finishes.

Lily's heart is giving long, drawn-out thuds. She feels as if she may very easily stop breathing. The euphemism sounds odd to her. It feels like something she's either never heard or hears every day. She can't quite remember what it's supposed to mean. He pronounces it with a heavy, almost ironic emphasis. She stares at him, baffled, her brain resisting whatever it is he is trying to tell her. His mouth is twisted into what might, under other circumstances, pass as a smile, and she is experiencing a variety of impulses: to shout, 'What on earth do you mean?', to place her hand comfortingly on his arm, to laugh. Somewhere behind them a bluebottle rattles, butting its head again and again against a pane.

Marcus raises his eyes to hers. It's then that she knows, and horror crawls over her skin like ants.

'How did she . . . ?' Her voice sounds strange to her, as if someone else is speaking through her. 'How?' she whispers, as if sound itself might hurt him, injure him.

But Marcus cannot speak. Lily hears herself saying she is sorry, she is so so sorry, and presses his hand between both of hers. To touch any other part of him at that moment would have seemed inappropriate, a trespass.

Lily pushes through the ticket barrier at Warren Street. A fine drizzle hangs in the air, suspended. She can't be bothered to walk down to the pedestrian crossing so she dodges the traffic, weaving between the cars that slough past her, slicked with rain.

Sarah's art school is a grey building arranged round three sides of a square. As Lily walks across it, the spiked green casings of conkers split and crack under her feet, revealing swirled, polished brown. She bends and breaks them from their impossibly white pods. There is something about their weight, their firm temperaturelessness, the way they fit exactly into the curve of her palm that pleases her. She fills her pockets, aware of them as she climbs the stairs, shifting and resettling inside her clothes.

The corridors remind her of her primary school – the high, white-timbered windows, the wide grey worn concrete floors, the scent of paper and paint and chemical-heavy cleaning fluids. When she reaches Sarah's studio, she peers through the marbled glass of the door, and spots her, bending over a pot on the floor, stirring energetically. The rest of the room is empty.

'Hi,' she says as she unlatches the door.

Sarah turns. 'What are you doing here?'

'Laurence has a cold,' Lily says, 'and his mother's convinced it's pneumonia, which means . . . I get the day off.' She holds up a carrier-bag. 'I brought some food. Have you had lunch?'

'You,' Sarah says, 'are a psychic marvel. I'm starving. But I've got to do this first. The plaster'll dry out otherwise.'

Sarah is making a body cast. She's been talking about it for weeks. Next to her, Lily now sees as she moves towards the window, is the framework, dangling on a string — a female form in frail, twisted wire, its hands resting on its hips. With the light directly in her eyes, it had been invisible. Lily places the conkers in a row on the window-sill, watching as Sarah soaks gauze strips in the wet plaster and wraps them, carefully, concentratedly, around the curves and planes of the framework. She works quickly, chewing the inside of her cheek, her fingers moving over her creation, deft and capable.

Lily unpacks some of the food, and feeds Sarah torn strips of bread. Some other students pass through, pausing briefly to watch, then moving on down the long, thin room. Sarah is older than most of the other people on her course, a mature student, although she prefers to refer to everyone else as 'immature students'. Lily drinks from a water bottle, rubs a conker into the dip of her hand and watches as the woman emerges, feet first, like a lone parachutist, waiting for the earth to come up and meet her.

'Gypsophila,' Sarah says at one point. 'Great word.' Lily pokes at the wet, creamy tub of plaster with a fingernail. It is the consistency of cake mix or mud. Sarah tells Lily about a lecture she went to that morning about male nudes, and about two people on her course who are going out together and insist on holding hands throughout the tutorials.

'How's Laurence's French coming along?' she asks.

Lily grins. '*Très bon, naturellement.*' She shakes her head, thinking of Laurence's mother, a tall, anxious woman with prematurely whitening hair and not enough to do. 'That woman is mad, really mad. How is it you need a licence for a dog but anyone can have a baby? It shouldn't be allowed.'

'And how's the new flat?'

Lily concentrates on peeling the tight, pungent skin of a clementine in one long, coiling strip. 'It's fine.'

She feels Sarah looking at her. The possibility of telling her about Sinead opens somewhere, like a window in another room. But something is blocking her. Some kind of loyalty to Marcus, maybe, or a reluctance to reduce it to small-talk, or to make real these nebulous fears she's been having. It seems too new, too undigested in her own mind, to speak of it easily.

She swallows a clementine segment, neat and contained as a goldfish. 'It's fine,' she says again.

'And have you bedded the landlord yet?'

She removes the white web of pith from her clementine, frowning. 'There's been a bit of a new development on that front.'

'Oh, yes?'

This all seems wrong. Sarah's using the flippant voice with which they do all their chit-chat. How can she sit here, munching her way through a clementine, discussing the death of a woman as if it means nothing at all?

'Um,' Lily begins, wondering how to go on. Then it comes out in a jumbled rush. 'You know the girlfriend I told you he had? The one whose room I've got? Well, she died.'

There is a short, shocked silence. When she looks up, she sees Sarah on a chair, standing beside a perfect white replica, her hands dyed the same colour. 'Are you serious?' Sarah steps down with a thud. 'My God. How come? I mean, how did she die?'

'I don't know. He couldn't really . . . talk about it'

'When did he tell you?'

'Last night.'

'My God,' she says again. 'How long ago was this?'

'Not sure. I think pretty recent.'

'Jesus, the poor guy.' Sarah picks a dot of dried plaster from her shirt and crumbles it between her fingers. 'You've got to be careful, Lily.'

Lily doesn't say anything.

'I mean, that's a big situation you've got there.' Sarah holds her arms wide, as if measuring it. 'You need to think carefully about whether you want to . . . take it all on.'

She comes in to find him watching a film on TV. They don't say much to each other and she sits down next to him, pressing her shoulders against the sofa, and discovers that there is no way of sitting so that their bodies aren't touching. The film is an old black and white one. An orchestral score surges as a woman is creeping along a corridor towards a big ornate door, the tempo of the music becoming more and more frantic.

Lily tips back her head and looks around the huge room. Rusted steel girders transect the ceiling, and by the window hangs an old, ropeless pulley. It seems peculiar to her suddenly that they should be living in this space: a hundred years ago it would have been a garment factory, where immigrants from eastern Europe stitched fabric into human shapes and practised getting their tongues around the muted diphthongs of English. This is what Lily loves about London, that every building, street, common and square has had different uses, that everything was once something else, that the present is only the past amended.

She swallows a yawn. Marcus's thighs are encased in jeans. She imagines that if she were to let her hand drop on to them, they would feel taut and warm, the muscles close under the material. It would be so easy: all she'd have to do would be to let her arm relax, and it would fall naturally, her hand coming to nestle close to his groin. She then realises that Marcus is looking at her, saying something. 'Sorry?' she says.

'He had more money for this one.'

'Pardon?'

'He had more money. He went to the States.'

Lily has no idea what he's talking about. 'Really?'

'Yeah,' he says, and turns back to the screen. 'It was his first Hollywood-backed film. Have you seen it before?'

'No.'

'Oh. Well, I won't spoil it for you then.'

A few minutes pass. The young woman is descending

a staircase in a frothy white dress and a big hat. An aristocratic man in a tuxedo stands at the bottom with his back to her.

'How was your day?' Lily asks after a while.

He glances at her. 'Good, actually.' He nods. 'I've got moved on to a new job. Project Architect.'

'Oh.'

'It's means being in charge of everything,' he explains, his eyes fixed on the screen.

'Right. That's great.'

'I suppose so.'

'What do you mean, you suppose so? It is great. Really great.' She touches his arm, wanting to press her point home.

'Mmm.' He shifts around so that he is facing her, and sighs. 'You're right.'

'Is it not a good project?' she asks, confused by his lack of enthusiasm.

'No, no, it's a great project. Really interesting – a bus terminus. It'll be . . . it'll be . . .' he rubs his forehead '. . . great.'

She looks at him, puzzled. They are sitting close together in this huge room, knees touching.

'I don't know,' he says, and gives a funny little laugh. Lily sees that he is trembling, his jaw muscles clenched. 'Life's just hanging on me a bit heavily at the moment. I don't know . . . I don't know what I can do to make myself feel better.'

'Do you . . . would it help at all to talk about it?'

'I don't think so, no.' He gets up and walks away quickly,

closing his studio door behind him. Lily sits where she is, her hands tucked between her knees.

The film still plays in the corner. An evil-looking woman seems to be trying to persuade the girl to jump out of a window. Lily wonders if she should switch it off.

It's Sunday afternoon. Lily is having a hibernation day. She has to do this about once a month. It's the only way, she tells herself, that anyone can remain sane in this city – lock the doors, put on the answerphone, don't leave the house, don't even think about going on public transport, just surround yourself with silence and do nothing.

At this precise moment, she is lying on her bed the wrong way round, her head tipped over its end, her legs crooked at the knees. She teases knots out of her hair with her fingers; she peels away loose jags from around her nails; she presses her eyes, then shuts them to see technicolour sparks behind her lids.

She sits up. Her head swims with the quick movement. She has no idea what time it is. Hunger tears like paper in her stomach. She should probably return the message Sarah left her earlier but can't quite make the move to do so. The day is ebbing away, the sky that blank, whitish, shut colour.

Lily stands, wanders to the window to look down into the street, and reaches up her hand to unfasten the latch. She encounters not cold metal but a dry crackle. She stands up on tiptoe to see a folded piece of lined paper, jammed into

44

the join. Lily tugs it out and opens it. It's a list of things: *hairgrips* is first. Then:

> *notebook*
> *stamps*
> *hair serum*

In a different column, with slightly neater, more thought-out handwriting, as if the person had shifted position or moved to a table or readjusted the pen:

> *pick up photos*
> *call I*
> *shoes?*

Shoes. Question mark. Was she going to buy shoes or not? Had she seen a pair she liked but wasn't sure about, and maybe needed to try on? Or did she need some and was just reminding herself to have a look? The writing is spiked, sloping. The bottom of the *g* a deft, straight line. No loops, the dot of the *i* pulled into a dash in her haste, her *e*s missing a space in their top half, the taller letters dwarfing the smaller. Who is 'I'? 'Call I' seems strange, as if it had been a reminder to place a telephone call to herself. What kind of hair needed grips and serum?

The paper feels crisp and brittle. Lily holds it to her face and sniffs. The floor beneath her shakes, as if a washing-machine is on somewhere else in the building. There is a rumbling sound in the next-door room like a radiator digesting heat.

She wrenches open the window and, without thinking about it, lets the paper fall from her fingers. It floats down in a straight line, and she thinks suddenly of the paper fish her father used to make her by looping a strip of paper into itself. He would stand her on a chair and hand her the delicate curl of paper: Lily would hold her arm up above her head and release it; there was always a moment when you could see it twist and spore like a sycamore helicopter into a fish shape before it hit the ground and became just a loop of paper again.

She leans out of the window, wanting to catch that moment when it meets the ground but as she does so, the window-ledge seems suddenly lower; her body swings far further forward than she intended, her feet sliding on the boards. Her heart convulses, blood cooling her chest, and she has to grab for the window-frame to steady herself, her nails scraping against the woodwork, her fingers scrabbling for a hold. The courtyard, street, cars, Tarmac, cobblestones wheel and tip beneath her, looking at once far away and sickeningly close. Her mind seems to split away from her body and she seems to see herself or maybe someone else fall, limbs flailing, hair arching behind her, hitting the ground with a crunching thud. She imagines that final, immovable, hard kiss of stone as she is moving back into the room, into safety, into balance. Then she grips the window-frame with both hands, standing up very straight. She doesn't shut the window, but keeps the breath of the street moving around her. She is aware of the swell of the room at her back and the rush of the drop in front of her, and she stands there for a while, thinking.

That evening, Lily sits at the table, her dinner in front of her, half reading a book. Her eyes keep straying from the tight blocks of printed text, floating upwards to rest on Marcus. Across the room, he is murmuring into the telephone, his face turned to the wall. Another black and white film plays out, unwatched, on the TV.

Lily turns a page. Marcus dials a number, hangs up, dials again, hangs up, redials, speaks inaudibly into the receiver before dragging the phone on its extension lead into his room. The white cord rattles after him like a snake.

With one hand, she winds strings of tepid spaghetti around a fork. Marcus's film, freeze-framed to a moment where a man in too-short trousers is vaulting over a low wall, continues to flicker in the corner. She puts the fork back on the plate and starts clearing the table of her dinner things, stacking the plates on each other, balancing her mug on top of them. As she walks around the table towards the sink, she sees, she is sure she sees, out of the corner of her eye, something in the bathroom – a movement, a flicker, the greenish glass bricks refracting and splintering it.

And then suddenly it is gone and the space behind the glass is empty and clear. She'd blinked or looked straight at it and it had vanished. Lily slides the stack of plates on to the counter and moves towards the bathroom. The light is on and the window wide open. Rain flecks the curtain and the sill. There is the faint, sickly scent of jasmine in the air. The hinge is stiff as she tries to shut the window; she pulls hard on the catch and the curtain billows and reaches for her, the dampness clutching at her. It must have been what she saw, moving in the wind.

But she inspects the shower. It is dry, pristine, unused for hours and hours.

The next day, Marcus is out of the flat before she even wakes. As she's leaving her room, her bag on her shoulder, struggling with one arm in and one arm out of her coat, hooking her foot into her shoe, she sees on a chair outside Marcus's room the patterned shirt he was wearing when she first met him. It is draped, its material creased and rucked, the geometry of its pattern interrupted, one arm flung across the chair back, the other dangling to the floor. The top three buttons are undone, as if he pulled it over his head in a haste to be undressed.

Lily stands a few feet from it. She takes a step forward, but a movement at the corner of her eye makes her stop almost guiltily and flick her head towards the rest of the flat. It's empty. Of course. Who does she think might be there?

She covers the last two steps in a rush and seizes the shirt in both hands, as if someone is about to snatch it from her. As she does so, there is a sense of something being spilt inside her. She presses the shirt to her nose and mouth, trying to adjust. It is an unaccountable feeling, like the sting of sunburn you weren't aware of happening.

She's in love with him. This is not good. She doesn't want this.

Lily thrusts the shirt from her, looks away, out of the window, and sees for the first time that the green cones of shoots are pushing up out of the black soil in the window-boxes. She frowns. It's far too early, or perhaps even too late, for them. How come they're growing now, just as winter is beginning? Lily steps to the window, staring down at their green tips – waxy, speared and determined. Beneath them, she knows, are the paper-dry cortexes of bulbs, and inside them, the germ of flowers, folded and folded into themselves. Sinead planted these bulbs, she thinks. There's no way Marcus or Aidan would have. Sinead packed in their parchment bundles with powdery peat, watering them, placing the boxes here where no one has touched them since. How long can she have been dead? Two months? Three? How long ago did she plant these bulbs and would it have crossed her mind that she wouldn't see them flower?

She turns away. The flat seems sticky with Sinead's fingerprints. She doesn't know what to do.

She arrives at work late. Natasha, the lingerie supervisor, who Lily knows for a fact wears padded bras, gives her a narrow-eyed glare as Lily tries to skulk into the back room, unnoticed.

Sarah bursts in as she is stripping off her jeans.

'Shit,' Sarah says, flinging off her coat and struggling out of her sweater. 'I overslept. Through two alarm clocks. Can you believe it?'

'Natasha's on the rampage.' Lily yanks her shirt over her head. 'Did she see you?'

'Don't know.'

As they struggle into the green nylon skirts of their uniform, bumping into each other in the hot proximity of the tiny windowless room, Lily says, 'I have a question.' She stops, unsure of how Sarah might take this, then decides just to launch in. 'If you wanted to find out how somebody died, how would you go about it?'

'*What?*' Sarah straightens up from lacing her shoe. 'Who on earth—?' Her face clears. 'You mean the girlfriend. Whatshername. Lily, you can't be serious.'

'I just want to know.' She shrugs. 'That's all. Satisfy my curiosity.'

'But you can't go poking around behind his back! Lily, that's – that's devious and dishonest. It's stalker territory. If you want to know, you have to ask him.'

'I can't.'

'Just ask him. It's not an unreasonable demand. He tells you, he cries on your shoulder, you fall into each other's arms, you live happily ever after. Simple.'

Lily drags a brush through her hair. 'I don't feel I can. He's so . . . wrapped up in his grief. Most of the time he seems fine, and normal, but when she's mentioned, he just clams up. Won't say another word – about anything. And it's not exactly hard to imagine why, is it? I'd feel like some horrible ambulance chaser if I forced the issue. It's much easier this way – on everybody.'

'Can't you ask the other guy? The flatmate film man?'

Lily snorts. 'Yeah, he talks to me a lot.'

'So what are you going to do?'

'Don't know. Go to the Public Records Office? I've no idea how you go about these things.' She meets Sarah's exasperated gaze. 'Look, this is something I have to do. Once I know I'll be able to—'

'What?' Sarah demands. 'Sleep easy at night? Know what you're dealing with? What?'

Lily doesn't answer.

'Just what are you hoping to gain from this?' she persists.

Lily scrapes her hair back into a band, avoiding Sarah's eye.

'I don't understand you!' Sarah cries, still cross, crushing her clothes into a tight bundle. 'Why can't you just let it lie? Leave the poor woman alone.'

There is a tense pause. Lily pushes stray strands behind her ears and straightens her skirt. Then Sarah sighs: 'OK,' she relents. 'I shouldn't do this. I really shouldn't do this. But I have this friend. An investigative journalist on a tabloid. A real door-stepping, garbage-sifting rat. Nice guy, though, otherwise. He'll know what to do.'

Lily grabs her hand and squeezes it.

'Don't,' Sarah says, snatching it away. 'I'm only doing this to shut you up. This doesn't mean I agree with it.'

'I know.' Lily grins.

Sarah shakes her head. 'Just . . . give me her name.'

'Wilson,' Lily says. 'Sinead Wilson.'

Aidan is drifting, his mind running over thoughts like

water over stones. If he does buy a flat in Kentish Town should he spend a bit more for the one with a garden? Does he have time for gardening? He can't quite picture himself digging and planting things somehow. He'd have to start visiting those funny places . . . what are they called? They smell of peat and compost, and have rows of plants with roots bursting out of black plastic containers. Garden centres. Would having a garden involve the purchase of a wheelbarrow? Then he has the alternative vision – alternative to the one of him in wellies in the pissing London rain shovelling clods of manure around – of him in a deck-chair in summer. Behind him, someone is tending a barbecue, and music floats from his open ground-floor windows . . . He must remember to get that CD Jodie wanted. What was it called? He has it written down in a notebook back at his hotel. Something FunkMasters. Or FunkMasters Something. And he must call Sam when he gets back. What else is on that list? Something about—

At the sound of his name, Aidan jerks his swivel chair round from the window and the Tokyo skyline, its monoliths gleaming in the sun, and looks at the row of faces around the table, all angled at him expectantly. The man next to him is clearing his throat with a discreet, scraping sound. Was it him who'd been talking? Or someone else? Who'd just said his name? And what had been said during his little zone-out? He tries to arrange his face into a thoughtful, rather than panicked expression, busying himself with stabbing a drink carton with the sharp end of a straw.

'So,' he says, in what he hopes is an unruffled voice, looking round the table, 'shall we just run through that once more?' He leans back in his chair, raises the carton to take a drink, and misses his mouth with the straw.

Lily is balanced on a display pedestal, embracing an armless dummy. She can't get the bra fastener done up behind it. She wrestles with the two strips of elastic, her knees aching, her face pressed against the steel-hard fake tits, but the hooks refuse to connect with the eyes.

She yanks the bra off the dummy and examines the label. She's brought the wrong size up from the storeroom: a 30B, for God's sake. What was she thinking? Shop dummies are always a 32C. Temper tightens like a coil inside her. She doesn't like knowing things like that, doesn't like the fact that this job is, no matter how much she tries to resist, filling her head with useless, pointless crap. The average width of stocking tops. The number of bras British women buy per year. Which manufacturer caters for which type of figure. How to recognise those figures at a glance. The pros and cons of underwiring, adjustable straps, front fasteners, seams.

Lily climbs down from the display, leaving the dummy naked, and stamps over to the storeroom, the 30B hooked around her wrist like a catapult. Minutes later, she emerges with the same but ever so slightly bigger bra, this time stretched between both hands. This sour, furious mood, she's aware, is fuelled by an impatience for information about Sinead. The desire for it moves within her like a pulse.

She hitches up her skirt and climbs on to the display again, pins gripped between her lips, just in case. The bra slides easily over the dummy's shoulders, but she has to struggle with the back fastener again. She has just managed to hook it together and is straightening the cups over the hard swell of the fibreglass breasts when she notices a man watching her, his head on one side. He is wearing a tailored woollen coat and suit, and has a long, furled umbrella clamped under one arm. He smiles and arches his eyebrows when she catches his eye. She is pulling back her lips in a snarl and, as she does so, forgets all about him and all about the bra and the dummy and all about the humiliation prickling at her because she is suddenly struck with a thought. A thought so obvious and so thrilling she doesn't know why it hasn't occurred to her before.

She runs most of the way from the tube. By the time she pounds up the stairs, her legs feel like liquid and her lungs like fire. When she throws open the front door, the flat is dark and Lily almost cheers. She needs the place to herself.

She knows exactly what she's looking for. She scans the bookshelves first – art books, novels, random magazines, CDs. Nothing. She opens the long, thin doors of the cupboards opposite the kitchen, and finds shoes, coats, a dismantled desk, boxes of tools, a tent in a bag. She's going to have to do what she was hoping she wouldn't.

She stands on the threshold of Marcus's room. It's exactly like her own, but reversed, like the reflection of a room in a mirror. Two plan chests sit in the corner, with architectural models, sheets of cardboard, tins of paints, pens and cutting tools heaped on top. The walls are a bright magnesium white. Bits of paper, plans, diagrams, sections, maps, are stuck around the area where he works. It has a slightly temporary, unlived-in feel: an unshaded bulb hangs from the ceiling; clothes are stacked in boxes; electrical flexes criss-cross the floor like tripwires. He lies on that bed every night, she thinks. Then she recognises it as the bed that used to be next door, in Sinead's room. Shoving that thought aside, she strides across the room and sits at his desk. Surprisingly comfortable chair. Slightly splintered edge to the desk.

She cocks her head, listening out for any tell-tale noise, then leans over, pulls open the drawers and begins sifting through the contents with bent, anxious fingers: staplers, pens, stanley knives, screws, batteries, rulers, set squares, glue, erasers, bills, postcards, letters addressed to Marcus Emerson (Lily can't bring herself to open these, but peers briefly into their folded, inked depths before putting them back). Files containing A3 sheets of drawings. Folders stuffed with tracing paper, bits of newspaper articles, contracts, official-looking letters. At the bottom of one drawer, she finds among paperclips and pencil shavings, face-down, a business card: 'Sinead Wilson, Lecturer, Department of English Literature'. She holds it between her fingers. It's light, flimsy card, the letters raised. If Lily pressed hard enough she could push them back into themselves. But she doesn't. She looks up, looks round the room, and sees her own face outlined in the grey of Marcus's shut-down computer screen. Then she turns towards the shelves, and sees what she's been looking for – the gold and red spines of photograph albums, five of them, arranged in a row.

Lily pulls down the first. It's one of those flip ones where you slot photos into little plastic sleeves. She opens it, starts flicking through it. Her initial apprehension melds into disappointment: buildings. It's just buildings, one after another after another. She skims through them, faster and faster. Gutters, windows, flooring, staircases, doorhandles, paving slabs, marble walls, light fittings, ceilings. A large, undulating, silver building, all waves and shimmering expanses. A low, white, angular one with a gap in the middle as if a bite's been taken out of it. She shuffles through them, perplexed. Then something makes her stop, go back two to a black and grey building with wide steel girders on its exterior. At the building's base, near the entrance, very small and very far away, legs blurred as if she was walking too fast for the camera's shutter, face angled towards the camera – or its owner – a rucksack on her back, her hands pushed into her pockets is a thin, tall woman with dark hair. The black dots of her eyes stare out at Lily, fixed, inquisitive.

She replaces the album, takes down the next. It's more buildings. She puts it back, tries the next. More buildings. She replaces it and opens the last and as she does she gasps and has to clutch the album so as not to drop it. The top photograph is the woman from the other photograph at the bottom of the building, the woman who used to live in this flat, the woman who helped create this flat, the woman who wore the blue-black dress that is now hanging among Lily's clothes, the woman who is now dead.

She and Marcus are on a pavement somewhere. A city that isn't London. It's evening-time; angled rhombuses of sunlight lie over the street and gutter. Cars pass them, frozen into blurs. She has her arm curled round his neck, her fingers in his hair, her nails a dark red. The person behind the camera has just said something funny because she is facing the lens, eyes wide, laughing, the coils of her hair swinging into her face so that it's partially obscured. Wherever it is must be hot because she is wearing a red dress with thin straps over her shoulders. It has beads sewn into the material filled out by her breasts. Her lips, painted the same red, are parted to show sharp, precise teeth. Sinead was beautiful. Lily sees this, sees the length and turn of her neck, the dark, rather wide-set eyes, the narrowness of the waist, the long, long legs that end in shoes that tie around the ankle. Marcus is side-on to the camera, slightly behind and to one side of her, his hand is held flat against her solar plexus, as if he is holding her upright, as if he is holding her to him. He is looking at her, ignoring the camera, ignoring the photographer, ignoring everything else going on around them. His face, unlike hers, is solemn, intense.

Lily shuts the album, pushes it back into its space on the shelf. Terror, inarticulate and obscure, is surrounding her like a force field. She bolts from the room, through the flat, out of the door, down the stairs and out into the darkening streets. She twists round to look up at the flat as she leaves, and its windows look blank, innocuous.

She gets back late. She's been sitting at a corner table in the pub down the road, tearing beer mats into the tiny, identical squares of confetti. When she opens the door, Marcus is walking from the kitchen past Aidan's door.

'Hi,' he says, 'good day?'

'No. Shit actually.'

'Oh. Well. You're back now, at least. Don't bring the office home with you — that's what Sinead always said.'

Lily, caught in the act of taking off her coat, panics. She's never heard him refer to her voluntarily. Does he know what she's been doing? Has he sensed it? Did she leave signs? She can't have done — she remembers replacing the album, shutting the drawers, pushing the chair back under the desk. She did. She knows she did.

Marcus, also, seems taken aback, confused, blinking rapidly as if he can't quite believe what he just said. They stare at each other in mutual shock. Lily looks at his hands, resting on his hips and she suddenly sees, suddenly understands, their sinewed strength, their flex and power. As she looks, she finds she is wondering at their stretch and capability.

She goes into the bathroom and picks up her toothbrush. Her arm is shaking slightly. Her face looks out at her from the mirror — porcelain white beneath the remnants of her summer freckles. She makes herself pick up the toothpaste, keeping things normal, keeping herself calm, and squeezes out a length on to her brush and starts scrubbing at the flattened tops of her molars. She rinses her mouth, spits, rinses and spits again. The splashing of the tap echoes round the boxed-in room. It's all gleaming metal and reflectiveness, like an operating theatre. Or a morgue. Nothing would leave a mark in here that couldn't be washed or sponged away. Stainless steel lines the walls, seamless concrete covers the floor. Male things are lined up on the shelf — shaving foam, deodorant, razors. Half of it is noticeably empty. Lily wonders what happens to the cosmetics of the dead.

She is about to go back into her room when she stops, turns and presses open Marcus's door. He is sitting at his desk, writing something on a pad of paper and he looks up, surprised.

'You know,' Lily begins uncertainly, 'my grandfather died two years ago.'

He looks startled. 'Oh,' he says, and crosses his legs. 'I'm sorry . . . I'm sorry to hear that.'

'Yes.' She waits. Marcus looks at her. She looks back. What is he thinking? What does he keep wound up behind that brilliant, fathomless blue gaze?

'I'm sorry,' he says again.

'It's OK. I didn't . . . it wasn't as upsetting as . . .' She tails off expectantly.

Marcus doesn't seem to know what to say. His hand moves slightly on the paper.

Lily sighs. She's never been any good at the softly-softly approach, never been one for pussy-footed game-playing. 'Look,' she says, 'I just wanted to say that if you ever wanted to talk to me about Sinead, you can. I . . . I'd be happy to listen. Or to help. If I can.'

The pen drops from his hand and rolls away from him on the sleek surface of the desk. He makes a grab for it, managing to catch it just as it is falling to the floor. When he is holding it fast, trapped by four curled fingers, he looks at her again. 'What do you know about Sinead?' His voice is steady, toneless.

'Not much, but—'

'Well, there you are, then.'

Lily turns on the pivot of her heel. 'Fine,' she says. 'OK.

See you later.' Her foot strikes a box of nylon-tipped pens on the floor, their coloured casings skittering away over the boards, but she doesn't stop. As she is reaching for the handle she thinks she hears him say: 'Don't go.'

Two words. Just like that. So quiet that Lily is convinced she imagined them. But her hand hovers over the door-handle, and without looking round she tries to gauge the silence behind her. It stretches, elongates and swells. Lily presses the cold metal of the door-knob into her fingers. He said nothing, he said nothing. She imagined it. Must have done. But she half turns. He is looking at her, uncertain, almost shy.

'Did you . . . did you say something?'

'I said don't go. I don't want you to go. I'm sorry,' he says. 'I don't mean to be . . .'

Lily has left the door and is crossing the floor towards him. He pushes the letter he is writing into a drawer. *You always*— Lily catches sight of before he closes the drawer and stands up. He puts his hands around her neck, his fingers in her hair. His breath is hot on her face. He lifts her arm and presses his mouth to the blue river delta of veins at her wrist.

They reach the bed quickly, her hands finding their way through his clothes to the hard smoothness of his back, his mouth against her neck, her cheeks, her hair, her eyelids, her throat. There is the sweet burning, the confusion of limbs and fabric before the relief of skin upon skin. He feels his way about her, his face intent, concentrated. She shuts her eyes against the glare of the electric light, lifts herself from the mattress to allow the layers of clothes to be peeled away.

The weight of him on her is a relief, a release. As he arches the upper part of his body away from her to pull off his T-shirt, Lily opens her eyes to take the shortest glimpse of him, to store the snapshot into her memory. What she sees, though, makes the blood stop in her veins.

Standing beside the bed, near enough so that Lily could reach out and touch her, is a girl with black Medusa curls and an angular white face. She is looking straight at Lily.

Lily jolts as if electrocuted, and she screams, the noise stretching at the walls of the room. It seems easy to push Marcus off her and to turn away and leap in one fluid movement from the bed. The thing is behind her then, as far away from her as possible and she can't see it and she never wants to lay eyes on it ever again.

'What the hell . . . ?' She hears Marcus say and she looks back at him. She doesn't want to, she wants to keep her gaze and her face and her body – naked and cold now the warmth of Marcus's is leaving her – averted, but she cannot ignore his voice and the sound of it drags her eyes to him. Marcus is kneeling on the bed, staring at her, dishevelled, perplexed. Beneath him, between his thighs, is the imprint of her body. She's left a kind of negative space behind her, a vacancy where, if she'd kept her eyes closed she'd still be lying. The room is empty apart from the two of them.

'What's the matter?' he says, his face flushed. 'Are you OK?'

Lily blinks, looks down at the crumpled outline in the sheets below him. There is just Marcus in front of her, the air behind him blank, clear, hollow. It was nothing. She imagined it. It was nothing. 'I saw . . . I thought I saw . . .'

He reaches out to her. 'What?'

At that moment, there is a swift knock at the door and someone outside saying, 'Marcus?'

Marcus struggles over the bed to get to the door. But Aidan opens it before he reaches it.

'Marcus, I——' Aidan stops short on the threshold and stares at them – semi-clad, clothes strewn about the room, the thrashed-about bed. Lily bends to gather up her things, holding them to her front. Aidan says nothing and doesn't move, just turns his head to look Marcus full in the face.

'How was Japan?' Marcus says.

There is a pause. The two men's eyes are locked on each other. Lily walks towards the door.

'Excuse me,' she says.

Aidan steps aside and she passes through into her room. She gropes for the lamp on the desk and switches it on. It sparks blue, the bulb filament exploding with a hollow pop, pain streaking up the fibres of her arm. Through the dark air of the room she can make out the black outline of her reflection in the mirror. She stares at it wildly: in it she has no face, no features, no dimension. She moves and it moves with her. She feels a bit crazed, light-headed, and struggles with a desire to burst into giggles. This is ridiculous! What *was* that? Did she really just see Marcus's dead girlfriend? During sex? Or did she imagine it? Was it real? And what does 'real' mean, in terms of a dead girl?

At a noise behind her, she leaps into the bed, scrambling beneath the covers, pinning them to her with her fists. Her mind gallops, falling over itself. I don't even believe in ghosts, she wants to shout.

Aidan presses his forehead to the cold, slick glass, and peers into the distance at the four pale columns of Battersea Power Station rising above the low city skyline. It's weird, unaccountable and bizarre. He's known this city all his life and suddenly everything looks rejigged, Battersea Power Station north of the river, Harrow-on-the-Hill in Leytonstone. Someone has clearly moved the river.

He's in a glass capsule of the London Eye, a huge white wheel that circles slowly next to the Thames. He'd had an hour to kill before meeting his friend Sam and, curious about this strange structure that's appeared since he was last here, bought a ticket and climbed on.

People line the sides of the oval capsule, taking photos, unfolding maps. The wheel is surprisingly silent and slow. He'd been expecting a faster, more fairground ride, not this rather sedate amble through the skies of London. As they approach the apex, two American girls leap up from where they were seated and indulge in a frenzy of photographing each other. They approach him with their camera and he takes it, trapping them together in the viewfinder, clicking the shutter.

Aidan looks out at Canary Wharf tower, glinting like mica in the sun. When he'd left London, three years ago, it had been alone on the skyline, a tall, shimmering blip in the levels of buildings. But now other structures, half built, are crowding in next to it, blurring its outline. A friend of his died in the bombing there a few years ago. Sam, who'd also known him, said recently that he sometimes still forgets he's dead, still gets the urge to call him, to tell him things. Ridiculous, he said, isn't it?

Aidan turns northwards again and, as the city rises to meet him, thinks about how he nearly slipped from a high-level footbridge as a child. His father caught him by the straps of his dungarees just in time, and he saw his feet swing out over lanes of traffic, parks with children on climbing frames, roofs of houses, fishponds in back gardens, people shopping on a busy street.

Shuffling out of the capsule and back through the barriers, he sees Sam waving at him. Next to him stands a woman whose eyes are still searching the crowd. Lisa. Sam's been seeing her for almost a year, but Aidan's never met her before.

When Sam introduces them, with a mock-formal flourish, Lisa grips his hand in hers and says, 'At last, the elusive Aidan.' They talk about where to go, what to eat, the geographical dislocation you get from being in the Eye, how cold it's suddenly become.

As they are walking to the nearest pub, Sam asks: 'How's Marcus?'

Aidan sees Lisa glance up at him quickly, then look away. Sam's told her, he sees. Not that he minds. He just forgets sometimes that couples, like body cells, have a kind of permeable barrier between them.

'Don't ask,' says Aidan.

'And I said to him,' Diane, Lily's mother, is saying, 'I said, Graham I really don't think it's on if I'm here for the evening and she calls up and you spend three-quarters of an hour on the phone to her. I mean, it's not that I'm jealous because I'm not the jealous type, am I, but I think basically that it's just not on.'

Lily holds the phone to her ear with one hand and, with the other, twirls a length of hair around her index finger. The office is empty, the agents out at lunch. She's supposed to be sending out a stack of letters to casting directors, but has phoned her mother instead for a chat.

'. . . and he replied that I shouldn't feel threatened. That it's not an issue for him any more . . .'

Lily is being calm today. Very, very calm. All this shit about ghouls and ghosties is just nonsense. Nonsense. She knows that. It was just a product of an overwrought mind – she was having sex with Marcus for the first time, she'd just looked at those photographs (and how stupid was that, she can't believe she did that, what an idiot), the whole affair with Marcus has that discombobulating feeling of turning into something big, and so on and so on. Nothing to worry about. It won't happen again.

She stares at the hair wound around her finger. Her nail is filling with blood, turning a bright pink. She releases her hair and it unravels quickly, settling back into place. What is it that makes hair curl anyway? Isn't it something to do with the follicles?

'Did you ever see your father after he died?' She hears herself interrupt her mother's monologue.

There is a short silence.

'What?'

'Um . . . Grandad,' Lily says. 'I mean, do you think ghosts . . . er. Nothing. Forget it.'

'Ghosts?'

'It's nothing. I didn't mean it.'

'Why are you asking me that?'

'No reason. Sorry. Carry on with . . . with what you were saying.'

'Well,' Diane doesn't need a great deal of encouragement, 'anyway, so after that he decided to buy an answerphone. And I said . . .'

Lily zones out again. Lights hum above her head; phones ring in rooms down the hall; outside, cars wait in line for the lights to turn.

She walks fast, her feet skimming the pavement, her lungs filling and emptying. When she'd reached the turning into the courtyard, the flat was obviously empty, its windows dark and hooded. Something failed her. She couldn't go in, she just couldn't. She'd stood there for a while, tussling with herself. This was ridiculous. She was being stupid. There's nothing there. It's all in her imagination. All this alarmist shit about ghosts and apparitions. She needs some time out, a holiday maybe. She doesn't really believe she saw anything. Does she? Before she was even aware of deciding to do it, she had turned on her heel and run back down the street.

Cars pass, lifting her hair with their backdraught. At the end of the road, she turns in the opposite direction to the tube station. She passes a Victorian iron bridge that drips cold, slimed water into her hair, a milliner's shop with hats poised on featureless, smooth dummy heads, a closed flower stall, the ground strewn with severed stalks, a church with its façade illuminated in greenish light and 'Ever thought about what might happen after death?' emblazoned on a sign outside. She finds it hard to understand how small turn-of-the-century terraces, industrial warehouses, huge powering roads and bars filled with boys with mobile phones can all exist together in one space.

She returns clutching a carton of milk against her jacket. A triangle of light is slanting out from the warehouse window. Marcus must be back. Relief opens out around her like wings.

Before letting the front door close, Lily is careful to turn on the light. It lasts just long enough for her to make it up the narrow staircase to the first-floor landing where she turns on the next. As she is climbing the flight of stairs that leads to their door, she hears, or she thinks she hears, something behind her. Later she'll go over and over it in her mind, trying to identify it, reclaim it, clarify what it was. But at the time, she stops on the stairs and turns her head. And as she does so, it's as if a very fine mist is brushing over her face, leaving the surface of her skin cool and moist.

I am not afraid, she tells herself, I am not. But her

legs move under her like pistons and she hurls herself at the door.

Aidan had heard the footsteps pounding up the stairs, but the door crashing open still makes him jump. Lily bursts into the room as if she's been pushed, losing her footing, stumbling to her knees. Aidan stares at her, astonished. A second ago he'd been deep in his book and now there's a woman sprawled across the flooboards in front of him.

'Are you all right?' he says, after a moment. He wonders if he should go over and help her up, but he hardly knows her for heaven's sake.

'Yeah,' she says, getting up and dusting down her skirt. 'Sorry about that. I must've . . . er . . . I must've tripped or something.'

'Right.'

She brandishes a milk carton at him in the manner of a terrorist with a hand grenade. 'Do you want something to drink?' she asks, her chest still heaving from her run up the stairs, the words jerking out between breaths. 'Hot chocolate?' she demands.

He hesitates. 'Um . . .' This girl really is quite odd.

'I'm having some.'

'OK.' He nods. 'Why not? Thanks.'

He hears her banging through the cupboard of pans, then the milk gulping out of the carton. He steals a surreptitious sidelong glance just as she is striking a match against its box – one, two, three times. When the flame catches, she puts her thumb quickly into her mouth, wincing. It must have burnt her.

She stands above the cooker, absorbed in watching the simmering milk, blowing her fringe away from her eyes. Her attraction, Aidan decides, as he watches her across the room, lies in her embodiment of opposites. The way her fragile, slight frame and her apparently meek silence are belied by that restive, elf-like glimmer in her eyes. She may not say much, but Aidan reckons she keeps an awful lot to herself; he's seen her with Marcus, listening to whatever he's saying, her lips shut and expressionless, but her eyes veiled, moving about his face, her mind churning over, thinking, thinking, always thinking.

Suddenly she's there beside him, handing him a mug with oiled, coloured bubbles at the rim. He takes it, looks up to thank her, and as he does so sees that she's young, can be no more than twenty-two, twenty-three. He gives a minute shake of his head as she takes a seat opposite him.

'Aidan?' Lily says. She is aware of the air around them, like a kind of soundless buzzing, but she doesn't care. She has to ask. This division in herself, between the rational and the irrational, has to end. She has to put a stop to it. And the only way to do that is with hard, immutable facts.

'Yes?'

'What happened . . . with Sinead?'

His head jerks up from his book. He looks at her for a moment, then starts blowing on the surface of his drink.

'How much do you know?' he says quietly.

'Nothing.'

'Then that's something you'll have to talk to Marcus about.'

'I don't feel I can. Can't you—'

'Lily,' and his voice is sharp-edged, 'I don't . . . I hardly know you. It's really none of my business.'

She looks at him. His eyes are so dark that his pupils are lost in the liquid ebony of the irises.

'What was she like?' She can't help herself.

Aidan sighs. His fingers work at a dog-ear on his book's cover, his nail flicking at the white-creased triangle. He's not going to tell me, she thinks, then something is released in his face. His fingers stop flicking. He gets up, shoving a bookmark into the pages.

'She . . .' He places the book on the table, carefully, as if it's a fragile artefact, and pushes his hands into the back pockets of his trousers. 'The kind of woman people fall in love with. Just like that.' He pauses, then adds: 'The kind of woman who collects broken hearts.'

Lily doesn't know what to say. Jealousy clots inside her like frog spawn, and she is surprised by it, discomforted.

He gives a little expellation of air, like laughter, yet not. 'Look,' he says, 'what I will say is this. If you have any sense you'll stay well away from Marcus.'

Later, Aidan and Marcus stand in the pooled light of the kitchen, Marcus stirring something on the cooker, Aidan clattering dishes around. Lily sits at the table, a newspaper spread before her, her fingerprints stained with its ink. Her mind clings to what Aidan said and images of those hearts keep appearing in her head. She imagines them, small, damp and pulsating, lying at the bottom of a handbag, or skewered together in rows on a kebab stick. Lined up on a windowsill like pot plants. Packed into the glovebox of a car.

'So if you wanted to render it in 3D, you'd have to — what? — use Quark?' Marcus is saying.

'Nah,' Aidan replies in a monotone. 'Quark wouldn't do it.'

There is a silence.

'So what would?' Marcus prompts.

'You could design it in Quark, if you wanted to. But CAD is what you need.'

'CAD and what else?'

'An animation package. But if you're going to download that — which you can off the internet — you're going to have to get a memory upgrade. It'll just keep crashing otherwise and you can't have that while you're rendering because it'll just get fucked and pixellated every five mintues.'

'How much will that be?'

'Couple of hundred quid. Maybe more. It depends.'

'Lily,' Marcus says suddenly. She is deep in an article about a woman who disappeared the previous month, so that when she looks at him she feels disconnected and distracted. 'Have you eaten?'

'Not yet, but I'll cook when you've finished.'

'Have some of this. There's plenty. I've made far too much for just me.' He gives a short, mirthless laugh. 'Can't seem to get used to cooking for one person,' he mutters, more to himself than either her or Aidan.

'Well . . . if you're sure.'

'I am. It's curry. Do you like curry?' He is looking at

her, eyebrows raised, the muscles in his arm clenched from his stirring.

'Lovely. Curry. Yes. Thanks very much.'

Aidan swills water over a plate in the sink. Their terse and incomprehensible conversation seems to have come to a standstill. Marcus walks from the fridge to the table and holds out a green bottle. 'Beer?'

She raises her eyes to his. His mouth is curved into a half-smile. As she looks, it splits into a full, expansive grin. She looks away, smiling herself, and sees two things happening simultaneously: Aidan seeing them and his face contracting in something like disgust, dropping the plate into the sink; and, in the reflection in a chrome bowl on the table, an elongated shape, behind her.

Marcus nudges the rim of the fridge-cold bottle into the flesh of her upper arm. 'Beer? Lily?'

'Um.' She is twisting around, despite herself, to see behind her. Where is it? Where does it go when it's not here, when she can't see it? Does it lurk behind doors or – the idea horrifies Lily – in other rooms, waiting for her? 'Beer. Er, yes. Please.'

Aidan passes them, heading for his room. The walls of the huge space boom and resound as he slams his doors shut.

Marcus heaps rice then yellow curry on to two plates. He is talking – something about the curry and a place in Kerala, but she is finding it hard to concentrate on what he's saying. The room around them seems live, dangerous with possibility, like a severed electrical flex. As she is raising her first forkful to her mouth, she feels his thigh against hers and she lurches back, food falling off the fork.

Marcus laughs, 'You're very nervy, aren't you?' And he moves in closer, his voice dropping to a whisper. 'Are you afraid of me?'

There are curry-stained grains of rice scattered around Lily's plate. She plucks at them. 'Afraid? Of you?' From here she only has a vista of the end of the warehouse, half of the kitchen and the door to the bathroom. There's a whole mass of air behind her, stretching to the long windows and the bedrooms, that she can't see. She casts a quick look over her shoulder. 'Afraid?' she repeats. 'No. Of course not. Don't be ridiculous.'

'What went wrong, then?' His voice is a murmur now, and his hand is pressing down on her thigh.

'Um, well.' Lily does a swift all-round check. Still nothing. 'I thought I saw . . . I thought I saw something.'

'What?'

'Er. Well, I'm not sure.' She looks again over her shoulder. The end of the room is in darkness. It's the black void that frightens her. There could be anything in it.

'Marcus.' She turns back to him. His face is inches from hers. He is looking at where her shirt opens at her throat. This has to stop, she tells herself, you have to know the truth. 'Can I ask you a question?'

Something alters in his expression. Tiny muscles round his eyes tighten. Lines appear at the side of his mouth. 'Sure,' he says, leaning back, 'ask away.'

'Well.' Lily swallows. The roof of her mouth feels dry. Her fingertips clutch at the cold, wet column of her glass. 'You see, I was wondering—'

Two feet away, the phone rings. They look at each other. She closes her mouth.

''Scuse me,' Marcus says and gets up, walks away from the table, lifts the receiver. She hears him say, 'Hi. How's it going?'

Lily lifts the food to her mouth and chews. Then, with that kind of sentience where information is elided with knowledge, when even without any proof or warning you just know something to be true, she realises that Sinead is sitting in the chair next to her. Lily swallows, the lump of food scraping at the soft part of her throat. There is a strange, collapsed feeling at the front of her face, like tears or hayfever. Her hand, grasping a fork, shivers in mid-air. She has never felt colder. She glares down at her plate, lecturing herself fiercely and rapidly with words like gunfire: This is nothing, get a grip, come on, Lily, this is nonsense, you know it is.

She slides her eyes inside their sockets. Sinead is there at the table, opposite Marcus's abandoned plate. She is staring, with great concentration and intent, into Lily's face, one hand covering her mouth.

Then Marcus is pulling back his chair with an atonal scrape against the floor. 'Sorry,' he is saying, 'it was some guy at the office who's having a problem. They've got this big hand-in and they're all gearing up for an all-nighter and—' He breaks off. 'What's wrong?' he says. He leans towards her, his face creased in concern, putting his hand over hers. 'You look . . . What is it?'

Lily looks from Sinead to him and back again. Sinead has removed her hand and her lips are moving, as if she's speaking, as if she's trying to tell her something. Marcus can't see her. *He can't see her.* He doesn't know she's there. How can she tell him that sitting opposite him is—

'Nothing,' she says, with an attempt at a smile. He mustn't know. He mustn't ever know. 'I'm fine.'

Lily stands at the basin. Marcus has disappeared into his study to take another call from the office, and Aidan has stayed in his lift-shaft room since dinner. She has listened for him coming out to make a cup of tea or to go to the toilet even. But nothing. What on earth is he doing in there, and what is it animators do anyway? And why would he say that about Marcus? Marcus is supposed to be his best friend.

She has a length of waxed cotton wound round each finger and she is sawing it through the gaps in her teeth. She makes herself hum fragments of a song she heard earlier in the day on the radio at the office. Without warning, something falls from the top of the bathroom cabinet, striking her on the head. The floss jerks up to cut into her gum. Red soaks quickly into the white string. Lily looks down. In the basin is a a medicinal-looking foil-covered strip with the word 'Femodene' emblazoned across it, days of the week connected by tiny black arrows. She picks it up. The strip's purple foil crackles in her hand. Tiny round pills rattle inside their sealed foil holders. About a third of them have been punctured from their casing.

Anger swarms at the back of her head, unexpected and potent. 'Right, that's it!' she shouts. 'I've had enough of you!'

She flicks the blood-stained floss into the toilet bowl and, with both hands, twists the foil strip until it cracks. Pills pop out and bounce around the basin's curves, disappearing down the eye of the plug. She pushes any remaining pills out of their cases and turns on the taps full so that the basin is flooded with icy water. She imagines the tiny white pills dissolving into milkiness as they are flushed far, far away. Then she crumples the strip into itself, piercing her palm as she does so, and flings it into the bin.

'See that?' she cries to the empty room. 'See that? I'm not afraid of you! I'm not! So just – just piss off!'

Her voice sounds reedy and weak to her, the high ceiling above her swallowing her words. The shower curtain moves slightly.

Lily pushes out through the door, not wanting to look back into the room, not wanting to see the mirror – she has this fear that the reflection thrown back might not be her own. She marches down the dark warehouse and through Marcus's door. In the semi-light she can see that he's lying on his back in bed, his face turned away.

'Marcus,' she whispers, climbing into the bed and wrapping herself around his warmth. He's naked and she is wondering if he always sleeps naked, if he never gets cold in this unheated crypt of a flat, if he always slept naked with—

And she is keeping her eyes shut tight because she doesn't care if she's there, she doesn't want to see, because this way even if she is there she is winning because she's not going to open her eyes to see.

'Hang on a sec,' he says, and leaves the bed, and the surprise makes her eyes lift and she sees the darkened room and it seems to be tilted slightly but maybe it's only because her head is tipped back on the pillow, and there is only her on the bed and Marcus leaning over a drawer in his desk. She turns her head fractionally and before she can clamp her eyes shut again she sees a minuscule draught run along the wall, lifting the papers stuck there, one by one. But he is back, and she is going to do this, she will do this, this will happen. And then he is inside her very suddenly, it seems all the way, and the shock makes her gasp and before she realises it her mouth and her eyes are stretched wide open and she can't shut them again because everything is happening at once, and right beside her, crouched down next to the bed, is Sinead, her head angled to look right into Lily's face, her features as clear as if she were real and alive and flesh.

Lily has to clamp her mouth shut and press her face into Marcus's shoulder, which is damp with salt and moving over her. It's as if she's split into two separate existences, one that can only feel and the other that can only listen to the other's breathing and think of the thing crouching right next to her. But she is in the grip of determination to do this thing, to get it done, to have it out of the way and behind her. Somewhere in her mind is the conviction that, after the first time, she'll go, she'll leave them alone, she'll vanish and never come back, that the very act of Marcus sleeping with another woman will make her disappear.

When it is finished she waits until she feels back in herself before she opens her eyes. It takes a while for her to be able to see anything through the thick, pitchy dark that surrounds her. Then objects start sinking into grey – the chair in front of the desk, the window frame, Marcus's form next to her, asleep. Nothing else.

Because she's not sure if she should stay, she returns to her room. She puts her hand to the wall next to her bed. The paint feels ridged, unreadable as Braille. Sinead painted these walls. Those imperceptible ridges were made by the fibres of her brush dragging through the paint. At some point, Sinead stood on this very spot and daubed wet, vibrant blue colour on to these walls, utterly unaware that Lily would ever sleep within them.

Lily would like to scratch them with her nails, over and over, scraping off the paint, paring them back to the bare, colourless plaster.

When she returns to the flat the next evening, six or seven people are sitting around the table. Plumes of blue smoke rise to the ceiling and low, throbbing music plays in the corner. Marcus turns. 'Hi,' he says. 'This is Lily,' he tells them all, 'our new flatmate.'

They nod or say, 'Hi' or 'Nice to meet you.' Lily nods from the door then walks around them to the kitchen.

She pulls two slices of bread from a bag, their texture damp and spongy, and slots them into the toaster, eyeing the group. A woman with a short red bob and black hipster trousers is saying: 'Frankly, Tim, I think they should be paying you at least five grand more. I mean, you got your Part Three – what was it, two years ago? You want to know what I think? I think you've long outgrown their design strategy.'

Lily smears butter on to her toast. The knife edge rasps against the crisp surface. Bob-haired woman glances her way.

'Has anyone seen the new Parks and Simpson building in Manchester?' says a man in a grey army fatigue shirt. 'Designed by some year-off students, apparently, and signed off by one of the partners.'

'And you can tell,' says Marcus, standing with a wine bottle gripped between his legs, pulling at the cork with a slim, steel handle. 'Looks like a self-build scheme.'

Everyone laughs. Lily swallows down clods of toast, watching as the gathering breaks up into smaller conversations. From the other side of the room is a shrill, insistent ringing. The phone.

'I'll get it,' she says, putting down her plate. Marcus glances up at her and smiles. As she walks towards it, she hears the grey-shirted man ask him, 'How are things?'

Marcus's back is towards her so she can't make out his reply. She hears him say, 'Well,' but the rest is lost: she can make out 'she' and 'me', then 'she' again, and 'each other'.

She lifts the receiver. 'Hello?'

'Lily, it's Sarah.'

'Hi, how are you doing?' The connection crashes and wanes. 'Sarah? Are you still there?'

'Yeah. Can you hear me now? I can't talk long, I'm about to go into a film. But I spoke to that friend of mine.'

'What friend?'

'The journalist.'

'Oh.' Lily glances back at Marcus, but he's standing up, cutting up something on the table with a long silver knife in each hand.

'He says there's nothing on her. Nothing at all.'

'Really?' She turns back to face the wall, whispering now. 'Are you sure? You got the name right?'

'Yeah. Wilson, Sinead. He couldn't find any deaths registered under that name. He went back two years.'

Lily bites her lip, pressing the phone to her ear.

'Lily? Are you there?'

'Yes,' she says, 'I'm here.'

'He says that it could mean she died abroad or . . .'

'Or?'

She hears Sarah sigh. 'Or that her death might be unresolved.'

'Unresolved?'

'If the coroner's still investigating it. Or the police. Or if they haven't got a body yet, in the case of disappearance or . . . or murder.'

Lily stares at the framed picture in front of her. It's made up of rows and rows of people's faces, all grinning for the camera. So many teeth, strung across their faces like necklaces. 'Right,' she says. 'I see.'

'Listen, I have to go. You'll call me later, won't you?'

'OK.'

'Promise?'

'Yup.'

Lily wakes to feel Marcus's hand on her breast, his mouth on hers. She turns over, the sheet tightening around her. She is aware of being very hot. Things seem to be quite far on: Marcus is naked and so is she. She can't quite work out in the dark the orientation of his body in relation to hers. Bits of him float and collide, disembodied, against hers, and her hands flail like webbed feet against the sheet, searching for a hold on him.

She hears his breath next to her ear and she forgets, in her vague and bleared state, that she has to close her eyes.

But there's nothing there. Her room is empty. The walls, the ceiling, the door, the windows all look blissfully as they should. Her mind is a sheer, measureless blank as she comes; he holds her to him very tightly, cradling her head in his hand, as if comforting her.

She sits bolt upright suddenly, decisive, determined. Marcus is stumbling about the room, trying to locate some clothes, muttering about needing the toilet.

'Marcus,' she says, 'I have to ask you this. What happened to Sinead?'

The name makes him flinch as if she's slapped him, and he freezes. 'Why do you ask?'

'Why do I ask?' she repeats, her impatience leaking out. 'Marcus, for God's sake, we're living together,' she gestures around the room, 'sleeping together and . . . I mean, this was a huge thing that happened in your life and I know nothing about it. Nothing at all.'

He ties the dressing-gown cord slowly, and she sees that his hands are trembling. 'Well,' he says, 'the thing is . . .' In one movement he reaches his palm towards the bed and lowers himself on to a corner of it. She can see only his profile, etched against the glow of the streetlight outside the window. 'It's quite difficult to talk about.' His voice is even, level, reined in. He doesn't look at her, but winds the cord round and round his wrist. 'When something like that happens it's hard to . . . to organise it . . . in your own thoughts so that you comprehend it, let alone trying to put it into words so that somebody else can. I'm sorry.' He shakes his head as if he has water trapped in his ears. 'Do you know what I mean?'

'Sort of.'

'I will . . . I will tell you . . . at some point. I promise. Just not at the moment. If that's OK with you.' He grips her ankle through the duvet. 'Is that OK with you?'

'Yes,' she says, struggling to sound kind and understanding, when what she really wants to do is yell, no of course it bloody isn't, just tell me. 'Of course.' She pulls her face into a strained smile.

He gets up, stopping in the doorway. 'I'll be back in a sec,' he whispers.

She looks up. He is framed by light, half his face illuminated, half invisible in dark. Behind him, at the window where the building falls away to the pavement, a black-haired girl hovers, moving, shifting, crackling, agitation simmering in her face, her hands pressed to the xylophone bones of her chest.

Aidan waits in line, a newspaper in one hand and the money to pay for it in the other. A man at the front of the queue is paying by credit card, and making very heavy weather of finding a pen to sign his name. People around Aidan tut and sigh and shift from foot to foot.

From his back pocket his phone gives a single, plaintive cheep. Aidan pours the coins into the hand clutching the newspaper and pulls it out. He has a deep love, combined with a certain admiration and gratitude, for the items of technology in his life that he would never admit to anyone. He believes the person who designed his phone a genius: sleek but durable aluminium casing, tiny aerial, curved but unslippery buttons, and a blue light that comes on when he touches the keypad. The tiny screen tells him that he's got a text message from Marcus.

Aidan looks around the cramped shop. An undergrown teenager with hair shaved down to his skull is standing by a stand of CDs, staring straight ahead of him. There is something oddly fixed and static about him. Then Aidan sees that with one hand, he is shovelling CDs into his coat. Their eyes meet for a second: the boy's arm hesitates, then reaches to button his coat. Aidan looks away, looks back at his phone. The boy flits past him and out of the door. Aidan hits the erase button on Marcus's message.

'There's a bar that's just opened, done by someone I really like. I'm going there now to have a look.' Marcus is pulling on his jacket. 'D'you want to come?'

In her room, she kicks off her shoes and slides her feet into a different pair. She pulls off her sweater, which smells of the Underground and traffic fumes and air-conditioning, and puts on a cardigan from a pile beside her bed. It's just been washed so she has to stretch and resettle it to the shape of her torso. Her hair crackles with static as she walks back towards Marcus, standing by the door.

She is heading for the road to the tube, but Marcus reaches for her hand. 'Let's get a cab,' he says, nodding towards the main road.

The bar has a floor made of glass bricks, lit by bulbs from the basement. The expanse of light underneath her and no discernible floor makes Lily feel giddy and malcoordinated. She has to suppress a desire to cling gecko-like to the grey walls, has to force herself to balance on this skinless block of light.

They sit at a table in the corner and she touches the angled join where the walls meet. Marcus has placed in front of her a tall glass filled with pink liquid. Cubes of ice shift and jostle in its depths. She puts her lips to its surface and her teeth and tongue fill with the bitter tinge of citrus fruit, then the afterkick of vodka. Marcus is drinking beer from a bottle, its neck foaming around a sliver of lime.

He has met someone he knows. A man with very tight green trousers. The corner of his mouth drools a cigarette. His ash falls in flecks to the surface of Lily's drink until she moves it out of his way. At her eye level is his exposed navel. A very neat line of black hair, so neat it could have been drawn on with a marker pen, runs from his belly button to disappear into the waistband of his trousers.

'I've never been to Dallas,' Marcus is saying.

'You must go,' the man says, with a kind of religious fervour, and, as if to emphasise Dallas's wondrousness, touches Marcus on the shoulder with his cigarette hand. A snake of grey ash is left on Marcus's sleeve. He doesn't notice.

Dallas. Funny word. Backwards, it spells 'salad'. Almost. She takes in another mouthful of her drink and looks at Marcus. His brow is creased and he is holding himself slightly away from this man. He doesn't like him, she sees.

'But have you seen the one in Reykjavik?' Marcus asks.

Reykjavik? He's been to Reykjavik? When did you go to Reykjavik? she wants to shout. Her mind is filled with an image of him and Sinead swimming naked, hair slicked to their heads, in a steaming, sulphurous pool. She thinks: I don't know anything about you.

'Sorry about that.' Marcus turns back to her when the man finally leaves.

'Who was he?'

'Oh, some bloke.' He flicks his hand in the man's direction. 'He goes out with someone I used to work with.'

'When did you go to Reykjavik?'

'Reykjavik?' He has to think. 'Two years ago? Something like that.'

'Right.' She nods. 'How old are you?'

'What?'

'I said, how old are you?'

Marcus laughs. 'Why? What is all this?'

'I just realised I hardly know anything about you. So I thought I'd ask.'

'Oh.' He smiles. 'Well, I'm thirty.'

'Where were you born?'

'France.'

'Any brothers or sister?'

'A sister.'

'Younger?'

'Older.' Marcus laughs again. 'Anything else?'

How did your girlfriend die? Lily thinks. 'When did you decide to become an architect?' she asks instead.

'When I was nine.' He up-ends his bottle, taking another swig. 'I was ill, off school, lying on a sofa. My mum had, you know, brought down the duvet while I watched TV. I had chicken pox. Anyway, I saw this Open University programme about architecture, and that's when I decided.'

'I envy you,' Lily says.

'Do you?' He is surprised. 'Why?'

'You've got a vocation.'

'But doesn't everyone? I mean, on some level?'

'No.' She shakes her head emphatically. 'Not at all.'

He looks confused, as if he wants to ask more but is unsure what. Lily doesn't want to talk about it, so she says, 'Do you like this place, then?'

Marcus looks up at the ceiling, his throat whitening with the tilt of his head, then at the wall ahead of them. 'It's very fashionable, all this brutal, utility stuff. And I do like it. But this place,' he rubs the underside of his wrist with his fingers, 'is too contrived. It's a bit formulaic.'

'Is it?'

'Well, it's like they've got a list of all the elements a trendy bar should have and ticked them off one by one. Exposed pipes, distressed concrete walls, iron banisters, back-lit bar, glass brick floor, aluminium furniture. You know?'

'Yes,' Lily looks around again, 'yes. I see what you mean. What are your buildings like then?'

Marcus laughs. 'My buildings? Non-existent. I haven't built anything yet, only bits of buildings. That's how it works. The one I was working on in New York – I designed the staircase and the ceiling.'

'Right.'

'You need to set up on your own if you want to build your own stuff, but I'm not really ready to do that yet. Got to put in a few more years in other offices first and do competitions in my spare time.'

Lily plucks a peanut from the bowl on the table between them and drops it into her mouth. 'Tell me about Aidan,' she says, then coughs. The peanut is covered in a kind of dusty coating.

'Aidan?' His eyes flick over her face quickly. 'What's he got to do with your interrogation?'

'Nothing,' she croaks, still coughing. 'I'm just interested.'

'Well, what do you want to know?'

She tries to swallow, but she keeps on coughing. Marcus

asks her if she's OK. The peanut bounces around the inside of her mouth. She takes a swig of her drink. When she's gulped it down, the peanut has disappeared. She's so relieved she grins at him. 'How long have you known him?' she asks, with her new, empty mouth.

'Years. We were at school together.'

'Are you good friends?'

'Me and Aidan?' Marcus shifts in his seat, picks at the label on his bottle. 'Yeah. He's my best friend.'

Without warning, a violent cough erupts from her oesophagus. She hacks and splutters, water springing into her eyes, her hand clamped over her lips, her lungs labouring for air.

'Are you all right?' she hears him ask, concerned. 'Do you want me to bang you on the back?'

'Nh-nh,' she manages, shaking her head. The peanut seems to have reappeared in her mouth. She pushes it with the end of her tongue between two teeth and crunches it into powder. She breathes in deeply, then says, as if nothing has happened, 'How long has he lived with you?'

'Not long. A couple of months. He'll be moving out soon. He's been living all over the place for years – the States, Japan, Germany – and now he's moved back here permanently, and he's bought a flat. He's only staying with me until he gets the keys for his new place.'

'Oh. I find him . . .' She pauses. 'He's a bit . . . unapproachable, isn't he?'

'You think?' He considers this. 'Perhaps. He's . . . he's been slightly . . . going through a funny time recently.

Moving back here and . . . and everything. He's a very talented man, you know, our Aidan.'

'Is he? What does he do exactly?'

'He's an animator.'

'I know, but what does that mean? What does he do all day? Draw cartoons and stuff?'

'Well, a bit of that. But he works on films mainly. Animated feature films. That kind of thing.' Marcus drains his bottle swiftly. 'Another drink?' he asks, getting up.

In the cab on the way back, he reaches over, takes her hand and folds it into his. She stares at her hand in his lap as if it is no longer connected to her. How did it get there and what is it doing there? He leans over and his lips brush her face. Tarmac rumbles beneath them. The taxi dips in and out of cones of orange light. In the rear-view mirror, Lily sees the eyes of the driver swivel towards them, then away. Marcus lifts her hair and presses his mouth to her neck. It's an expansive gesture, and there is something about it that makes her uneasy. The ends of her hair fall back into his face too soon. His hand travels up too far into empty air. She thinks: My hair is too short for that. She thinks: that gesture belongs to Sinead.

At the flat, he pulls her into his room and takes off her clothes one by one, dropping them to the floor.

'Let's turn the light off,' she says.

In the morning she is waiting for Lily, sitting on the washing machine. Lily nearly cries out, but clamps shut her mouth just in time. Her throat is prickly with thirst after the alcohol last night, but she cannot bring herself to go near her. The kitchen taps are only a short reach from the washing-machine, and to get to the bathroom, she'd have to pass through the gap between the counter and the machine. What if she reached for her, touched her, grasped her?

Lily brings her clothes into the big room and dumps them on the floor, getting dressed with Sinead sitting just ten feet away. Lily stares at her and she stares at Lily as Lily slides on her underwear, yanks a sweater over her head, pulls up the side zip of her skirt. Dressing in the bedroom while this is out here would be worse. At least she knows where it is if she keeps her eyes on it. One foot dangles over the washing-machine's convex, eye-like door, the other is tucked underneath her. Her fingers rest in her lap, twisting, curling, knotting into each other.

After that, it gets worse.

Lily wakes with a jolt, knowing somehow that she's been standing there for some time. She is lying in the sarcophagus hollow made by Sinead's body in the mattress. Marcus sleeps next to her, the covers pulled up round his shoulders.

Sinead is standing, pressed in between the bed and the wall. Lily's leg lies alongside her. She is dressed only in a vest and knickers. Her arms and legs are pale and smooth as soap. Lily's breath rattles in her throat. She's been staring at them while they slept. Her face is drawn, the texture of candle-wax, a small V between her brows. Lily cannot look at it for long, but she sees more misery there than she can ever imagine.

The moment stretches. The room is jagged with the dark mounds of furniture; a vase looms on the table, the lamp's face is angled towards her. Sinead seems to be breathing, the blunted peaks of her breasts rising and falling beneath the vest.

'Please, please, please.' The muttered words break from Lily's lips. 'What is it that you want?' She clenches her eyes shut, her fingers gripping Marcus's shoulder. He sighs and turns towards her. Everything is icy: her hands, her hair, her limbs. The heat from Marcus fizzles out as it reaches her skin. She can feel, metres and metres below the infrastructure of the building and the streets, the shaking of the first Underground trains of the morning.

When she opens her eyes again, she sees that Sinead is creeping in slowed-down, mesmeric steps, as if walking through water, towards the door.

Lily moves her dry tongue over her lips. Her teeth are

93

banging against each other with the cold, trapping wedges of her mouth. There is a swelling pressure in her bladder, but nothing, nothing would persuade her to leave this bed.

Then she is everywhere: leaning against the fridge, behind doors, reflected in the windows, standing at the basin, crouched in the wardrobe in the morning, hanging around the flat door, sitting straight-backed on the sofa. She is always watching Lily, fixing her with a look that seems to veer between sadness and a kind of soft frown, almost like confusion or concern.

And it seems to Lily that the flat itself is conspiring against her. Doors swing back in her face. Locks stick around her key. Plugs spark under her touch. The refrigerator refuses to open, then yields easily to Aidan's hand. The hot-water taps give only cold water then scalding, skin-peeling jets. Stacked arrangements of tins crumble and clatter if she so much as passes. The blue flame of the cooker ring gutters out, leaving wreaths of sour gas hanging in the air. The phone rings then cuts dead. A bike in the hallway crashes to its side. Her clothes slip their hangers and lie in creased, lifeless heaps at the bottom of the wardrobe. Stair-edges seem to shift and multiply beneath her feet, tripping her, leaving a grey-mauve line along her forehead. Table corners leap out at her. The kettle boils but won't switch itself off, filling the kitchen with burning billows of steam that condense in a transparent slick on the walls that makes Marcus tut and run his finger down it.

It's as if she seethes from every door lock, every cupboard hinge, every lightbulb, every nail, every brick, the putty holding in the windows, the water that circulates in the radiators.

Sleep eludes Lily. Waking hours gnaw at those she spends unconscious. Violet shadows leak into the hollows under her eyes. She tears at her nails until the skin is pale, peeled and raw, her fingertips tender, her fingerprints blurred. Headaches pincer her temples by the afternoon. She dozes on buses, misses her stop, and trips as she stumbles off to the pavement. She finds she has begun forgetting words: in the middle of a sentence, she'll be pulled up short by a blank in her mind. She'll know the shape of the word, she'll be able to envisage the object, but its syllables aren't where she usually finds them.

She is sitting on her bed one morning, getting ready to pick up Laurence, bending over to tie her trainers when her nose catches a scent: faint, sensual. Jasmine? But she knows it – it clings to the room she lives in, to certain cushions on the sofa, to a shelf in the bathroom. She doesn't move, but crouches over her shoes, waiting. The air around her seems to thicken and curdle. The scent becomes stronger. She feels it scorching a path along her nose and the back of her mouth until she can almost taste it, feel it smarting at her eyelids. She blinks, water rimming the edges of her vision. In front of her there seems to be a shadow. Or less of a shadow than a shape, as if oxygen is densifying, its molecules buzzing faster and closer and closer together. She can't see it if she looks straight at it, but if she blinks at it askance, the elements in the atmosphere seem to be pulling themselves into a shape. A definite shape. The shape of a pair of feet, standing on the boards before her.

Lily gulps at the air, but the scent is so strong she almost chokes. She wants to shut up her lips and nostrils like a seal under water. She can't look up, can't raise her head to see what she knows will be towering above her. Her fingers fumble with her laces, which have become as slippery as liquorice between her frozen knuckles. She doesn't wait but makes a run for the door, laces snagging at her feet.

'Relax,' Jodie commands, her body curved like a comma over the steering wheel.

'I am relaxed,' Aidan replies and, as if to prove it, spreads his fingers out on his thighs. 'I'm calm.' He pulls his face into a fixed, false grin. 'I am enjoying myself,' he says, in the robot voice they invented as children.

His sister shoots him a look. She is clearly trying to come up with a retort.

'Eyes on the road, please,' he incants, in the same voice.

'You are so—' Jodie begins, and the car veers towards the line of parked vehicles at the side of the road. Aidan puts out his hand and nudges the wheel.

'Get off!' she shrieks. 'I'm driving!'

'I know you are. I just don't want you to take all those wing mirrors with you.'

'Like scalps,' she says, with relish.

'Er, perhaps. Hang a left here, would you?'

'*Hang* a left?' she repeats, mocking. 'You've spent too much time in America.'

'I'd never deny it,' he says quickly, then: 'Handbrake.

Into neutral. OK. First gear. Foot off the clutch.' The car leapfrogs forward then judders to a halt. Someone behind blasts their horn, three perfect semi-quavers.

'You impatient bloody bastard boy racer!' Jodie yells at the rear-view mirror, yanking at the handbrake, then mutters to herself about the restarting procedure.

'Road rage,' he warns.

'Shut up.'

'Foot off the clutch slowly,' Aidan says, 'slowly, slowly. That's it.' The car glides forward in a steady curve. 'Perfect.'

Jodie pulls the gearstick back into second. 'I have to pass this time, I have to,' she moans softly.

'You will.'

'I have to,' she repeats. 'I'll never get promoted otherwise. And I really don't want to be one of those women who can't drive. You know the ones.' She sighs and slumps down in the driving seat. 'Oh, God. I'm never going to be able to drive.'

'Stop being such a doom queen,' he says, eyeing a beige Mercedes approaching down the middle of the road. 'Cut your speed for Mr Swanky up ahead.' Jodie presses the brake. 'You're going to be fine. Is Rory taking you out much for practice runs?'

'Ha,' she barks.

'What do you mean, "ha"?'

'Ha.' She shrugs. 'Just ha. You know.'

'No, I don't.'

They pull up rather abruptly at a zebra crossing. Her face, when he looks across at her, turns from orange to pale and back again in the flashing Belisha-beacon light.

'Oh,' she shrugs again, 'I just didn't think it would do our relationship much good, him teaching me to drive.'

'Mmm.' Aidan puts his head on one side, watching her. 'I can see that.'

People stream in front of the bonnet, pushing prams, bikes, scooters.

'He's being a bit . . .' she scratches at the raised red parabola of an insect bite on her upper arm '. . . wearing at the moment.'

'In what way?'

'I don't know.' Her fingernails scrabble at her arm. 'Too attentive,' she says at last.

'Too attentive?'

'Yeah.'

'How?'

She considers this while she moves the car over the zebra crossing and out into a river-like expanse of empty Tarmac. 'The other day, for example . . . you know I've just moved into my new flat?'

'Uh-huh.'

'Well, he goes out and buys me an Ordnance Survey map of the area from 1884 or something.' She looks over at him, pointedly. 'And the house is on it.'

Aidan frowns, puzzled. 'Yeah?'

'Well,' she sighs, exasperated, as if he's just said something really stupid, 'don't you think that's just a little bit . . . too much?'

'It sounds nice.'

'Nice!' She pounces on the word like an aggravated

cat. 'Nice! Exactly! That's exactly my point.' She sits back, satisfied.

'But, Jodie—' He stops. They are pulling up behind a car at a large junction. A building site looms up on one side of them; a park sweeps away from them on the other. Coming out of the green, curlicued gates of the park is a figure that makes his words evaporate, dissipate into his lungs. A familiar figure is walking along the pavement, arms crossed over a bag held in front of her. The low, cold wind blows her hair flat against her head. Aidan watches as she waits for the pedestrian crossing lights to change.

She passes within six feet of the car. He is nervous, afraid that she might turn her head and see him, sitting, hands idle, in the passenger seat of his own car. And as she comes closer to them he sees that her lips are animated, moving slightly, almost imperceptibly. For a moment he thinks she must be listening to her headphones and mouthing the words to a song only she can hear. But he sees her hair, stretched sleek behind her ears. No headphones. She looks white, gaunt, ill even. Her lips conduct a secret conversation with something or someone, her eyes fixed to the paving stones in front of her.

'Co-pilot Nash,' Jodie is shouting, 'calling co-pilot Nash.'

Aidan turns, blinking, towards his sister. 'Sorry,' he says.

'What's up with you? You look like you've seen a ghost. Who is that woman?' Jodie demands, leaning forward to look after her.

'Oh,' he says. 'No one.' He claps his hands together,

rousing himself. 'Green light,' he points up through the windscreen. 'Let's go.'

As the car pulls away, he looks into the side-view mirror and sees Lily's back receding into the distance, moving away from him. He feels somehow ashamed at having seen her here, as if in some way he's violated her privacy, her secret self. Then the car moves around a corner and she is gone.

Lily's lost her. She'd been right there, right beside her, just a few seconds ago, saying something about how her sister has torn the ligaments in her ankle. But now Lily has found herself suddenly alone in the crowd, a man with a toddler on his shoulders to her right where Sarah should have been, and in front of her a woman with a large wicker basket hooked over her arm.

Lily hefts the weighty terracotta pot holding the lemon geranium from one hip to the other and strains up on tiptoe in search of Sarah's red-hatted head. They are in a Sunday-morning flower market near the flat. The pavements are lined with stalls, plants, shrubs, star-faced flowers, trays of herbs, ferns, bunches of holly. People seethe along the road in groups and currents, holding foliage and blooms aloft. Music pumps from one stall and a young boy thrusts a cluster of pink petals into her face. 'Gladioli!' he yells. 'Four for a pound!'

She turns round, turns back, then heads for the pavement, which is lined by the bare wooden backs of the stalls, where the crowds are thinned out. Sarah's lemon geranium is covered in fine, invisible hairs, which prickle and itch at her. She walks the length of the market, then back, along the other side of the street. No sign of Sarah. The sun strains through the piled, grey cloud and beneath her feet there are stray, blackened flowers, flattened to the pavement. When she reaches the place where she'd last seen her, irritation overtakes her. She stamps down the pot and sets her fists on her hips. This is ridiculous. She'll never find her again. She'll take the bloody geranium and go back to the flat and hope that Sarah follows her there.

She lifts it again and starts forcing a path through the people, sidestepping bodies, turning sideways to get through. And suddenly she sees her, standing beside a stall crammed with lurid, sharp purple flowers.

'Where were you? I lost you,' Lily says when she reaches her. 'Here, take this,' she hands her the geranium pot, 'it weighs a bloody tonne. Where did you . . .' she falters, then stops. Sarah is gazing at her, frowning. 'What's the matter?' Lily asks.

Sarah sighs, looks up the road, twiddling her hair, then back at Lily. 'What's the matter with me?' she says. 'Nothing. Absolutely nothing. Apart from the fact that my closest friend never tells me anything.'

Lily is taken aback. 'What do you mean?'

'You. I mean you.'

'What about me? What haven't I told you?'

'You haven't told me anything!' Sarah cries.

Lily is baffled. 'About what? I don't—'

'I want to know,' she cuts across her.

'Want to know what?'

'What's wrong.'

'Nothing,' Lily shoves her hands in her pockets crossly. 'Nothing's wrong. Why are you being so weird?'

'*I*'m not being weird.'

'Neither am I!'

The two girls glare at each other. Sarah crosses her arms and then, just as quickly, points her finger at Lily's face. 'Something's going on with you,' she says.

Lily swallows. 'This is ridiculous. Come on,' she turns round, 'let's go.'

Sarah holds her ground. 'There is,' she asserts. 'Something's going on. I know it.'

'Know what?'

'I know it,' she says, 'because I know you. I was standing here and I saw you before you saw me, and I was watching you come along the road. And you looked . . .' She hesitates.

'I looked what?' Lily scoffs.

'Hollow,' Sarah says, quiet now.

'Hollow?'

'Yes. Hollow.'

'That's bullshit. Hollow? You can't look hollow.'

'You did. You looked . . . empty and . . . and worn out and . . . you looked hollow, I'm telling you. Like a part of you was gone or missing or something.'

'Oh, for heaven's sake, it's too cold to stand around having a stupid conversation. Let's just go.'

Sarah seizes her wrist. 'What is it, Lily?' Lily tries to withdraw, but Sarah holds her tighter. 'Is it Marcus?'

Lily pulls her wrist free. 'No.' She looks down at her feet. 'No, it's not.'

'What then?' Sarah sighs. 'Look, Lily, for weeks now you've been . . . all funny and preoccupied. And you look like death warmed up. And I can't take it any more. What is it?'

Lily shrugs, silent.

'It's Marcus, isn't it? It must be.'

'No,' Lily says, 'it isn't him, it's . . .'

Sarah leans closer to her. 'What? It's what?'

'Well . . .'

'Yes?'

Lily closes her eyes. 'It's his girlfriend.'

'Sinead?' Sarah says.

Lily nods.

Sarah takes her arm. 'Let's get a coffee.'

They sit on a wooden bench in a narrow alleyway filled with hard-edged winter sunlight. Sarah has bought coffee and rolls from a small kiosk in the brick wall behind them.

'But, Lily,' she is saying, 'everyone has a past.'

'I know that,' Lily says.

'And the people who haven't aren't interesting enough to bother with.'

'I know, I know.'

'Then what is it? That you still don't know what happened to her? Is that still bothering you?'

'No,' Lily says, then: 'Yes. I don't know. I suppose,' she leans her head on the back of the bench, 'I suppose it's that it doesn't feel like she is past.'

Sarah looks at her. 'You mean you don't think he's over her?'

Lily flicks crumbs from her lap. 'Mmm.'

'Well, she did die, for God's sake. I mean—' Sarah stops. 'What I mean is, it's not a situation . . . I mean,

it's unusual. However she died, it's unusually difficult . . .
not difficult . . . heavy. It's an unusually heavy situation for . . . him to be in. For you to be in.' She fiddles with the zip of her coat, agitating it up and down
its track. 'What I mean is,' she says again, 'that you
shouldn't worry.'

'I shouldn't worry?'

'You shouldn't worry that you worry.'

Despite herself, Lily smiles.

'It's a big, huge thing. Bigger than anything you or I have
ever faced. And of course he's going to take time to . . . to
get right.' Sarah drains her cup and regards her friend. 'And
he's worth it, isn't he?'

'Worth what?'

'The wait. Worth allowing him a bit of time. I mean,
you like him a lot, don't you?' She zips her coat all the
way up to her throat. 'I've never seen you like this about
anyone. You're in deep.'

Lily shakes her head. 'Nah.'

'Yes, you are,' Sarah says, accusing, turning on her.

'I'm not,' Lily protests.

'Yes you are.'

'No, I'm not.'

Sarah leaps to her feet and strides off down the alley.
'Are too,' she throws over her shoulder.

Lily gets up and, struggling with the pot, shouts, 'Am
not!'

'Are too.'

'Am not.'

They run through the crowds, shouting to each other

and, at the edge of the market, Sarah has to stop, breathless and laughing.

A note on the table:

> Dear Lily and Aidan,
>   I've had to go away for a couple of days – maybe more. Work stuff, mainly. The project's going to tender and I've got things to sort out and it looks like I'm going to have to be on site. See you both next week.
>   Take care of yourselves, M x

She picks it up. On the back is an architectural drawing, or part of one; a slip torn from a larger sheet. It's a bathroom from above. She is amazed at the detail: the oval sweep of the bath, the sunken dip of the sink. Taps, shower-head, plug-holes, door handles. Two toilets. Two? Why would anyone need two toilets in one room? Then she realises that one is a bidet. She wonders if Marcus did this drawing. If this arrangement of bathroom appliances is his design. If he laboured over every measurement, every angle, every inch of the flooring.

Turning over the piece of paper, she runs the words around her head. Tender. Going to tender. On site. Work stuff. Mainly. Things to sort out. Take care. She lets it drop back to the table surface and looks about her, letting her coat slide off her back. The buttons clunking on the metal of the chair makes her jump. The air movement caused by the coat pushes the note off the edge of the table and down to the floor. She bends over and it's only after she's put it back on the table that she notices a long coil of black hair attached to its corner.

She holds up the hair between fingerpad and thumbnail at arm's length. She moves towards the kitchen where she gropes on the surface for matches, never taking her eyes away from that sinuous black spiral. She strikes the match and holds the flame to the hair. On contact, it sparks and sputters upwards into nothing, leaving only a bitter scent in the air.

She seizes the broom by its neck and sweeps each floorboard in long, skating movements. The brush-head clunks like a croquet mallet against the skirting boards. What she collects in the metal dustpan — an aerated clot of dust and hair and indefinable fluff, from the quick glance she allows herself — she empties into the steel sink and drops in a lit match. The flames flare blue, briefly. From under the sink she gets a bucket and a tall, squeezable bottle of fluid. She squirts a thin, green stream into the ridged bottom of the bucket and directs a jet of hot water after it. Foam froths and masses around the top. She pulls on a pair of pink rubber gloves, their insides furred like moleskin, and she cleans. She scrubs the table, the counter surface, the sink area, the front of the washing-machine, the cooker hob, all the door-handles, the shower, the toilet seat, the bathroom mirror, the shelves, the window-sills, and then gets a mop and, starting from one corner and backing towards the opposite one in the way her mother always taught her, cleans the floor in wide, damp sweeps of the string-headed mop.

When she's finished, she perches on the arm of the sofa, her feet buried in the cushions, watching the floorboards lighten in unexpected patches.

She is tired out by love, tired of love.

He's hot in the sun, which is pouring in through the large frosted-glass window. He'd quite like to move out of it, into the shade, but there are no other chairs. The solicitor who's dealing with Aidan's house-purchase has disappeared with a sheaf of paper, leaving Aidan sitting there with nothing to do but fiddle with the cap of his pen, and think — follow trails of thought like a dog does smells. It's like trying to keep a virus at bay, he decides, trying not to think about it and what happened. If you feel the warning signs of an infection filtering through your body, you take drugs, stay in bed, keep warm. But this is like a more virulent disease than anything else Aidan's ever experienced.

At the back of the solicitor's office two men are baiting another, younger man. The victim, still in his late teens, is sitting at his desk, eyes fixed on his screen, giving the impression that he is working so hard he hasn't noticed what the other two are saying. A deep red stain rising from his collar to his cheeks betrays him. Aidan sees that if they carry on much longer he might burst into tears.

'Why haven't you got a girlfriend, Matthew?' one of the men with an even fuzz of sand-coloured hair covering his head is demanding. 'Just tell us, Matthew. We're interested. Is it because you're boring? Is it because you're ugly?'

'Or is it because you're gay?' the other one joins in, flexing a ruler between his thin, white hands.

'Are you gay, Matthew? Are you? Just tell us, Matthew. We want to know.'

Aidan shrugs himself out of his sweater and shoves it into his bag, which is lying at his feet. Tell them to fuck off, Matthew, he wills him, tell them to fuck right off. Matthew, shrunk into his keyboard, mutters something soundlessly, his hair stuck into sweaty strips across his forehead.

'What was that, Matthew?' The one with the ruler. 'We can't hear you.'

Aidan gets up quickly, unable to stand any more. The two men, sensing a movement in the room, shift and turn towards him, their faces wary, defensive. Aidan holds their gaze for longer than necessary, until they look away, until one of them puts down the ruler. Then Aidan walks very slowly and deliberately across the carpet to the water cooler. He pulls a paper cup from the holder and fills it, silver bubbles streaming up into the inverted bottle. He drinks. The three men watch.

Aidan's solicitor bursts back into the room, shirtsleeves rolled back, shuffling pages in his hands. 'Sorry about that, Mr Nash,' he says, as he passes him. 'I think we're all set now.' He stops midway to his desk, looks back at the men. 'Have you boys got no work to do?' he demands.

Aidan sits again on the hot plastic of the seat in the sun, watching as his solicitor collates pages and staples them together. It is ridiculous, he decides: he tries all the time not to think about it, not to dwell on it, not to be always ruminating on the 'if I had' or 'if he hadn't'. But even today, when he's completing on his new flat, when he can finally move out of that accursed warehouse, when he should be the happiest man in London, he can't shake the unease that's rooted itself within him.

Lily is watering Marcus's plants, which are lined up in rows along the kitchen shelves. She knows they probably aren't his at all, but is choosing to call them Marcus's plants all the same. She found a little, sharp-snouted watering-can at the back of a cupboard behind cloths, old newspapers and cleaning-fluid bottles, and every few days she gets it out and drips water into the dried-out soil.

She is standing at the sink, the CD-player turned up loud, refilling the watering-can when, suddenly and without warning, the flat is plunged into darkness and silence.

Lily freezes, her hands under the tumbling water of the tap. It's as if she's fallen down a hole. The dark is so black and so dense that she can't tell if her eyes are open or not. She feels for the tap and twists it off, trying to ignore the adrenaline kicking at her ribs. It's the key, she tells herself, the blue electricity key that Marcus showed her when she first moved in. It needs to be taken to the garage down the road and recharged every couple of weeks or so. That's why the electricity has cut out. It must have run out. No other reason.

No other reason, she mutters to herself, turning in the black, fathomless space, no other reason at all. She is, she estimates, facing the length of the room now. All she has to do is walk through the kitchen, between the counter and the units, past the table, through the living area and down to the electricity meter, which is in a small, high-up cupboard on the wall outside Marcus's studio. That's all. Simple. She knows the flat. She could do it with her eyes closed.

Putting out her hand, she touches the counter top more quickly than she imagined, and she snatches back her hand in shock. She rubs her palm against her hip, feeling its definite fleshiness, its corporeal realness. It was just the counter, that's all, it just means she is further to the right than she thought.

Lily shuffles her feet and shunts forward a few inches. She battles silently with herself about putting her hand out in front of her. She doesn't want to *touch* something there, to feel anything brush up against her palm. But, then, she doesn't want to walk face first into anything either. She dithers, rubbing the edges of her shoes against each other then stretches out her arm into the black beyond and edges forward, the other hand resting on the counter edge.

At the end of the counter she lets go of it. To her right now should be a dining chair with her coat over the back. She gropes towards it, just to feel the cool solidity of its metal spar. Nothing. Her hand flails in a black void. Panic jags at her chest. To her left should be the fridge and she pushes her hand towards it, and almost falls sideways when she comes into contact with nothing, a vacuum.

Her breathing is fast and shallow now and she steps back, hoping to regain her bearings by finding the counter end and starting again from there. But she steps back and back and back again and there is nothing behind her. Just space and more space.

Lily whirls round and then whirls back, not wanting to lose the way she was facing, the way to the electricity cupboard, the way to light and release, but she is so disoriented now that she can't remember which way she's facing and which way she should be going. She's experiencing a kind of inverted, negated perception. Usually, it's her environment and the people in it that seem firm and immutable, while she just passes through it, wraith-like. But now it feels as though the flat has dissolved into a black miasma and she is the only live, complete element in it.

She stands on one leg and moves the other in a semi-circle around her, to see if it comes into contact with anything. Nothing. Her heart is beating so fast and hard that she feels dizzy and breathless. She tries clearing her throat, tries humming the song that had been playing, but can't remember it and what comes out of her mouth sounds so disjointed and echoes around this sightless space so much that it, too, frightens her.

She shakes her head, presses her hand against her leaping heart in an attempt to calm it. All she has to do is walk in one direction and she'll come across something that will tell her where she is. It's simple. It's easy. She does live here, after all. It's only electricity.

She strikes out in the direction to her left. She expects any second to encounter the fridge or the bookshelves. But nothing happens. She keeps moving, one hand held in front of her, knees bent. She thinks about how ridiculous she must look. Then the idea that she is being watched plants itself in her head, spreading deep, gnarled roots. Watched by something that can see in the dark. Or something that doesn't need light, is beyond light.

Still nothing, and she continues to shuffle in her chosen direction, a small whimpering noise escaping into the air every few seconds, and, knowing it's coming from her, she chooses to ignore it.

Then her fingers meet something. She flattens her palm against it. A cold, smooth, hard surface. Glass. Which means she's reached a window or the mirror near the door. She doesn't get the chance to move her hand up or down to find a window latch or a mirror edge because there is a tingling, stinging feeling at the centre of her face. The very back of her nose. A familiar, dreadful scent is itching at her.

Lily has never experienced pure fear. She thought she had, but realises now that it was some weaker, poorer relation of what she is feeling now. Pure fear is clean, flawless and contourless, almost tipping you over into the sensation of nothing at all. It doesn't so much take over your whole body as deprive you of one.

The scent gathers in the air around her. Lily screws up her eyes, trying to see something, anything ahead of her. Nothing. She can see nothing and all the time the smell is getting stronger, closer. It's as if her heart has stopped beating now and Lily wonders if she's going to die, if that is what this has all been leading up to, what it's all been about. Maybe she should dart aside, run, struggle, fight it, but her mind seems to be divorced, elsewhere. She wants to say the name aloud, just so it knows that Lily knows it's there, just to hear it, just so both of them hear it together. Lily is drawing in breath, her mouth ready to form the strange word when something light and damp seems to wreathe her ankles. Balance, then body tension desert her; her hand slides down the cold skin of the glass and her last thought is that her head is cracking against what, for a micro-second, she believes is the wall but is in fact the floor; and everything doesn't go black but blank – formless and infinite.

Something is touching her stomach and Lily leaps the rest of the way to consciousness.

Aidan is leaning over her, his hand flat on her front, his other hand holding a torch, which he is directing not at her but near enough to her for them both to be in a capsule of yellow light. His face is shocked, concerned. Lily tries to sit up but her vision merges everything together.

'Don't,' Aidan says gently, his hand pressing her down, 'just stay still for a bit. Lie flat.'

He puts the torch down on the floor next to them and pulls himself out of his leather jacket, which he spreads over Lily. The heat left in it warms her hands and she moves them under it.

'Are you all right?' he asks, picking up the torch again. 'What happened?'

'I – I – the electricity key ran out and . . .'

He is shaking his head. 'No, the whole street's out. Didn't you notice? There are no streetlights. They're digging up the pavement down the road and they cut through the electricity cables by mistake.' He laughs but it's shaky – pent-up and relieved at the same time. 'You scared the life out of me, Lily. I'd been in here for a bit, looking for the torch before I found you. I thought you were . . .' He bites his lip. 'Can you sit up?'

He helps her upright against the wall, his hand around her arm. Then he rests his thumb and index finger across her cheek and peers into one of her eyes, then the other. Lily has never seen him at such close range and finds she wants to study his face.

'Well, I don't think you're concussed. But did you just faint or did you hit your head?'

His hands are exploring her skull, gently moving her hair aside as his fingers search and press different sections of her head. His touch is so assured, so tender and so unexpected that it seems to hit some exposed spot in her. Her throat closes and liquid swims into her eyes.

'Oh, no,' he is ducking down to look into her face, 'I didn't hurt you, did I?'

'No, no, not at all.' She rubs her hand over her face. 'I'm fine. I really am.'

He leans back on his heels. 'Well, there are no lumps. But I think you might have a big bruise here tomorrow.' His thumb brushes her cheekbone.

'Yeah. I think . . . I think I just passed out. Fainted, I mean.'

'Right.' He nods, frowning, then asks: 'Do you faint much?'

'Er . . . no. Don't think so. Can't remember having fainted before.'

'My sister does.' He moves off into the kitchen, the cone

of his light bobbing over the walls and ceiling. 'She faints all the time.'

Lily follows the jittering beam of light. Relief is ebbing through her. She is indeed in front of the mirror behind the door, and she can't believe that the flat is all still here, still intact, still existing. 'Does she?'

'Yeah. Always has done. Always will probably. She has low blood pressure.' He wedges the torch on top of the fridge between a pile of magazines and a jam jar. 'It takes an hour or so to fix,' he is saying, as he moves about, opening drawers and rattling boxes of matches, 'or so they said.'

'What will?' Her brain is disordered: she seems unable to follow the thread of the conversation. Does he mean his sister?

'The electricity. Idiots,' he mutters, as he stands two half-melted candles on the table and holds a match to them. The wicks catch and vertical shadows reach up and touch the ceiling. He comes back over to where she is propped up. 'You know, you ought to go to the doctor. Get yourself checked out. Just to be sure.'

Lily moves her feet, preparing to stand. Aidan leans down and, grasping her by both forearms, pulls her up. She sways, her legs feeling frail. But he catches her round the waist and, his arm supporting her, walks with her to the sofa. When she sinks into it, he remains above her, standing. 'You must go to the doctor,' he says again, looking her over, 'tomorrow. You really must. You're white as a sheet.'

'I will,' she lies. 'I promise. But I'm sure it's nothing.'

'Yeah, well, let the doctor be the judge of that.' He

turns and goes to his doors. 'Right. I'm going to pack, but if you need anything just shout.'

'Pack? Are you going away?' she asks, hearing the dismay in her voice and hating it.

'Not exactly.' He pats his trouser pocket and a metallic clink answers. He smiles. 'I got the keys to my new flat today. At last.'

She watches as he walks to and fro in the quivering candlelight, piling up by the door suitcases, bags of books, and boxes of computer screens, leads, hard drives, scanners, CD-ROMs. A cup of tea appears at her elbow, heavily sugared, and, feeling guiltily better, she gets up, laying his jacket carefully over the arm of the chair.

'Do you want a hand with anything?' she calls.

'No. I've just about finished.'

Keeping the bathroom door open to catch the flickering of the candles, she washes her face, examining the faint mark on her cheek. As she comes out of the bathroom the lights rise up to meet her as if she's just walked on stage. Aidan is standing at the table, hands shoved into his back pockets. Behind him, the CD clicks and whirs in the machine, and then loud, inappropriate trip-hop fills the space between them. For some reason, they both laugh.

'Let there be light,' he says.

'Power to the people,' she returns quickly.

'If music be the food of light,' he says, just as quickly.

'And so put on the light.'

'It's lighter than air.'

'Here's some light relief.'

'*Eine kleine lichtmusik*.'

That makes Lily giggle. 'Er . . .' she can't think of one. 'Let them eat cake!' she blurts wildly.

Aidan laughs. 'I win,' he says. Then: 'Look, I'll . . . I won't go tonight. I'll take my stuff over to the flat in the morning.'

'Oh.' She is suddenly sober, knowing she should protest, that he should go, but she can't find the words, for him leaving now seems like the worst thing that could ever happen to her. 'Thank you,' she says meekly, 'thank you so much.'

'No, it's fine.' He scratches his head. 'Marcus'll be back soon. So you'll be . . . fine.'

The next morning their awkwardness is back. Aidan stands at the door with a cardboard box.

'I hope . . . you'll be all right,' he says, holding out his hand. She is set off balance by the formality of this gesture but she takes it anyway, presses it in hers, knowing that she should say something. He drops his eyes, easing his hand out of hers, turning away.

Lily realises that she'll probably never see him again. She wants to ask him for a phone number, or an address, whether he'll be happy now. But she doesn't.

'Good luck with . . .' she can't think how to end the sentence '. . . your new flat,' she adds in a moment of inspiration.

'Thanks,' he says, and without looking back, ''bye, then.'

The instant the door closes, she whips round to face the

room. The tap drips, water tap-tapping into the well of the sink. Underfoot, a central-heating pipe sighs and shudders. At the far window, a breeze fills a shirt with her shape.

She stares at it for a second then jerks herself into action, running towards her room, fear tightening her scalp. She seizes her bag from the floor and starts snatching up objects to shove into it: tube pass, purse, book, keys. Where are her keys? She storms about, lifting clothes, magazines, books and hurling them in to the air. No sign of them. She leans around her door. The flat looks impossibly long from this perspective, the bathroom and kitchen stretching away into the distance. She makes a sudden dash across the floorboards, her footsteps crashing and bouncing off the walls. Keys, keys, keys, she is intoning to herself. Where the hell are they? Not on the table, not on the sofa, not by the door. Keep looking, Lily, she tells herself, they've got to be somewhere, can't be far away.

In another part of her mind, a terrible thought is growing. She is struggling to ignore it, keeping her mind on the search, but it's getting louder and louder. If she can't find her keys, she can't open the door, which is fitted with a stupid self-locking mechanism. If she can't open the door, she can't leave. If she can't leave, she'll be stuck in here all day. And all night. And all the next day. And the next. Until Marcus gets back.

And around her the room is suddenly quiet and still, the kind of stillness she has come to hate. The tap is silent, the sink dry. Her shirt is pressed flat at the window. She darts a glance at the door, six feet away. Maybe it won't be locked after all. Maybe, just maybe, it didn't lock after Aidan. She almost tries it, just to make sure, just on the off-chance that the mechanism hadn't worked for once. But the idea of her tugging in vain at an unyielding handle isn't a good one. She runs briefly through other means of escape – the lift shaft, the windows – and then a very cold focus descends on her brain: I have to get out of here. I have to find my keys.

She scatters objects from the table to the floor – unopened mail, Marcus's note, newspaper supplements. She wrenches open the kitchen drawers and ransacks their contents. She runs her hand along the shelf where the plants sit in a neat row. She empties out the chrome bowl on the counter and matchboxes, elastic bands, corkscrews, a tiny silver earring, some hairgrips scatter over the Formica and on to the floor.

'Come on!' she shouts to the air. 'Where have you put them?' Then mutters, 'Bitch,' as she strides to the bathroom and pulls open the cabinet. By the sound system, she pulls CDs from their shelves. She hurls the sofa cushions to the floor. She lifts up the corners of the rugs. Then she walks slowly and deliberately to the large windows at the end of the flat, where the bulbs are pushing up through the soil.

On the sill is a mug. Lily has seen it before but never really thought about it. It has a black 'S' printed on its side. She pushes her fingers into its cold porcelain mouth and lifts out her keys.

Laurence has found a stone and is bashing it against the hollow iron leg of the swing. He takes his steadying hand away from the swing for a moment to look back at her, delighted.

Lily smiles at him and waves. 'That's a good noise, Laurence.'

He turns back to his labours and the dull, metallic thud rings out again over the misty park. A mother in a pink bobble-hat, bouncing a miserable-looking child on a see-saw, glances at her disapprovingly. Lily is tempted to stick out her tongue.

She feels light-headed and edgy, and a heavy knot of dread is tensing her stomach, like the feeling before an exam. What is she going to do? She can't go back to the flat, and she can't very well move out either. How would she explain it to Marcus?

Laurence is coming over the grass towards her, with the emphatic, solid stagger of a toddler, grinning. His mother has dressed him in so many clothes that he is quite spherical.

'Hi,' Lily says, 'what happened to your wonderful stone?'

His fists grip the material of her coat. He extends the index finger of his hand towards the bench she's sitting on and looks up at her enquiringly. He's going through what his mother refers to his 'acquiring verbalism stage'.

'Bench,' says Lily.

He points again.

'Bench.'

He points up.

'Sky.'

And behind her.

'Tree,' Lily says. 'Tree. You try.'

He points instead at the mother beside the see-saw who is involved in a struggle with her child. It is weeping piteously and trying in vain to get off the see-saw.

'Horrid lady,' Lily says.

He points again.

'Silly hat.'

Laurence jiggles at her leg. 'Up,' he commands, in his throaty growl. 'Up.'

Lily scoops him off the ground and on to her knee. 'Shall we go home?' she asks him. 'Are you cold yet? No, probably not. You're dressed for a Himalayan expedition, aren't you?'

He twists round in her arms to gaze at her. She sees his slate-grey eyes fix on the bruise that has bloomed on the side of her face.

'What do you think will happen?' she asks him, straightening his hat on his soft, blond hair. 'Eh? What's your view? What am I going to see next? And the million-dollar question: am I losing my marbles?'

Laurence extends his finger towards the bruise, frowning.

'Wouldn't you like to know?' she says, pressing her face into the silky skin of his neck. He wriggles, laughing his emphysemic old-man laugh. 'You ask too many questions, that's your problem.'

'How much does he earn?' Diane says, attempting to hold up a burgundy shirt against Lily. Lily pushes it away from her. She is regretting telling her mother about Marcus. She's spent the night back in Ealing and, in a weak moment, Diane had extracted a promise from her to be a shopping companion the next day.

'I don't know. I haven't asked him, have I?'

Shoppers flow around them, bumping bags and umbrellas and elbows. Diane places the shirt back on the rack. 'Must be considerable. An architect.' Diane rolls the word around her mouth, giving it about five syllables. 'It's wonderful, Lily. I'm so pleased.'

'It's not . . . like that, really.'

'Not like what?' Diane demands. 'Serious, you mean? Lily, nothing is serious at first.'

Diane makes her way through the racks and carousels of clothing with the weaving gait of an expert department-store shopper, leaving Lily stranded among the cardigans. Nearby another mother and daughter study a blue angora twinset with religious intensity. 'Is it me?' the daughter asks.

'Well,' her mother replies, 'it could be.'

'I hope you're taking care of yourself, Lily,' Diane shouts, from the sock and hosiery department. Lily starts to calculate whether she can get to her mother's side quickly enough to stop her continuing in that vein. 'You are taking precautions, aren't you?' she bellows. 'What are you using?'

'Mum,' Lily hisses, stumbling to her side, plastic bags flapping from her arms like angel wings, 'for God's sake. Do you have to? Everyone can hear you.'

'Who?'

'Everyone.' Lily gesticulates around the shop.

'Well, it's important. I have to ask. You don't have to give me any details if you don't want to. Just tell me, put my mind at rest, are you being careful?'

Lily closes her eyes. 'Yes. Of course. Of course I am.'

Half-way through the morning they have coffee. Lily stacks up her mother's bags on a spare chair. Diane swirls white cream from a tiny carton into the black of her decaff, agitating the surface with a spoon. Lily watches the colour sink into brown.

'You don't look well,' Diane announces, peering into her daughter's face. 'What is it? PMT?'

'No.'

'When's your period due?'

Lily stares at her mother. 'Why are you so annoying?' She glances at the surrounding tables, but everyone is engrossed in shopper's conversations. 'It's . . . I don't know . . . two weeks or something.'

Diane flattens her fingers against Lily's brow. 'Are you

off-colour? Do you feel ill? What's that mark on your cheek from?'

Lily ducks away, 'It's nothing. I . . . I fell, that's all. Tripped. I'm fine.'

'You don't look it. You look like you've got tuberculosis.'

'Thanks.' She sips at the slick black surface of her coffee. 'He had a girlfriend,' she says.

'Really?' Diane is immediately there, listening. 'A serious one?'

'Yeah. I think so. They lived together.'

'How long for?'

'Four years? Five, maybe. Don't know.'

'How long ago?'

'Don't know.'

'Well, haven't you asked?'

'She died.'

'Oh.' Diane frowns as if this information is irksome to her. 'When?'

'I'm not sure. Quite recently I think. She's still . . . sort of . . . around the flat.'

'Around the flat? In what way?'

'Er,' Lily breaks the Danish pastry on her plate into smaller and smaller crumbs. 'Um. Well, all her stuff was still in my room . . . when I first saw it.'

'I see.' Diane considers this, displeased. 'What did she die of?'

Lily sees paving slabs, regular and neat as fields seen from an aeroplane. She closes her eyes. 'Don't know.'

'For heaven's sake, Lily,' Diane takes an exasperated

swig from her cup. 'Don't you and this Marcus ever talk to each other? Hold a conversation?'

Lily eats her Danish slowly, dipping it into her coffee until her mother tells her to stop that, it's disgusting. A waitress comes, an orange pencil gripped between her teeth, and slides the crockery on to a tray. Diane starts looking at her watch.

'She was really beautiful,' Lily says.

'Who?' Diane is searching in her handbag for something.

'The girlfriend. Marcus's girlfriend.'

'Ex-girlfriend,' Diane corrects her.

'Can you be an ex if you died?'

'Of course,' Diane snaps. 'You're his girlfriend now . . .'

'Well—'

'. . . so that makes her his ex.'

'Mmm,' Lily picks at a loose thread in the seam of her shirt, 'maybe.'

'Look, Lily,' Diane leans across the table and takes hold of her daughter's hand, 'don't worry about this, this . . . girl.'

'Sinead.'

'Sinead? What kind of a name's that?'

'Dunno. Irish, I think.'

'Well. Anyway. Don't worry about her. Put her out of your mind. She's gone. He's yours now. He's a good catch.'

'I wish you wouldn't talk about him as if he was a fish.'

Lily weaves in and out of the crowds on Oxford Street. Diane has gone home. Three hours' shopping is 'just her limit'. Lily's bought a blue shirt of sheer, flimsy fabric. She folds it up into a small, square parcel and crams it into her bag.

She walks down Charing Cross Road and, turning left, wanders through Covent Garden. It begins to drizzle and Lily realises she's forgotten her umbrella. At a pharmacy on a corner she stops and peers through the window at a woman having a makeover. She's tilted back in a chair like a dentist's, her hair pulled into a grey, clinical band. A woman in a grey overall and orange foundation is standing over her smearing something white and foamy on to her face. She's wearing a badge that says, 'Ask me about options for lips.'

Suddenly, something beyond the woman having a make-over, something through the window that faces out over the perpendicular street makes the depth of focus in Lily's eye flicker and stretch. Then her stomach drops to the pavement she's standing on.

Sinead passes the window without looking her way, a hood obscuring most of her face. Then the window is blank again, veils of grey drizzle sweeping across its greenish glass.

Lily edges to the corner and peers round. Is this how it's going to be now? That she's going to follow her everywhere? That Lily will see her everywhere – outside, in shops, at work, on the tube? Is this how it's going to be?

The figure is walking at a steady pace away from Lily. She has a rucksack on her back. A smaller woman with blonde hair is walking beside her. The blonde woman is saying something to her and now Sinead is nodding, unfolding her arms and turning her face towards her friend, her right palm upturned in a gesture of affirmation to whatever it is she's saying. They stop at a zebra crossing. They are still talking. The friend is shaking her head. Lily finds that her feet are moving under her and the scene where Sinead and Sinead's friend are standing waiting to cross the road is getting closer. Lily feels incredibly calm, as if somehow she had always known this would happen, had always seen this coming.

They cross the road. Sinead adjusts her hood, pulling it further over her face against the steady rain. Lily is five maybe four paces behind them. Sinead's jacket rustles as her body moves inside it. At the tube station they stop and face each other on the pavement.

'. . . but I should be back by Thursday,' the friend is saying. 'I can't believe it will take longer than that.'

Sinead nods. The two women embrace.

'So I'll give you a call, then. OK?'

Sinead says something Lily can't hear.

''Bye,' the friend calls from the station entrance, 'see you soon.'

Sinead watches her go through the ticket barrier, waves, then turns away. She walks fast when she's on her own, Lily discovers, weaving in and out of the Saturday crowds. She turns unexpectedly and quickly into a bookshop, and Lily leaps through the doorway so fast she almost falls into her.

The windows are steamed up. Umbrellas stand by the door, dripping pools of rainwater on to the black-tiled floor. Sinead wanders over to the fiction stands, pulls off her gloves, shrugs back her hood and gives her hair a shake, freeing it from the neck of her jacket.

Lily pushes her way through the groups of bent-necked people. And from somewhere a memory twitches then opens out in front of her – a day trip she took with her parents when they still had her baby brother Mark, before Lily found him in his cot, blue and cold as marble. Her father held him in a papoose on his chest and the family walked through a field of long grass. She doesn't know where it was exactly, but she can see it all clearly. It must have been a field near a cliff-edge because she remembers the sensation of a steep, sheer drop that she couldn't see to her left. It was sunny and the grass was washed in yellow-green. She had on open-toed sandals and in her hand was a green plastic dinosaur, which had come in a kit, in two hollow halves. Her father had glued it together, pushing the gummed edges against each other until they set. There was a ridge of bubbled, hard glue along the dinosaur's back, through its blank-eyed face, through the swell of its belly and along its tail. It was most comfortable to hold it by its upper tail. They all walked through the field, her parent's voices criss-crossing over Lily's head, the faraway sea – was there sea? there was definitely sea – throwing pebbles up on to the beach far below them, Mark breathing breathing in his papoose, the soft creases of his nose and mouth pressed to her father's sternum, and the grass swooshing, sussurating, cleaving open to her steps. Part of her was frightened. The grass came up to her neck. What if she was swallowed up and her parents couldn't find her again in this endless, rippling green sea? She held up the dinosaur until her arm ached. If she didn't allow the grass to touch it, everything would be all right. When she looked down, she saw the dense brown roots, clinging to the sods of dried earth, falling open for her, shrinking back at the pressure of her sandal; and in front of her opened a path through the field.

And this is how it seems again in the bookshop. As if surrounded by a negative magnetic field, people fall away from her, step out of her path. And she carries on walking through them, right up to Sinead.

She stands near her and breathes in. She can catch her scent – inky, musky, with a hint of hair wax, soap, rain and that perfume. Sinead trails her index finger along the shelf, draws down a book, flicks over the title pages and reads the front page. She shifts her weight from one foot to the other.

Lily circles her, stands on the other side of the shelf, peering through the books. Sinead's eyes flick from side to side on the page. Lily sees her swallow, cough, and swallow again. She rubs the heel of her palm against her head. Lily comes round to Sinead's side of the shelf, picks up a book, puts it down. Touches the cover of another. 'Sinead?' she says.

She turns, the book still in her hands. She keeps her thumbnail in the page she'd reached. Her eyes scan Lily's face, moving from her eyes to her mouth, over her hair and back to her eyes. Sinead is taller than Lily. Lily's brow reaches her shoulder. Her expression is open but perplexed.

'You're Sinead?'

'Yes,' she nods, 'I am.'

There is a pause. She's not Irish, after all. Her voice is modulated, accentless, placeless.

'Sorry,' Sinead shakes her head, 'I don't—'

'No, no. You don't know me. I mean, we've never met. Not properly. Well, we've never actually met at all.'

'Oh. So how do you—'

'My name's Lily. I'm—'

Sinead recoils as if she's been blasted by cold air. 'I know exactly who you are.'

Before Lily can absorb this, Sinead has twisted on her heel and walked off. Very fast. Lily sets off after her.

'Sinead, wait.'

She turns a corner, Lily pursuing her. Sinead has her hands around her head as if protecting it.

'Please, Sinead. I just want to . . .'

'What?' Sinead turns on her suddenly. Lily jumps back, striking the edge of her wrist on a bookstand. Several people turn round and stare at them. Sinead towers over Lily. 'You just want to what?' She is crying now, silver tears dripping into the raindrops on her coat. 'Leave me alone, for God's sake. What's wrong with you?'

That Lily has caused these tears appals her. She feels about in her pocket for a tissue. 'Don't cry,' she says, putting out a hand to touch her sleeve. 'Please don't cry.'

Sinead pulls away from her and for a moment in front of Lily there is just the space where Sinead had been. Lily steps through the door after her into the cold air of the street. Again there is that sensation of Sinead – on the pavement again, sobbing now with uncontrolled, deep, wrenching gasps, sobbing with her hands around her eyes – getting closer to her, not the other way round.

'I'm sorry,' Lily says, 'I'm so sorry. I didn't mean—'

Sinead wipes at her wet cheeks with the edges of her fingers. 'Go away,' she hisses, 'leave me alone.'

Lily stands there, outside the bookshop as Sinead lurches away from her. She watches as she makes her way through the crowd, and even after she can no longer see the shape of that head, she stares at the spot it disappeared from for a long time, just in case it might return.

He's back. The lights are on in his room. Lily hurtles up the stairs and into the flat, flinging aside coat, bag and keys, bursting into his room, breathless and loud. 'She didn't die, did she?'

Marcus starts, the wheels on his chair jerking backwards, and looks up from his computer, blinking as if he can't see her properly. 'Hello to you too,' he says, with a nonplussed smile. 'Who didn't die?'

'Sinead.'

His smile shrivels like burning paper. '*Die?*' He passes his tongue between his lips. 'No. Of course not.'

She sighs in exasperation, surprised to find she is close to tears. 'But you told me she did!' she screams.

Marcus stares at her, his face scrunched into itself. 'No, I didn't.' He shakes his head slowly.

'You did!' She is furious, spitting with outrage. 'You did! You—'

'Lily, why would I tell you—'

'You said . . .' She stops, thinks back, fists clenched at her sides.

'What did I say?'

'You said . . . you said . . .' She grapples with her memory, re-enacting in her mind that moment on the sofa with the glove stretched out beside them. She asked him what happened, and he said . . . Then she remembers: 'You said she was no longer with us,' she shouts, accusing. 'Those were your exact words. No longer with us.'

He is still staring at her, disbelieving. Then he clears his throat and crosses his legs. 'Lily,' he begins, 'I may have—'

'What?' she demands. 'You may have what?'

He shrugs, helpless. 'I may have used those words but—'

'You did!' she insists. 'You did use them!'

He holds his hands up, fingers spread, as if calming an excited horse. 'All right, all right,' he says, thinking. 'But I must have used them euphemistically. No one uses that phrase for what it really means any more. I meant it as . . . a figure of speech. A joke. I never thought—'

'A joke?' she yells. 'A joke? You think this is funny?'

'No,' he says. 'Not at all. But . . .' he sighs '. . . you . . . we obviously misunderstood each other. I certainly never meant to—'

'Well, what did happen, then?' she demands.

He seems to shrink a few inches. He looks away from her. His hands move from his keyboard up to his eyes then his forehead. He supports his bowed head, his back bent over like an arthritic man. 'She . . .' Lily waits. He looks out of the window, grips his fingers in his hair, inhales. 'She . . . she left.'

Lily steps forward into the room. 'Why?'

'I don't know.' He has to force the words out, as if they choke him. 'She . . . just left. She left me.' He says it as if he's trying to make himself believe it. 'God, Lily, I don't know.'

'But she must have said why. You must know.'

'I don't, I swear it.' He tugs at his shirtsleeve. 'She just . . . walked out. One morning. Wouldn't talk about it, and . . .'

'What?'

He shrugs. 'I really don't know.'

'But . . . was there someone else? Did she leave you for—'

'Lily, please!' he says sharply. They are silent for a moment, Lily staring at him closely, as if the reason might be inked there on his skin. Eventually, he looks at her again, rubbing his jawline, taking a deep breath like a man about to go under water. 'Things can change,' he begins, his hand circling in the air. 'People move on. And sometimes it's hard to nail down the reason for it. Sometimes there really isn't one. I never got a clear idea of why she . . . why she wanted to go. And I probably never will.' He stands and comes towards her. 'That's all I can tell you, I'm afraid.' He reaches her and he touches the ends of her hair. His face looks sad and distant for a moment, then he smiles. 'Now, is there anything else we need to clear up?'

Lily is silent for a moment, looking up at him. Then she says, 'No. No, I don't think so.'

But later, on the bed, with his head weighing down her shoulder, she thinks about Sinead's hands as they covered her head, and how the bones and veins and tendons made an intricate latticework beneath the white, pellucid skin.

At lunchtime, Lily wanders beyond the hinterland of the office. She's alive, she's alive and in this city. It makes Lily look differently at the streets she walks through: she could meet her at any moment, catch a glimpse of her, could be walking on paving stones that Sinead walked on last week or yesterday, today, this morning. London feels different all of a sudden – pulsating with a kind of stirring possibility. Street corners she passes every day look unfamiliar. Every dark-haired woman makes Lily's heart vault in her chest, half in dread, half in hope.

Back in the Covent Garden bookshop, Lily stands at the bookshelf, plants her feet where she estimates Sinead's shoes might have have been less than twenty-four hours ago, reaches for the book Sinead had been looking at. Lily opens it, her eyes sliding over the words, and looks up. Repeats the action. Opens the book, looks up at the gap through to the other side of the shelves. Then looks to her right. That's what she saw. This view is what Sinead saw yesterday – the corridor through to the children's section, the posters dangling in the air-conditioned draughts, people milling through the tables, the glossy display stand for thrillers.

This is all exactly what she saw when I said her name – except with my face in the middle.

Lily comes out of her room, magazine in hand, heading for the TV. But there is a distinct and recognisable change in the atmosphere – a kind of chilled stasis. She stops dead in her tracks, her teeth rattling against each other, scanning the flat. She can't believe it, she really can't.

Something flits and twitches in the unlit recess beside the front door. Lily treads slowly over the boards, rolling the magazine into a truncheon. She can glimpse a restless, ceaseless motion. Something is moving in the dark.

She feels for the light switch and snaps it on. Sinead is pacing from the door to the bathroom's glass wall and back again. When she reaches the wall she does a half-circle, then walks back with stiff, urgent steps to the door. At the door she puts out her hand as if to open it, but hesitates, withdraws it, then turns away and walks to the bathroom. Round and round she goes, as if on tracks. It makes Lily think of a cheetah she saw once in a zoo, circling back and back on itself as it trod the same section of cage, over and over again.

Lily slams the magazine against the wall. 'You're not real!' she screams. 'You're not!'

Sinead seems to glance her way, falter in her rhythmic steps. She pauses for a moment, poised. Then she turns and walks towards her.

Lily is crying now, sobs racking up from her chest. She stares at the apparition coming towards her, and batters her face and head with her fists. 'You're losing it,' she whispers to herself, 'you're really losing it.' Sinead is close enough now for Lily to reach out and touch her. Lily starts backwards, hitting her head against the wall. 'Oh, God,' she sobs, trapped, 'please leave me alone, please. You're not real. I know you're not. You're not even dead,' she yells, 'so just go away! Please! GO AWAY!'

When she peels her fingers away from her eyes, Sinead is still there. Lily stares at the face of the woman in front of her. She is talking, fast and insistent. But no sound comes out. Lily watches, transfixed. Sinead's lips move soundlessly, and she scans Lily's face, as if anxious for her to understand.

'I can't hear you!' Lily sobs. 'What are you saying?'

Sinead pauses, glances around them and leans closer, as if she doesn't want to be overheard. Her mouth is moving even faster, a secret flood of words pouring out. Lily bangs her ears in frustration. There is one word she forms over and over again. Lily watches her lips carefully: don't, she is saying, don't.

'Don't what?' Lily cries. 'Don't what? I don't understand! I can't hear you!'

Then she can stand it no more. With a strange, low cry, she steps sideways and darts past Sinead. Her whole body is shaking and her legs barely hold her. She seizes a chair and slides into it, crying and coughing.

When she looks round, Sinead is gone. The room feels as it should. Lily sits at the table. She wipes the tear tracks from her face, listens to her breathing slowing down. She knows what she has to do.

She can't believe how easy it was. She stands at the crossroads holding the piece of paper, still amazed. All she'd had to do was look in the phone book: and there it was, in black cramped letters on thin, grey paper. She doesn't know why it shouldn't have been there, but somehow, when she'd been running her fingers down through the columns of all the other places beginning with 'uni', she'd thought there'd be a blank or it would be missed out or it wouldn't exist. All she'd had to do was dial the number and an efficient-sounding woman answered and told her the address straight off, and the number she should ring for a 'lecture schedule'. It had been the easiest thing in the world. Two phone calls, a lie to the agents about feeling ill, and here she was.

Tall, neatly terraced houses surround her, most with a brass plate by the side of the door. To her left is a large bookshop. People mill around the pavements, talking, folders and books clutched in their arms.

Lily checks her watch and checks the piece of paper. Then reads the street sign again. This is the right place.

She takes a seat at the back, near the door, sliding into

the polished wooden bench. The room is huge, with long tiered benches full of people and, at the bottom, a lectern and a blackboard. Everyone is talking, banging open folders, fiddling with tape-recorders or waving at someone in a different row. The girl next to her is saying to her friend: 'And he got this squid and chopped it up. Just like that. Lengthways and, you know –' she gestures, bringing down her hand in a sheer cutting movement '– sideways. It got *everywhere.*'

Lily experiences a sudden surge of nerves. What is she doing here? All she wants to do is find her and talk to her, but why is she sitting here? She must be mad, thinking she can just walk in here. She should be back at work. She should leave.

The door next to her opens, and there she is, striding past Lily and down the central steps. She is wearing a grey skirt, split to the thigh, long black boots that zip close to her ankles and a soft, diaphanous sweater with horizonal ribbing. Her hair is up, coiled on her head and speared with what looks like a silver knife. At the front, she lays out her papers then looks up and surveys them all. Lily ducks down.

'Right.' Sinead announces, and silence falls over the room. '*Gawain and the Green Knight.* If you have the parallel text with you, you might want to open it at page seventy-three.' A scuffling motion passes over the room like a Mexican wave. 'Or, for the braver among you, you can follow from page fifty-eight in the original.'

Lily has nothing – no book, no paper, no pen. What was she thinking of? She must stand out a mile. She looks around, fear crawling up her neck, and inadvertently catches the eye of the girl next to her. She is pretty, with very straight brown hair parted down the middle. She gives Lily a half-smile and pushes her opened book towards her so that it rests on the bench between them.

'Thanks,' Lily whispers, and the girl smiles and glances back towards Sinead. Lily looks down at the book and sees a sea of incomprehensible words, some that look like English and some with letters that don't appear in any alphabet she knows. On the page opposite are stacked lines of text – in recognisable English. '*And I shall stand and take a blow from him, unflinching, provided I have the right to deal him another when I claim it,*' she reads.

'There is no clear evidence as to the identity of the person who is known only as the Gawain Poet,' Sinead is saying. 'A number of people believe the Pearl Poet is also the Gawain Poet. Now, I'm not going to speculate here about the whos, whys and wherefores because, to be honest, I don't really care. It got written. By someone. That's all. But what I do believe is that the so-called Gawain Poet was a woman. Which might explain why she wanted to remain anonymous, her kind not being taken very seriously in those days. Now,' she says again and, lifting the book, reads: '*I declare he was the biggest of men, and the handsomest . . . for although his torso, back and chest were thick-set, his stomach and waist were attractively slender.*' A stutter of laughter circles the room. 'What self-respecting bloke is going to write that?'

Lily crosses and recrosses her ankles underneath the bench, pushing each hand up the opposite sleeve. Around and in front of her, rows and rows of heads are bent over notes, arms jerk with quick note-taking; one or two people are whispering something in their neighbour's ear. Lily is amazed by the rapt concentration in the room, how everyone is listening to the words that flow from Sinead's mouth, how this one woman is the vortex of everyone's attention, the reason they're all here. People are concentrating and transcribing her every word in a notebook, or trapping the rises, falls and modulations of her voice on a tape-recorder. This is not how she remembers university.

'What we have to realise,' Sinead reaches up to pull down one half of the blackboard, and the sweater lifts to reveal the bottom rung of her ribcage, 'is that Gawain is caught in the workings of a social machine that is beyond his ken. And doesn't even know it. What he ignores, or doesn't have the nous to take notice of is in fact the clue, the key to the whole plot in which he is ensnared. What appears to be the periphery is in fact the centre.'

Lily leans, her hands flat on the glass, against the big bookshop window. Daylight is sinking into violet. The sky is lighter than the buildings. The clocks will be going back soon: in a few days' time, this hour of the day will be gloomy, orange-lit and cold. She sinks down and rests on her heels, making sure she is still tucked into a doorway, just in case. A group of men with briefcases, tight shoes and well-cut hair pass her. The hem of one of their raincoats brushes against her knee. 'Hello, darling,' one says and they laugh, but Lily doesn't react. Her eyes are fixed on the building opposite.

There is something about this woman that strains and tugs at some vital part of her, as if her heart, connected to Marcus's, is connected to Sinead. And at her very core is an unease of things not quite fitting into each other. Questions, small and insistent, whisper to her from corners of her mind. How does Sinead know about her? Can it be possible that Marcus really doesn't know why she left? What is she – or the thing that looks like her – trying to tell her? What can be so bad to make a live woman haunt another?

She's going to stop her, that's what she's going to do. She's going to just stop her in the street and ask her straight out. No messing about. Why did you leave? That's all. Simple. Tell me why you left. And Sinead will tell her. And then she'll know.

Students she recognises from the lecture leave, bunching outside the door to pore over maps or to chat or to look up at the sky. Two men in caretaker uniforms wander out and down the street, a few lone academic-types. But not the person Lily is looking for. Lights are switched off in an upper floor. An elderly man stands by the now-locked doors, gazing at passers-by – a woman with a double-seated pushchair, a couple in matching fleeces, a man trailing an empty dog-lead. Then, just as Lily's legs are becoming numb with cold and inactivity, Sinead appears.

Lily leaps upright. Something in the hinge of her knee catches and twangs, but she ignores it and moves swiftly over the pavement, never taking her eyes off the figure on the other side of the road. Sinead is carrying a bright red and purple woven plastic bag in the crook of her elbow. She walks fast, and Lily's knee sends arrows of pain up her thigh. Sinead crosses Gower Street at the lights, but Lily misses them and has to wait in agony, watching Sinead's back recede into the distance. As soon as the lights glow amber she is running over the tarmac and along the road in a kind of stumbling jog, her breath steaming out in front of her, careful not to get too close. By the time they reach Tottenham Court Road, Lily is ten yards behind her.

To her horror, Sinead suddenly breaks into a run, dodging cars, across the road. Has she seen her? Lily staggers after her, blood surging through her head. Sinead swings herself up into the back of a bus. Lily pushes herself into a sprint. Sinead is climbing the stairs to the top floor. Lily hears the ding of the bell and she stretches out her arm, making a lunge for the rail. Grasps it, thumb meeting fingers. Feels the bus powering away from her. Her feet scrabble for the platform. Her left foot makes contact and she hauls herself up.

'Good exercise, eh?' the conductor says, and winks.

She manages a smile, then, steadying herself like a sailor against the swell and roll of the bus, cautiously climbs the winding stairs.

It's quite busy, people sat singly on most of the seats. Sinead is next to a man in a baseball hat on the front seat, the one Lily doesn't like sitting in, the road eddying and rushing underneath her, and that teeth-smashing bar across the window against which she could be thrown at any moment.

She sits near the back, in an empty double seat. Leaning towards the window, she can spy Sinead's profile through all the other heads. She is reading something, her bag propped on her knee. Lily is suddenly aware of the loud labouring of her breathing. A few rows ahead, a teenager chirps into a mobile phone and a red-haired man opposite is muttering to his girlfriend, who is staring fixedly out of the window. Otherwise, silence.

Lily swipes a sleeve through the condensation and a fan-shaped segment of the street appears – computer shops, a big stationer's, a window full of futons. Her breathing is returning to normal when the bus judders to a halt. Feet thud on the boards. People clomp down the stairs. The baseball-cap man stands. Sinead moves her knees aside to let him pass. Lily folds her body in half, her face almost buried in her lap, her finger plucking at the heel of her shoe.

The bus jolts forward and swings left into Euston Road. Lily peers up over the top of the seat. Sinead has moved next to the window and is looking out. There are four other people. The bus has picked up speed and is rushing along Marylebone Road. For the first time, Lily wonders where they are going.

She could speak to her now. It would be so easy. Too easy. All she'd have to do is stand, walk a few paces and slide into the seat behind her and say – say what? Remember me? Hi, how are you doing? Great lecture, by the way.

Lily turns her head away and gazes out of the window. Huge corporate buildings skim past. Thin darts of horizontal rain fleck the glass. Her own reflection – large-eyed, wild-haired, staring straight at her – makes her start.

At Bayswater, Sinead shunts herself along the seat and stands. Lily bends, fiddles with her shoe, her tights, her buttons until she hears her descend the stairs. Then she gets up.

They stand on the landing board together. Sinead leans right out, one hand holding the pole, hair and drizzle whipping across her face. Lily could push her. She could peel those fingers away from the pole and release her into the blasting flow of traffic. The thought, which appeared unbidden in her head, shocks Lily so much that she almost forgets to jump off after her.

Sinead strides up a side-street, tugging her coat around her, shifting her bag on to the other arm. Then she turns into a doorway. Lily hesitates outside. There are double glass and dark wood swing doors, with a kind of wooden kiosk beyond, where Sinead is paying and being handed something large and white. Above the doors, in twisted, unilluminated neon, are the words 'The Spa'.

Lily pushes at one side of the door and steps in. She hands over the money to a large, florid-cheeked woman, who slides two towels across the counter towards her. Holding them to her, she goes through the second doors.

Everything is very still and very cool. She is in a huge, high-vaulted room. People lie on rows of reclining chairs, draped in towels. No one speaks. The walls are gilt and stained-wood panelled, with lamps throwing circles of dusky yellow upwards. Reflections of water oscillate on the ceiling. The centre of the room is missing and people stand at the crater's edge, looking down into the floor below. As she walks through the room, people turn their eyes to her then look away.

Sinead is standing in a corner, stepping out of her skirt. Her hair is loose to her shoulders and her spine stands out from her back like beads on a thread. She folds her clothes into a narrow metal locker, wraps herself in a towel and descends the stairs. On the other side of the room, Lily does the same, the building opening out to her as she drops below street level.

There are women everywhere, naked. Milling from hot-room to showers to loungers to a steel drinking fountain to a small kidney-shaped blue pool, they step on crinkled, bare soles over the damp tiles, hair twisted to necks. Everyone is graceful and slow. Sinead slides between the vertical, heavy plastic slats of a doorway and is swallowed by steam. Lily follows.

The air is whited-out and heavy with the medicinal tang of eucalyptus. The hot, wet smell stings the edges of her lips. Through the mist she can make out figures, lying or sitting, and wooden benches running around the walls. Lily moves through the steam and lowers herself down. She peers around. Sinead, barely visible and recognisable only by the mass of her hair, is sitting at right-angles to her, her feet on the floor, hands on knees, her head tilted back on the china tiles. Lily is mermaid-wet, the towel soaked. Hot drips fall on to her face and hair from the ceiling. Every muscle seems to flex and droop, her limbs socketless, her head weighted on her neck. The pain in her knee fades. The steam machine hisses and sighs somewhere near the floor. Two people in the corner murmur to one another; the woman next to Lily rubs her hand over her skin in long, methodical strokes. Sinead hitches one heel on to the bench and leans her arms on her knee, her hair falling over her face.

Suddenly the heat is too much – sealed in around Lily's nose and mouth. Every breath seems to take in only more heat, and when she moves her eyes they scald her lids. She stands and pads over the floor, through the plastic slats, and gulps at the cold, still air in the shower room.

She walks around: echoing, empty hot-rooms linked to a further, hotter twin; another steam room; showers with three jets; the small, seething box of a sauna; a belching, spitting jacuzzi; an icy plunge pool with a glassy surface. She finds it strange that just above this warren of heat and cleanliness is a road where cars and lorries and taxis power to and from Westway, the city's arched concrete spine. When she returns to the first steam room, she almost walks straight into Sinead.

She is coming out between the slats, her cheeks pinked by blood, her body gleaming with sweat and moisture. She walks up some steps and around a corner. Lily raises her eyes over the small, surrounding wall just in time to see her lower herself into the freezing plunge pool. Feet first, her body disappears into the turquoise water like a woman swallowed by quicksand – calves, legs, buttocks, waist, back, torso, neck, head. For a moment, all that remains on the surface are the ends of her hair; then they, too, are pulled down. Lily waits. And waits. Counts to five, anxiety brimming. Counts past seven, then eight, then nine.

Sinead explodes up through the surface, an emphatic column of flesh, gasping and shivering. She reaches for a towel and rubs roughly at her stippled skin. Lily looks at her, a delicate white all over; she looks at the small, tilted breasts, the dark arrowhead of hair, the thin, muscular arms, the twelve, evenly spaced ribs. She pictures Marcus's hands and how they might fit in the dip of the waist, or curve over the buttocks, or how his fingers might slot between each of the ribs. There is a scar pleating the flesh of her upper arm. Lily imagines it would feel like braille under your lips.

Upstairs, she watches in a mirror as, across the room, Sinead, dry and in a robe now, settles herself back on a lounger, picks up a book, opens it, places the bookmark inside the back cover. And she watches as she tries to read it, tries to go over the same paragraph, again and again. She watches as something keeps tugging at her attention and as she lets the book fall closed. When the tears come, they don't surprise her. They don't fall like Lily always thought tears did – out of the corners of the eyes and one by one. Sinead's all seem to come at once and from every pore, flowing down her cheeks and nose and chin as if her whole body is crying, as if they will never stop.

It is dark. Her wrists are pinned to the bed. Something is travelling over her, something cold and inquisitive, sucking and sniffing at her so vigorously she feels as though she's being vacuumed.

'What do you smell of?' Marcus is demanding, pressing his nose to her arms, shoulders, the cleft between her breasts, her stomach.

'Nothing,' she says, trying to turn away from him.

He places his hands on her shoulders, buries his nose in her neck, inhaling. 'What is it?' His hands are strong and insistent on her limbs. She wriggles, turning this way and that, trying to get away from him, but he holds her fast.

'Marcus,' she says, cross now, 'get off. You're hurting me.'

Suddenly he stops, his hands disappear from her skin.

She opens her eyes, uncurls her neck. He is above her, staring at her, his brows drawn together. 'It's eucalyptus,' he whispers, his voice low and barely audible. 'Why do you smell of eucalyptus?'

Lily thinks of an avenue of eucalyptus trees she once drove through in Portugal, the wind turning their leaves silver. 'I don't know.' She turns her back to him, pretending to be asleep.

But for the rest of the night she lies on her side watching the dark soak into grey, while Marcus, next to her, thrashes around as if he can't find a way to get comfortable.

'What you have to recognise,' Sinead says, one hand raised to waist-height and turned upwards, 'is that they are two halves of the same personality.' She pauses and walks to the other end of the platform as if to allow time for the furious scribbling around her. 'She represents all that Jane has been forced to suppress.' Her eyes travel the room, veer close to Lily, pass over her, and – is it Lily's imagination? – return, linger, then move on. Sinead turns on her spike heel, walks the other way, and moves the tip of her tongue across her lips. 'And as for him . . .' she continues.

Sinead has stopped on a corner, looked up and down the street and checked her watch. Is she waiting for someone? Lily leans against the wall of the doorway she is concealed in. She's going to approach her tonight, definitely. No more messing around. She just has to wait for the right moment, that's all.

Sinead folds her arms, as if she's cold, takes out her phone and starts pressing at the buttons. At the sound of someone approaching, she looks up quickly but when she sees a woman in a red mac looks back down at the phone.

Soho seems empty tonight, the café doors closed against the cold and the windows steamed over. People don't loiter at this time of year, but hurry along the usually thronged pavements, coats hunched up around their ears. Lily feels her feet begin to numb and she tries to curl her toes inside her shoes. Sinead is also cold, Lily sees. She stamps her feet against the concrete, pulls her scarf more tightly around her face.

Suddenly her head snaps round and her whole body flexes expectantly. She smiles. 'What time do you call this, then?' she shouts. A man in a leather jacket, tall, big, with dark hair, is running towards her down the middle of the road.

'I'm so sorry, I'm so sorry,' he is saying over and over again. 'The tube stopped in a tunnel for about three years.'

Sinead steps off the pavement and they meet near the kerb, Sinead saying something Lily can't hear and the man bends over to kiss her cheek. Sinead brings her hand up to curl round his shoulder and he presses his hand to her back like a tango dancer. It's only when he pulls away that Lily recognises him. The shock is like the shock of infidelity. She has to put out her hand to steady herself against the wall.

Aidan. It's Aidan. Running towards her, late. Kissing her on the cheek. How come Aidan is meeting up with her? Does this happen a lot? And does Marcus know?

They are moving off now. He is pulling something from his pocket and showing it to her, and their heads are bent over it together as they walk. Lily hurries after them, watches them stroll along pavements, skirt puddles and parking meters, cross roads, exchange sentences, brush against each other, hand a magazine back and forth between them. Outrage floods through Lily, and she isn't quite sure why. They stop at a cinema and wait in line to buy a ticket, standing close together as they talk. There is nothing serious in their demeanour. Sinead is talking, animated, in a long spurt, Aidan listening intently. The noise in the foyer means she has to lean on his shoulder and speak into his ear. He bends down to hear her, his hair falling into his eyes, and then he throws back his head and laughs, clutching at the arm she'd laid on him.

They reach the counter, buy a ticket then disappear down the stairs. Lily is left standing on the street outside, still unable to believe it. Seeing them together seems incongruous, ridiculous. She wants to go up to them and demand an explanation.

After saying goodbye to Aidan at the cinema doors, Sinead walks quickly through the city. Lily keeps about fifteen paces behind her, the city moving beneath them. The high, narrow streets of Soho give way to shops and boutiques, and by the time they reach Leicester Square, Lily is wondering how long they'll be walking. But there's no stopping. They pass the crowds outside the Hippodrome, the people streaming out of the theatres, the National Portrait Gallery, and take a left towards Charing Cross Station. Sinead turns in her direction once before she crosses the road and once more when she stops at a shop window and glances up the street. Both times, a cold fear closes around Lily's heart and she looks down, hiding her face in her scarf.

Sinead walks on past the station and down the side road towards Embankment. Lily can smell the river now, over the chalkiness of a building site and the doughy odour of a streetside pizza place – that fetid, dank heaviness of air. They pass through the tube station, and on the other side, Sinead inexplicably speeds up, the rucksack bouncing off her back as she weaves through the crowds. She must be late for something. People tut and sigh as Lily shoves her way past them, desperate not to lose sight of the tall figure ahead.

Sinead starts up the metal steps to Hungerford Bridge. By the time Lily reaches them, a large group of people is coming down, five abreast. She darts from one side of the staircase to the other but, drunk and unhurried, they don't let her through.

'Excuse me, excuse me,' Lily says. The people mill and sidestep, chatting and calling to each other; Lily stumbles through them and, as she turns to go up the second flight, she looks up.

Sinead is standing on the bridge, looking down.

Lily doesn't move, poised like a cat. Sinead turns and disappears from view. Lily leaps up the stairs two at a time. Did she see her? Was she looking at her? Did she imagine it?

When she reaches the bridge, it is busy, people ambling, holding hands, roller-blading, pushing bikes and buggies. There's no sign of Sinead. She's lost her. Lily shoves her way through the crowds, searching for the woman now so familiar to her.

Then, without warning, she's there, bearing down on Lily, her eyes flashing fire. 'Why are you following me?' With every word, Sinead gives Lily a shove until she's pressed up against the barrier, the metal pushing into Lily's back.

'I—'

'What is your fucking problem?' Sinead towers over her. 'Leave. Me. Alone. Do you hear me? And tell . . .' she falters '. . . tell your boyfriend as well.'

'Marcus?' Lily says, the word coming out more loudly than she'd planned.

'Yeah. *Marcus*. Every time I turn around it's either you or him. Is stalking a thing for both of you?' Her bravura cracks. Lily sees her face collapse, tears spring down her cheeks. 'Leave me alone,' she whispers. 'I want nothing to do with either of you.'

There is a kind of ringing, like tinnitus, in Lily's head. 'Do you mean Marcus has been . . . in touch with you?'

'In touch?' Sinead repeats hysterically. '*In touch?*' She holds the barrier for support. 'Christ! He— he phones me twelve times a day. He follows me to work. He follows me from work. I'm surprised you haven't bumped into each other.'

There is a pause. Sinead presses her hands to her eyes. 'Look,' she says, more quietly, 'I don't know what you want from me, but . . . but I really have nothing to say to you.' She walks off.

'Wait!' Lily goes after her. 'I just want to know what happened. I thought you were—'

A train thunders past them, overhead wires crackling, lighted windows throwing bluish light on to Sinead's wet and furious face, its roar swallowing Lily's words.

'What?' Sinead yells.

'I thought you were DEAD.'

'Dead?'

'Yes!'

The train rattles past, receding into the night. Sinead is incredulous, disgusted. 'Is that what he told you?' Her hands are shaking, Lily sees, as they tug at imaginary folds in her jacket. Below them the Thames twists black in the dark.

'No . . . he . . . no.'

'Then why on earth would you think that?'

'I . . . I . . .' Lily stammers '. . . he . . . I don't know.'

'Well, I'm not,' she says. 'Sorry to inconvenience you,' and she moves away again.

'Sinead,' Lily catches up with her, 'please tell me what happened. Please. You have to.'

'No, I don't.'

'Please. I just . . . I need to know.'

Sinead stops and gives a short laugh. 'You *need* to know?' she repeats. 'Well, why don't you ask him?' She spits out the last word as if it tastes bad. 'Why haunt me?'

Lily blinks and a part of her almost laughs. 'I'm . . . he doesn't . . . he won't talk about it.'

'Well, that's really not my problem.' She is walking faster now, sidestepping people. Lily hurries after her, the butt of blows from people's shoulders and bags.

'I know,' she says, breathless, 'I know it's not. But, *please*. What happened? Just tell me what happened.'

Sinead stops, her teeth set against each other. Fury seems to have flared again within her. 'Look,' she almost shouts, 'I refuse to have this conversation. This is nothing to do with me. You are nothing to do with me. I don't want . . . I don't want to . . . to see you ever again. *I want you to leave me alone.* Just . . . just go away! OK?' Without waiting for an answer, she dives into the crowd.

Lily follows, blind now, and seizes a fistful of her jacket sleeve. 'Listen—'

'Get off!' Sinead splutters, appalled, trying to wrench her arm free. Lily sees a kind of panicked astonishment in her still-wet eyes, feels the hardening of sinew and muscle beneath her grip. 'Let go of me!'

'No!' Lily grips her arm with all her strength, aware that this is her last and only chance. 'I want you to tell me. Please!'

A sob tears from Sinead's mouth, her fist batters Lily's hand, then scrabbles, trying to peel away her fingers. 'Why are you doing this?' she whispers hoarsely. 'You're *mad.*'

Lily feels the fabric of Sinead's sleeve slipping from her grasp. Sinead gives one final, vicious wrench to her arm: she comes free and reels backwards, colliding heavily with the rail. There is a dull clunk as the side of her pelvis impacts with the metal. She gives a small, bewildered, 'Oh', bends away from the pain, her hair swinging over her face, then tries to straighten herself, one hand pressed over her back, and limps away.

Lily watches, shoulders slumped, tears aching in her throat. 'Sinead!' she calls after her.

She doesn't look round, doesn't falter.

'He told me you walked out on him!'

She takes two more strides. Then another. Then her left foot slows, hesitates, and comes to rest next to her right. Lily moves forward. When she reaches her, Sinead is turning slowly towards her. Lily waits. Her eyes lock with Lily's, flick from one to the other. She frowns slightly, appears to be thinking.

'He told me that one day . . . you just went,' Lily says quickly, the words tagged to each other. 'That he didn't know why.'

Sinead swallows. She looks down at the river for a moment, then back. 'He said that?'

'Yes. That you . . . just walked out.'

'I just walked out?'

'Uh-huh.'

'He said I just walked out?'

Lily nods.

Sinead touches her forehead with her first two fingers, stretching the skin next to her hairline. 'So . . . you have no idea why he and I . . . why I left?'

'No.'

'None at all?'

'He won't talk about you. Not to me anyway. He just told me you left him. That's all.'

Sinead stares again at the river. 'If I tell you,' she begins, and Lily's pulse quickens with something between excitement and triumph, 'will you promise never to come anywhere near me ever again?'

'Yes.'

'Or to any of my lectures?'

'Yes.'

'Do you promise?'

'I promise.'

'All right.' Sinead nods. Twice. 'I'll tell you.'

part | two

If I told you the whole story it would never end . . . What's happened to me has happened to a thousand women

FEDERICO GARCIA LORCA, *Doña Rosita*

The shower-head gasps as she turns it off and the silence of the empty flat rushes in on her. She grips handfuls of wet hair and squeezes rivulets of water down her body, shaking herself like a dog, misting the glass bricks with spray. Then she steps out of the steam and, winding a towel around her, leaves wet soleprints marking out her route, which are already evaporating by the time she reaches the bedroom.

Sinead towels herself roughly, tugging a comb through her hair, grimacing as the teeth snag on knots. Then she pulls open her desk drawer and rummages about for a pair of scissors.

The new dress hangs on the outside of the wardrobe. She bought it weeks ago when, numbed by the idea that she was not yet half-way through the allotted two months of their separation, she'd gone on a shopping spree. She'd returned to the flat with that heady feeling of glee and guilt that comes after a major spend to find Aidan and his friend Sam cooking huge amounts of food in the kitchen. They'd taken an amused interest in the contents of her various plastic bags, and made her hold up her purchases one by one as they sat at the table and ate their way through their labours. 'God, I'm so glad I'm not a girl,' Aidan had said after a while. 'It's so *complicated*.'

With the scissors, she clips off the price label and flings it into the bin behind her. Humming now, she pulls the dress over her head, drawing the zip up through the fabric. Then she wanders through the flat, turning the CD-player up to volume ten, filling the air with sound.

Her bloodstream is full of bubbles, tiny pockets of pure oxygen hammering round her system. Marcus is coming back.

My birthday fell almost exactly half-way between the Christmas and Easter vacations, when post-grad students like me had a break from the carousel of giving lectures and tutorials, and had a chance to catch up on the supposed real matter in hand – the thesis. February in that city was the worst time, the fog rolling for miles over the flat, ditched fields to collect in the hollow where the city cowers. Icy moisture hung in the air. It rained constantly, the streets wet and polished like sealskins, the sky getting dark at half past four. I lost my gloves and my bare hands would ossify round my bicycle handlebars in the freezing damp air as I cycled from my house to seminars, tutorials, the faculty. I had to insulate my books in layers of plastic bags to keep them dry on my rides to the library. When I arrived, I headed for an out-of-the-way wing, piled my books into a towering ziggurat beside me and risked chilblains by resting my wet feet on the tepid, vibrating pipes. As I flexed my back up from the desk, I could see my face thrown back at me in the window opposite, teeth biting the inside of my cheek, left index finger twirling my hair.

I was, at this time, bored with my life. I was teaching two days a week, giving three lecture courses, and I was, on and off and usually more off than on, seeing an art historian called Antony who lugged great A3 illustrated books around everywhere he went, and refused to cycle because he couldn't buy a bicycle basket big enough to fit them in. It was the second year of my Ph.D. I'd given up the freedom, and the mind-crushing tedium, of an underpaid job to come to this insular city to study. At that very moment I couldn't think beyond or around the five-thousand-word chapter I had to write by the beginning of March. Thesis hand-in, in two and a half to three years' time, seemed like a distant, mystical grail. This annoyed me. I wanted to be able to project myself beyond these lodestones, which sucked all my thoughts towards them and repelled any others from my head.

I wasn't sure about this city, about this university, about this library, about the people who taught me or the ones I taught, about being here among stacks and stacks of spine-indexed, recorded, catalogued books that smelt of mice and rotting leaves. Could I see myself here for another two years, maybe more? Was this what I wanted when I'd vaulted that blind hurdle of my thesis?

I didn't know. All I knew was that when I read the late-medieval texts I was studying for my Ph.D., my mind latched on to something: it caught and sent a fly-wheel spinning somewhere, which then cranked another movement, slow at first, then bigger and bigger until it filled all space with noise and momentum until there was no space left at all, until when I looked up again at the window it was pitchy black outside and my face, puzzled and unfamiliar, was suspended out there in the dusky branches of the trees surrounding the library.

Three weeks before my birthday, I was sitting with my hands curled round an empty blue china teacup in the library café with my two housemates, Kate and Ingrid. Ingrid was slumped over, her forehead resting on the table's chipped surface.

'Get me out of this place,' she groaned.

Kate and I didn't respond, both staring into space, Kate jiggling her foot up and down on the spar underneath the table.

'Hello?' Ingrid said, raising her head. 'Are either of you two listening to me?'

Kate's attention zoned in on her. 'Huh? What did you say?'

Ingrid scrumpled up her chocolate wrapper viciously, and flicked it towards the bin. She missed, but didn't go and pick it up. 'Nothing. Sorry to interrupt your reverie. I was only attempting some, you know, conversation.'

'Do you know what I think?' I said suddenly.

Kate sat up, stopped jiggling; the cups, knives and tea-spoons were still once more. She looked at me, expectant.

'I think we should have a party.'

Kate and Ingrid were silent. They turned to look at each other, then back at me.

'Now that,' Ingrid said, 'is a fantastic idea. When?'

'My birthday.'

'Oh, yes,' Kate breathed, in her oddly feverish way, 'a party. Oh, yes.'

'God, that's such a good idea. Let's get everyone down from London. We need a really good—' Ingrid broke off, staring at something over my head. 'Hey,' she said, 'don't look now, but lover boy's just come in.'

I ducked down and rested my chin on my hands, folded on the table. 'Has he?'

'Yup. It's all off again, I take it?'

'Um. Kind of.'

'Well, I'm not surprised if he's taken to wearing those in public.' Ingrid pointed and, despite myself, I turned round. Antony the art historian was standing with his back to us and was wearing a pair of dungarees.

'Oh, my God.' I swung round again.

'He probably bought them in a spate of lovelorn grief over you. Think about it. You're sleeping with a man whose choice of garment is dungarees. What does this say about you? Oooh, he's coming over.'

'I quite like them,' Kate said.

'You would,' muttered Ingrid, then trilled, 'Hi!'

Antony dropped his books down on the table with a thud. 'Hello. Kate. Ingrid,' he nodded at us in turn. 'Sinead.'

'Hi.' I turned up my face to look at him. 'Are you going to sit down?'

He hesitated.

'Don't worry,' Ingrid said, 'we're off. Come on, Kate.' Ingrid seized a fistful of Kate's jumper and dragged her up off the seat. 'See you later, Sinead.' They disappeared, Kate protesting mildly at Ingrid's manhandling.

'So,' Antony said, 'how are you doing?'

'Not too bad.'

'How's medieval romance?'

'All right.'

'Have you got any further with it after that critical essay you were telling me about?'

I shifted impatiently in my seat. I had a policy of not talking about work during my tea breaks.

'We're having a party,' I said, hoping to distract him.

'Really? When?'

'My birthday. '

'I didn't know it was your birthday.'

'Well, it is.'

He emptied a small packet of sugar into his murky cup, releasing a fine spray of tiny crystals all over the table. 'You didn't tell me,' he said, looking down as he stirred his tea.

'I'm telling you now.'

'I see.'

For something to do, I flipped open one of the covers of his art books and pretended to be reading the frontispiece.

'Do you want to come?' I said, and realised the book was upside-down. I turned it round.

'To what?'

I glared at him. 'The party.'

He glared back. 'Do you want me to come?'

'Do you want to come?' I batted the question back at him like a forcefully aimed ping-pong ball.

'I want to come if you want me to come,' he said quickly, a smile beginning to curl his mouth. He was good at this, I remembered. I sighed and shut the book. This could go on all afternoon. I had work to do.

'All right.' I gave in. For now. 'I'd like you to come.'

'Great.' He smiled and, under the table, I felt his knee brushing mine. 'I'll come then.'

Sinead crams a carton of juice into the fridge door and a vodka bottle into the freezer, the ends of her hair brushing the layer of white, steaming ice. Then she slumps down on a chair at the table. She wonders where Aidan is and if he'll be in tonight. She thinks, idly, that she's hardly seen him since he came back from New York. He must be busy with his new job.

She lays out on the table a sheaf of student essays, some pens, and a volume of poems she needs to read for a seminar she's giving next week. She looks at her watch. Only seven fifteen. His flight doesn't even land until seven thirty.

She fiddles with the chair, getting a cushion from the sofa and settling it behind her back, shifting the chair towards the table and then back again by increments. She leans her elbows on the tabletop. Is she supposed to bend slightly or have a straight back? She can't remember and spends several minutes trying to conjure up those X-ray pictures that show bad positions for the spine. She picks up a pen and tests it several times on the back of an envelope by writing her name over and over again in a variety of different handwriting styles.

Then she gets cross with herself and slams down an essay in front of her, pen poised. '*Aphra Behn wrote in a time when women didn't write, about things that women didn't write about,*' she reads. Sinead frowns, shuffles the essay to the back of the pile, and looks at the next. *'What one must always be asking oneself is whether one's sexuality can be read and understood by one's'* – Her eyes slide away from the page and, putting down her pen, she examines her bare feet, her beetle-green toenails. Looks at her watch again. Rolls a mango from the fruit bowl beneath her hand. Jumps up again. Changes the CD.

I was standing in the hallway. This was the only reason. In the years in which I will look back at this moment and trace back why it happened and how it happened like it did, I will think: I answered the door, not because it was my party, but because I was standing in the hall. I won't be able to remember why I was standing in the hall. I just was. There are always points of collision – moments at which it is possible to say, yes, if I had done that differently or I had been standing slightly to the right or I had left the house two minutes earlier or if I hadn't crossed the road just then my life would have taken a completely different course.

So I was – for whatever forgotten reason, or maybe for no reason at all – moving through the hallway of the house I shared with Kate and Ingrid during the party celebrating my twenty-fifth birthday when the doorbell rang. And I moved towards it, ignorant of the effect it would have on my life.

I unlatched the lock and swung back the door. What I saw: two blokes, shivering in the fog-laden air, blinking in the light cast by my hall lamp. One was taller than the other, hanging back. Dark eyes with dark hair hanging over them. The other had short but soft-looking yellow hair, blue eyes, a duffel coat, and cans of lager under his arm.

'Yes?' I said. I had one hand on my hip and the other on the door jamb as if at any minute I might slam it shut.

The men shifted uneasily. The short-haired one transferred the cans to the other hand, then back again.

'Hi. We're friends of . . . of Sinead.'

I looked them over again, just for effect. 'Are you now?'

'Yes.' He nodded, gaining confidence. Even grinned.

'Well, I'm Sinead,' I said, 'and I've never met either of you before in my life.'

Their faces wilted. But I smiled. 'It's all right, you can come in.' I stepped back into the hall to let them in, they passed me, the cold from their bodies brushing my skin. 'Who are you anyway?' I called after them over the music.

'This is Aidan,' the short-haired one said, pointing at his friend, 'and I'm Marcus.'

She decides to do the washing-up, her hands disappearing beneath hot frothy suds, the glasses and plates knocking against each other under the surface. Water and stray bubbles slide from drying crockery down the draining-board and back into the sink.

Lying on her back on the floor, she calls Ingrid, leaves a message on her answerphone, and then calls her brother. 'Michael Wilson,' she says, 'it's me.'

'Hi,' he says, sounding surprised, as he always does. 'Wait a sec. I'll turn the music down.'

She hears the receiver drop to the table and his feet

slapping over the room and the music dim, as if it's been sucked into the distance.

'So,' his voice is back, close to her ear, 'how are you?'

'OK. I was trying to work but I appear to have the concentration of a goldfish, so I thought I'd call you instead.'

'Oh. Thanks. So I shouldn't be alarmed if you suddenly forget who I am and what you're doing on the phone to me?' There is a sudden cracking, crunching noise, followed by the sound of loud chewing. 'Anyway,' Michael says with his mouth full, 'I thought—'

'Are you eating?' Sinead shouts. 'How many times have I told you not to do that when you're on the phone?'

He laughs, chewing again. 'I know, I know. I only ever do it with you.'

'Is that supposed to comfort me? Or flatter me? It's foul. I feel like . . . I feel like you're filling my ear with saliva.'

'OK,' he swallows, 'sorry.'

She balances the soles of her feet against the wall, and they speak of their grandmother's operation, of when Michael will go home next, of a film Sinead saw last week, of meeting up for coffee on Saturday. And Michael tells Sinead how his girlfriend had a scan today and how the baby was lying in an invisible hammock, its thumb between its jawbuds, and how they could see the small, electronic flicker of its heartbeat.

There were walls of pounding music surrounding everyone and everything. I wanted to slice through the sound with a knife, pull its edges apart and step through into the silent beyond. The kitchen was crammed with bodies and flesh.

Kate had wrapped the lampshade in blue tissue paper, and people were swimming through the slow, aquarium room, holding drinks aloft, mouthing words, the music blanking out any sense of what they were.

On my razor-blade shoes, I slid round the walls, the skin of my bare back to the grain of the wallpaper. I'd put my glass down somewhere but had no idea where — I recalled the feeling of its hard curves leaving my palm, but couldn't dredge up where that happened or why or who I was with. I could also remember the sensation of the crackling, membrane-thin paper of a joint between my fingers. But that had gone too now.

Suddenly Antony was next to me, smoke wisping from his mouth and nostrils into the blue light surrounding his head. Then his lips were making a moist crescent shape on my neck, his fingers dragging through my hair. I slithered out from underneath him and through the doors into the garden.

It was cold. Mist hung just above my head. The back lawn, enclosed on all sides by an uneven brick wall, was full of people holding sparklers. The fizzing, crackling fires scorched trails of light on to my retinas, and I blinked, still seeing the streams behind my eyelids.

Holding up my dress, I climbed on to the wall and, holding out my arms, I stepped, one foot at a time, along the length of the wall, my heels digging into the loose plaster. The air felt clearer up here, I seemed to be above the mist and closer to the stars. Below me, people shrieked and laughed and the sparklers jittered through the dark like fireflies. I peeled my feet off the wall one by one and placed them in front of me; and I progressed gradually the length of our ramshackle and weed-choked garden. I'm twenty-five, I thought, twenty-five, I have existed in this world for a quarter of a century. When I reached the intersection with the back wall I heard a voice below me: 'Jump.'

I snapped my head around, and lost my balance: suddenly stars and tree branches and sparklers were swerving before me, and I didn't know which way I was facing or if I was falling. My arms whirled in the air around me. The scene stilled. Balance returned. I was amazed to find myself still on the wall. Below me was the man who had gatecrashed the party. The one with the blue eyes. Arms outstretched. Duffel coat open to reveal a slippery red lining.

'Jump,' he said again.

'No.'

'Go on.'

'Why?'

'Because I said so,' he said.

'That's not a good enough reason.'

'Because I want you to.'

'Neither's that,' I said.

'What?'

'A good enough reason.'

'Why do you need one?' he asked.

I was silent, flummoxed.

'Go on,' he urged again. 'Jump.'

He narrowed his arms to about the width of my waist, and then I was passing through the air, under the stars but above the sparklers and I felt the impact of his hands on my ribcage and my arms were about his neck and before I was even aware of it happening he was swinging me round and round.

I would remember this when, sometime in the dead hours of the next morning, I woke with Antony's arm heavy across me and the light grey behind the curtain. Antony's frame was holding the covers away from me, and there was a channel of freezing air between us. I got up, put on layers of clothes from my drawer, padded to the bathroom through the party debris and drank from the tap, holding the ends of my hair out of the flow. Looking into the mirror at my smudged face, I recalled not an image but a sensation of the gatecrasher's body imprinted on my front, and his fingers pressed into the spaces between each of my vertebrae.

When she puts the phone down from Michael, the roots of her hair are still damp so she opens the window in the bedroom, and leans with her elbows on the wide, stone sill, looking down into the street. Through the open door of the pub down the road, she sees the barman laying out mats on the tables and lifting down upturned chairs.

A group of people who live a few doors down pass below her. One of them jumps from paving slab to paving slab, avoiding the cracks, singing a song Sinead recognises. The rest laugh. She looks up, up over the roofs of the buildings opposite, over the dome of the Hawksmoor church two streets away and up into the sky where planes are circling over the city, pulling lines of vapour though the ether.

I walked down the aisle of a supermarket, pushing a trolley with wayward wheels. Antony trailed me, three or four paces behind.

'The thing is, Dr Jarvis just isn't a Vermeer expert at all,' he was saying, 'and that's the kind of person I need. I don't need some bloody cowboy like Jarvis. Do you know what he said to me the other day? Tony, he said, because remember I told you he always calls me Tony . . .'

I came to an abrupt stop in front of the pulses. Antony nearly fell into me, then wandered towards the cereals, still talking. To quell an urge to ram the trolley into his ankles, I snatched up a packet of red lentils and pretended to be reading the instructions.

'I wouldn't bother with those if I were you.'

I turned. My instant reaction was the thought that there was the most beautiful line between his lips; undulating, curved up at the ends. When he smiled, the pointed tips of his incisors showed – something I have always found peversely sexy.

'Why not?'

Marcus shrugged. 'Too much effort for too little taste.'

His face altered after he said that. His eyes slipped from mine. He seemed nervous and cleared his throat, as if about to say something yet afraid to.

'It's nice to see you again,' I said.

'Yes. I was thinking—'

But a proprietorial hand on the small of my back interrupted us.

'Hello, Marcus.'

I was appalled to find Antony next to me, leaning on the handle of my trolley, letting fall a box of cereal into its chrome meshing.

'Oh.' Marcus made no effort to hide his surprise. The beam of his vision swung from me to him to me again to our joined bodies, comprehension percolating through his face. 'Hi, Antony. How are you doing?'

'Not bad. Yourself?'

'Er.' He glanced at me again. 'All right.'

Antony didn't say anything further. I moved away from his hand, but it followed me across the new space between us. The three of us stared at each other, then Antony turned round and shoved at the trolley.

'Well, we must be off. See you.'

'Yeah, see you later. 'Bye Sinead.'

As we walked away, I asked, 'How do you know him?'

'He's an architect. Part Three, I think, or maybe diploma year. They're in the same faculty building as us. He thinks he's pretty hot shit. Doesn't deign to mix much with us *hoi polloi*. He lives in some derelict factory in London somewhere and commutes in when he needs to.'

At the end of the aisle, I turned, hoping to see him still standing there. But he must have walked away fast, because it was empty, the metres and metres of shiny grey lino stretching out underneath the strip-lighting.

I turned back to Antony, saw the way his hair grew away from the whorled flesh of his ear, saw his hands curled round the trolley handles, saw his lips moving over his teeth. Later that afternoon, in his high-windowed room, I told him our affair was over.

Sinead closes the window. Night air is settling over the city like a sheet of damp muslin. Further down the street, she sees a teenager lighting a sparkler, which spits sharp white darts into the gathering dark. He spins around, shrieking, a fiery dervish, his friend watching, a lit match in his fingers. The window sticks so she has to reopen and slam it closed three times.

She waters her plants, gives the floor a sweep, straightens the rug. She leans over the fridge and the cupboards, and takes out things she'll cook with later: a purple-black aubergine, hollow-centred and taut-skinned, onions, a limp sheaf of basil, a china mortar with a chipped pestle, a chopping knife with a thin, lithe blade.

If you lived for any length of time in that city, you knew that if you bumped into someone once, you'd bump into them again. But Marcus disappeared. I didn't go out of my way to find him: I could have looked him up on the post-grad directory, could have asked for him at the architecture faculty, could have reached him over the internal e-mail. But I didn't. That wasn't the way I did things; my pride prevented me. But that didn't mean I didn't look for his shape in the library or on pavements as I passed on my bicycle, or for the gleam of his hair in bars when I sat at night round tables with my friends. By April I'd given up hope of seeing him again; by May I'd banished him from my thoughts.

I was cycling along the main street. It was car-free so I could weave about in the middle. It was, I'd decided that morning, the first day of summer: my side-split skirt rippled and tugged like a kite around my legs as I rode; the students were all in post-exam frenzies so I could spend the day back at work on my thesis. I was heading for the library, which would be cool and silent and empty.

I was about to turn off into a cobbled laneway when I felt a restrictive tightness round my thighs. Then it was as if I'd hit a brick wall: my bike wheels screeched to a sudden halt, I nearly fell over the handlebars, my front wheel veering to the right. I had to slam my foot on the ground to stop myself toppling over. For a moment I thought I'd hit a fissure in the cobbles, but then I bent over to look down at the bike.

'Shit.'

The panel of my skirt had tangled itself up in the back wheel, winding its length round and round the hub. Not only was the bike now immovable but I was tied to it.

'Shitshitshit,' I cursed, through gritted teeth, as I lifted as much of the bike as I could, dragging it towards the kerb. Holding the handlebars with one hand, I tugged ineffectually at my skirt, but the material just tightened, pulling at the spokes.

I straightened up, assessing my options. Bicycles crunched past me, chrome glinting in the sunlight. The pavements were full of shambling groups of tourists, dressed in leisurewear, clutching maps and cameras. I calculated in my head the distance to the nearest cycle shop and whether I could prevail on any passer-by.

'Excuse me,' I wailed, in the general direction of the people on the pavement. A small man with a neatly clipped moustache and a blue cloth hat hesitated. 'Excuse me?' I repeated, hopefully, trying not to lean over and seize his arm. '*Excusez-moi? Français? Non?*'

The man frowned.

'*Deutsch?*' I hazarded.

He nodded, unsmiling; relief swept through me, then I trawled my mind for German phrases I hadn't spoken since I was sixteen. 'Um . . . *meine bicyclette* . . .' No, that was French. '*mein Fahrrad ist . . . ist kaput.*'

The man and his tight-lipped wife lowered their eyes to my bicycle, then looked back at me.

'I . . . er . . . *ich brauche* . . .' I felt sweat beginning to moisten my back. 'I NEED HELP!' I shouted, suddenly losing patience. Wasn't it obvious what had happened? '*Hilfe!* PLEASE!'

The Germans flinched, stepped back, then began sidling away.

'Wait!' I yelled after them. 'Don't go! Please! *Bitte!*'

Then, first wandering into my peripheral vision and now standing smack bang in front of me, was Marcus. He was wearing shorts and a grey shirt, holding a folder under one arm, sunglasses hiding his eyes, a half-eaten apple in his hand. All the blood in my body seemed to heat and rise to the surface of my skin.

'Hello,' he said, in a conversational tone, 'how are you?'

My relief and pleasure transmuted into irritation. 'How am I?' I shouted heatedly. 'How am I? Well, I'm great. Never better. How are you?'

He nodded, flinging the apple into a bin. 'Pretty good.'

Stepping forward, he lifted a book from the basket on the front of my bike and flipped it over in his hand. '*Maidens and Sorceresses: the Representation of Women in Medieval Poetry*,' he read, and grimaced. 'Is that what you spend your time doing?'

I snatched it back and slammed it into the basket. 'Much as I would like to discuss my work with you, right now isn't a good time.'

Marcus stepped up close to me, pushing back his sunglasses to rest on his cropped hair. 'Why not?'

'*Why not?*' I shrieked. 'Look at my fucking bike! I'm trapped! I can't move! I may never walk again!'

He considered me from our very close proximity. He had smooth, even-toned, blemishless skin. I'd forgotten about the curve of his lips. I felt the heat rising again to my neck and face, but was too cross to acknowledge it.

'Which one are you?' he said.

'What?'

'Maiden or sorceress. Which one are you?'

I ran through my head the pros and cons of slapping him: it would make me feel an awful lot better but he might run away without assisting me. I decided, on balance, against it. 'I need your help,' I said instead.

'What's happened to that boyfriend of yours, then?'

'What are you talking about?' I snapped, taken aback by the direction the conversation had taken.

'I haven't seen you for ages,' he changed tack again, ignoring his earlier question and my lack of answer, 'where've you been?'

'Here. I've been here. Where've *you* been?'

'Here too.'

'Look.' Flustered and completely wrongfooted, I attempted to take command of the situation: 'Marcus, will you please help me, please?'

He stepped back, surveyed the bike, my tangled skirt, the jammed wheel, then shoved his folder into my basket. 'Wait here,' he said – unnecessarily, I felt, as I clearly wasn't going anywhere. 'I'll be back in a sec.'

I stood, tethered to my bike, watching him go. If there had been a heat-sensitive camera on me at that point, you could have seen a plume of fiery red flaring up from the top of my head.

When Marcus returned, he was deft, serious and efficient – and clutching a monkey wrench. I tried to take it from him. 'It's all right, I can do it.'

'Don't be stupid,' Marcus said. 'It's easier if I do it.'

We fought over it, tug-of-war style, like toddlers over a doll.

'I can't let you.'

'Why?'

I struggled to formulate an answer. 'Feminist guilt,' I said eventually.

'Bollocks to your feminist guilt. Just stand still and shut up.'

Marcus pulled it from my grip and, squatting down, wrestled it against the wheel.

'So,' I said, not looking at him, 'have you finished for the summer?'

'No. I've finished for good.'

'For good?'

'Yep. That's it. Eight years of architecture training in the bag. Thank the Lord.'

Marcus rolled the wheel away from the bike and, lowering the back end, started unravelling the twisted, oil-smeared cloth of my skirt. It was concertinaed into black folds. There were translucent tears in its crosshatched fabric like stretchmarks. I plucked at it. 'Oh, God, look at the state of that. You don't have a penknife, do you?'

He dug into his shorts pocket and dropped into my hand a bunch of keys, attached to which was a red-cased penknife. The keys were warm, almost hot. The physics of it: the heat from the surface blood in his groin had heated the metal of the keys in his pocket, which in turn were now warming my palm. A chain of heat-agitated atoms.

He was reattaching the wheel to my bicycle, breathing hard as he turned the wrench. I examined the back of his neck and shoulders as I used the blade of his penknife to slice through the material of my skirt above my knee. 'There!' I exclaimed, balling up the ruined excess and chucking it into the bin.

He looked up, the wheel in place, and a rush of red fired his face. 'Oh,' he said, 'right. Looks OK. I mean it looks better like that, I think. I mean, I liked it before and everything but, you know, it's good. Yeah. It's great.'

I took the weight of the bike from him, balancing it against my leg. 'Thank you so much for helping me. You were brilliant.'

He was sheepish, looking down at his feet, which

he was shifting around on the pavement. 'That's fine. Anytime.'

There was a pause. Marcus scratched the back of his neck. I examined the plastic rimming of my bicycle seat.

'So,' I said eventually, 'er . . . what are your plans for the summer?'

He pushed something up to my face and for a moment I didn't recognise it.

'Didn't you have a look at this while I was gone?' he was saying. It was the folder he'd left in my basket.

'Er. No. What is it?'

He put it into my hands. I read the label on the front: 'The Beaufort Chinese Architecture Grant'.

'I'm off to Beijing tomorrow.'

'Beijing?' I repeated.

'Yeah,' his face was confused, almost apologetic, 'I got this grant to go to China. To study . . .' He was staring at me and seemed to lose his thread. I waited. He rubbed his thumb across his nose.

'To study . . . ?' I prompted.

'To study the processes of developing Chinese architecture. For three months. Initially. But then . . .' he trailed off again, but rallied himself '. . . it could be extended. I don't know.'

'China,' I declared loudly, as if preparing for a lecture on the subject. I swung my leg over the crossbar of my bike. 'China,' I repeated. 'I see. Well.' I was furious. I knew that. But I didn't quite know why. All I did know was that I had to leave. Fast. Or I might do something embarrassing. Something I'd regret. 'WellImustbeoffnow'bye,' I gabbled and leaned my weight on the pedal. The bike ground into movement agonisingly slowly.

'Sinead,' Marcus said, apparently alarmed that I was leaving, 'wait a sec.'

The bike picked up momentum. I waved in what I hoped was a cheery, carefree manner as I swept away. ''Bye! Have the time of your life!'

By the time I reached the library, the bones of my fingers were hot and sweat itched at my hair.

Four, or maybe five days later the phone rang late at night. I wasn't asleep but lying on my front on my bedroom floor reading a book I shouldn't have been reading – a contemporary novel. Nothing to do with post-feminist readings of medieval literature. The phone rang, four, five, six, seven times. I propped myself up on my elbow and peered at my watch. Eleven forty-eight. I returned to my book. The phone carried on ringing. Where the hell were Kate and Ingrid? It was bound to be Kate's boyfriend – an emaciated medic from Birmingham with a sparse goatee. After the fifteenth ring, I hauled myself to my feet, my finger still hooked into my place in the novel's spine, and pulled open my door.

'Bloody bastard phone, won't be for me anyway, who rings this late anyway, bastard,' I grumbled to myself, as I stomped down the stairs, slipping slightly in my socked feet. 'Yes,' I barked into the receiver.

'Can I speak to Sinead, please?'

I frowned. Didn't recognise the voice. The line blizzarded with static and distance. 'Yes. Speaking.'

'Oh. Hi. Sinead, it's Marcus.'

I clutched my novel so hard my finger popped out of my page. I looked down at it in annoyance – I'd never find my place again now.

'What?' I said, bizarrely, then tried again: 'Marcus. Where are you?'

'I'm sitting in a small glass booth in the Friendship Store.'

'The . . . ?' I shook my head, as if to try to understand what was going on. 'I thought you were in Beijing.'

'I am.'

'But . . .'

'The Friendship Store in Beijing.'

'Oh. OK.'

'It's like a supermarket for foreigners.'

'Right.'

There was a silence. I panicked, ran through the limited things I knew about China to think of a question to ask.

'Sinead?' said Marcus's voice, from a huge distance.

'Yes?'

'I realised I never asked you what you were doing this summer.'

'Huh? Oh. Staying here mostly. I've got work to do. You know – meetings to go to. Courses to prepare. That kind of thing.'

'Well, I was wondering . . . I mean, you can say no if you want. You hardly know me and everything – I mean you don't really know me at all. But,' Marcus said with emphasis, as if gathering courage, 'I just thought I'd call and see if you wanted to come out here to meet me.'

'To China?' I said. 'You're asking me to come to China?'

'Er. Yes.'

I would later try to convince myself – and all my friends, and all my family – that I thought it over, that I considered it, that I understood and assessed and came to terms with all the problems of abandoning my life and plans to go travelling in a developing country with a man I hardly knew. But I didn't.

'Yes,' I said instantly, 'yes, I will.'

She leaps on to a chair and by the time he's opening the door, she's standing on the table. The door opens and there he is. Her initial impression is his tan – his skin has been turned a warm, even colour by the American sun – and he's smiling. She wants to close her eyes, to still this moment, not let it pass, to let them wait there before they get their hands on each other.

He is laughing now at the sight on her on the table, slinging his backpack to the floor and coming towards her.

'Wait!' she cries. Marcus stops immediately. 'I have something to show you.'

He smiles. 'Do you want me to close my eyes?'

'No.'

Slowly, slowly Sinead raises the hem of her dress. Centimetre by centimetre it creeps up over her thighs, the tops of her legs, her mound of Venus, her hipbones. She is wearing new black lace knickers. He watches, eyes fixed on her hem. Neither of them breathes. Finally, she stands with her belly button exposed.

They stare at each other. He puts out one foot, then another and another, coming towards her slowly across the floor. 'You know what I think?'

'What?'

He is in touching distance now. If he raised his arm, his fingertips would brush her skin. 'I think that they look great, but there is one slight problem.'

She is covering her mouth with one hand now, suppressed laughter jamming up her throat. She knows what comes next. He is standing right in front of her now, looking up, his head on one side.

'I'm not entirely sure that they fit you very well.'

'Really?' she says in mock-concern. 'Do you think so?'

'Yeah. I'm actually very worried. In fact,' and he unfolds his arms and puts out his hand, 'I think I may need to check.' Very, very slowly, he puts his hand under the skirt at the back and rubs his palm over her left buttock.

'Hmm.' He frowns, puts out his other hand and runs both over her backside. The palms of his hands feel roughened and create a static frisson on the material. Sinead is holding her breath now. This is almost more than she can bear. 'Well, they fit OK at the back, but what I'm more worried about is round the front. If I could just . . .' He brings his hand up over her hipbone and it inches down. 'It's here that really worries me. I'm just not sure if they fit here,' and he plunges his fingers between the tops of her legs. Sinead gives a piercing shriek, Marcus buries his head between her legs, she leaps down on top of him, he grabs her round the waist. Entwined and paralysed with laughter, they crash backwards into the kitchen cabinet.

'Ow,' says Sinead, as their combined weight glances off her backbone, but it doesn't really hurt because they are kissing and kissing and pulling at each other's clothes. She has her legs wrapped round his waist and she is pulling at his hair and he is ripping down the straps on her dress and laughing and they are very good at this, very practised, their lips meet exactly and she remembers this even before she remembers remembering it. And all the time they are talking and the words come out a bit like this:

'Oh, God . . . how was . . . the flight . . . hey, it's so good . . . did you miss me . . . so good . . . this much . . . so good . . . I'm so glad . . . so good to see you . . . glad . . . those pants . . . you're back . . . where did you . . . your hair . . . get them . . . it's fab, I love it . . . it's great, it suits . . . and the dress, are they . . . you . . . new . . . Sinead, oh, Sinead . . . you don't look . . . are you hungry, are you . . . any different . . . jetlagged . . . God, I've missed . . . you smell the . . . you all the time . . . same, just the same . . . really? . . . my love, my love . . . you're back . . . I'm back . . . you're back . . . how was it . . . show me, tell . . . in New York . . . me everything you've done . . . did you take . . . since I went away . . . any photos . . . can't believe you're really . . . some, I'll show you . . . back . . . later.'

I stepped off the boat on to the small, rotted wooden jetty. It swayed and buckled, and I had to bend my knees so as not to stumble. I wanted to take my rucksack off my back. The muscles in my neck and shoulders were stretched like cello strings, but I was too afraid to put it down.

Behind and ahead of me were other people who'd been on the boat with me: men carrying woven baskets filled with hens, a pig on a leash, women with bright bundles strapped to their back and babies with faces like pansy flowers, a boy with a tyre, women balancing on their shoulders poles weighted with water, vegetables, bales of cotton.

Everyone was shouting and pushing. And staring at me. On the boat, four women had sat themselves round me in a circle on the floor as if I was about to tell them a story. But instead they were contented just to stare – not aggressively. They smiled if I smiled at them. I tried looking out of the window, getting out my book, fiddling with the straps on my rucksack. But everything I did was of interest to them. Their curiosity was entirely open and, it seemed, insatiable. The language wasn't as I had expected: it was soft, undulating, melodic, with lots of *sh* sounds and falling scales.

What I felt: tall. Sick from the boat. Afraid. Wet. Ungainly. Sweat down my back under my rucksack. A scratching in my throat as if I wanted to cough. Rich. Alone. My hair plastered to my head like seaweed.

What I could smell: riverwater. Boat diesel fumes. Animals. Feathers. Leather from my wet shoes. A milky, baby smell from the child in front of me. Woodsmoke. Damp soil.

Above me were towering columns of bamboo, creaking and bending in the wind, their ridged trunks the width of a man's thigh. Ahead of me, beyond the muddle of people who'd got off the boat, was a dirt path. Beyond that, I could see the village – grey buildings and a paved, wide street. Marcus. Marcus was in that village.

I elbowed my way through the small crowd, shifting the weight of my rucksack further up on my shoulders.

I didn't want to understand what the woman behind the blue-topped counter was saying.

'*Meyoh*.' She shrugged.

'Emerson,' I said clearly, 'Marcus Emerson. Are you sure he's not here?'

'*Meyoh-la*. No here.' She was wearing high-heeled turquoise wellingtons, I noticed, and a man's suit jacket.

I looked down at the piece of paper I was clutching. 'Traveller's Guest House,' I had written, 'Yangshuo.' I had written that just over two weeks ago while on the phone to Marcus. Only two weeks. 'Fly to Beijing, then Guilin. Boat to Yangshuo.' Confident, straight arrows between the words. 'M will be checked into TGH.' That meant Traveller's Guest House. Where I was right now. And this woman was telling me he wasn't here. I cleared my throat, felt again under my clothes for the pouch containing my money, passport and tickets. I had carried this scrap of paper all the way from the phone in my house.

'Could I have a room anyway, please?'

I sat on the side of one of the double beds – the room, for some reason, had two. It sagged under my weight. It was a few moments before I remembered the weight on my shoulders, and eased off the straps, letting the bag fall backwards on to the bed. I stared around the room. Chicken wire covering a small space above the door. A red flask standing in an enamel basin decorated with orange fish. A small shadeless bulb beside the bed. Mosquito nets bunched up above the mattresses like great grey puffball mushrooms. The window smeary. The mountains beyond. The mountains. I hadn't been able to believe what I was seeing as the boat wove up the river: vast, toppling, lumped rocks rearing up from the water, hung with mist. I'd always thought those Chinese silk paintings were of fanciful, mystical landscapes from the imagination of some artist. But they actually existed – weird, looming, almost top-heavy, planted into flat, river-threaded plains. Karst topography – the phrase, appearing unbidden in my head, thrown up from some distance geography lesson, surprised me. I smiled for a moment, then: he's not here, I thought, he's not here. Shit.

I woke with a start, sitting bolt upright. The cone of a muslin mosquito net surrounded me. It gave the room the kind of dim, nostalgic haze old romantic films had.

China.

I was in Yangshuo, China.

It was hot.

Marcus had promised he'd be here.

He wasn't.

It was hot. Very, very hot.

I kicked off the heavy quilted bedcover, rushed to the window and yanked it open, gulping for air. But the air that met me was the same as that in the room – heavy, heated, moisture-filled. I was wearing just pants, I was vaguely surprised to notice. Had I pulled off my T-shirt in my sleep? Around the room were scattered the clothes I'd had on yesterday – jeans, trainers, socks, hooded jacket, vest. I was wearing those when I left my house, I thought.

I picked up my clock. Three twenty. I peered at it. Three twenty? *Three twenty?* Confused, I looked out of the window. Definitely daytime.

I stood in the centre of my doubly double-bedded room in my pants, uncertain, disorientated. I thought: I've travelled non-stop for thirty-eight hours. I thought: Antony gave me these pants. I thought: I've taken a break from my Ph.D. I thought: I've come all the way to China to meet a man I hardly know. I thought: He hasn't turned up, maybe—

Then, without warning, a wave of exuberance sent me skipping across the bare boards. I'm in China! *China*, for God's sake! Who gives a shit about some unreliable man? I riffled through my bag, packed so carefully in Britain, tipping its contents out on to the floor, selecting a pair of shorts and a clean T-shirt. Must go out. Can't lie about in here all day. He might arrive at any moment. Don't want him to think I've been hanging around the hotel waiting for him.

I walked the streets of Yangshuo. Bicycles, tractors and things like big motorised lawn-mowers with seats slewed up and down the streets. I passed open-fronted shops crammed with tailored clothes, kettles, bright plastic buckets, farm tools, the pale globes of pomelos, electrical fuses, the hard, flinty green shapes of jade, stacks of red flip-flops, silk dresses. The women were ruddy-cheeked and dark-eyed, hair pinned up with coloured slides, dressed in navy Mao suits and high heels. The men didn't look like they deserved them – sitting in glum groups, smoking and drinking tea from jam jars. Everywhere I went people stared and pointed or shouted, 'Hello!' or '*Laowai, laowai!*'

I scanned the groups of white westerners sitting around café tables. But no one even resembled him. Approaching the guest house, I had to slow my walk because moisture was crawling down my body like insects. But the room was empty, the bed undisturbed, my clothes still in arcs where I'd left them.

I couldn't sleep so later I went out again into the unlit streets, shiny after a quick rainstorm. I couldn't remember the way to the river but followed the scent of its fecund dampness on the air. Down at the water's edge the top of the thick vegetation shifted in the hot breeze. I rested on the backs of my heels, arms folded over my knees. I watched as narrow rafts of lashed-together bamboo came gliding over the surface of the blackened water. Three of them. A man stood at the back of each with a long pole like a gondolier's; at the front sat a large woven basket. And around them, sleek-throated cormorants dipped in and out of the water.

The second day, I woke late again and lay for a while plucking at loose threads in the quilt, watching geckos dart across the ceiling. I ate in a café where I met two men from New Zealand. The three of us then went to a fan-maker's and watched a boy of about sixteen paint blossom on to the sanded surface of the fan slats. I told them about the fishermen and they explained that the cormorants have rings around their throats to stop them swallowing the fish.

They were going to Xian next, they told me, to see an army of terracotta soldiers, each with a different face. Did I want to come? I shook my head. I can't, I said, I'm waiting for someone. They nodded. As we parted, the taller one turned round to see me go.

The third day, I woke and my watch said only nine. I'd been dreaming about university and seminar preparation and the writing of my thesis. I got up immediately. I hired a bike, cycled out of the town along the dust road, which meandered between the bulk of the mountains, through glassy-surfaced paddy-fields, herds of crescent-horned water-buffalo, tiny villages where people would shout after me, amazed by this lone white woman on a bicycle. Away from the tourist zone of the town, people were living in shacks with animals, children worked in the fields, and ancient women hobbled on twisted, broken feet, carrying bundles of firewood.

The fourth day I was glum. I sat in a café. On the table in front of me was a mug full of shavings of ginger and scalding water, and an exercise book. On the first page, I had written 'Fact: he is not coming. Fact: you haven't got enough money for this on your own.' I had crossed out 'on your own' and written 'trip' instead. I had five mosquito bites the size of ten-pence pieces on my leg. They progressed up my shin in a meandering line like a child's dot-to-dot drawing. The New Zealanders arrived and started teaching me the Chinese numbers and the hand-signs that went with them: '*yee, er, san, si, wu, lui, chi, bah, jiu, xi.*' The broad palms and cracked fingers of the New Zealander curved, crossed and straightened. I copied them, repeating the words.

'What you writing?' one asked, nodding towards my book.

'Nothing,' I said, flipping the cover closed.

After they'd gone, I rested my head on my cupped hand. *Yee, er, san, si, wu.* He wasn't coming. *Lui, chi, bah, jiu, xi.* What was I going to do?

A week ago I'd been to see my supervisor, Dr Hilton. He was a tall, ungainly man with over-large hands and a barely audible voice. When I had described my Ph.D. to him he had murmured, 'I'm very excited indeed.' But on this day I sat in front of him and said, 'I've decided to go away. To China.'

His forehead had creased, his hands darting to the edge of his knitted waistcoat. 'China?' he'd whispered, as if it was a swear word. 'What for?'

'For . . .' I picked my words '. . . a break.'

'I see.'

There had been a pause. Dr Hilton had adjusted and readjusted the height of his chair. 'Sinead,' he'd said, then stopped. 'You are going to come back, aren't you?'

'Of course,' I'd said quickly. Was that too quickly?

'You must,' he'd said, 'your work is . . . very important. Very important indeed.'

I scratched at a mosquito bite with the ineffectual, heat-softened curve of a fingernail. I'd spent my living allocation for next term in coming here. A girl in a red tracksuit passed, waving at me. I uncurled my fingers in reply. I drew a line in green biro up my leg, connecting my reddened bites. The New Zealanders were away down the street, in conversation with a man with a cart piled high with striped melons. I recognised the bartering gestures. *Yee, er, san, si . . .* I carried on staring down the street. A man with sun-whitened hair was walking quickly up the hill, a rucksack on his back. In his hand he held a camera and a piece of paper. I uncrossed and recrossed my legs, knocking my ankle on the table. Then I stood up. Called his name. Watched him coming over the square towards me.

'Where in God's name have you been?' I shouted.

'Sorrysorrysososorry,' he was saying. Then his arms were around me and his mouth was next to my ear, the strap of his camera knocking against the green graph-line on my shin.

They topple on to the sofa. Marcus half falls on to the floor and Sinead holds him fast and he has his face stuck in her neck and she is grappling with the belt on his trousers when she realises she wants to look into his face. She wriggles backwards, making her back twinge a little because all their limbs are tangled up, and grabbing his head between her hands, pulls him away from her so she can look at his face.

His eyelashes part, Marcus opens his eyes and looks into hers. She wants to examine every feature, every contour, every millimetre of him. It's him, it's really him, she wants to gaze at his face for a very, very long time until she's had enough and can turn her eyes away again. His face is beautiful to her, but a strange, shifting kind of beauty. It moves across him like clouds over a landscape. The French have a word for it – *joli-laid*. Marcus has always had a protean quality about him: sometimes he can look quite different from one moment to the next, just the subtlest alteration in his facial muscles switching his features from a serene, absorbed beauty to a harder near-ugliness. It's never an unattractive ugliness, merely a recast version of his face. She's always found that—

Then he is arched between her legs, his hands behind her head. Her breathing sounds far off to her, as if in another room. She holds him to her, her hand in the dip of his back and his spine labours and flexes under her palm. Laughter bubbles somewhere inside her, which comes out into the air as shortened, staccato gasps.

Suddenly his back is still, straight, taut as a sprung trap. He rests on his elbows, motionless, his torso held over her. She waits, peers up, but can see only his neck, grizzled with stubble, and the wishbone curve of his jaw. She twists her head to try to see his face, but his elbow is leaning on her hair and she is trapped there. An image of Gulliver is flitting across her mind, making her smile, when he says something and she feels him shrinking inside her. He says the something again.

'Huh?' she says.

'Sinead, we need . . . we need . . .' He rears up above her, straightening his arms. 'We need to talk.'

This is not what Sinead was expecting. 'Do we?'

He nods.

'OK,' she says, 'but later, all right,' and goes to pull him towards her.

'No.' He adjusts his balance, and she feels him pulling away from her. 'Now, I think.'

Sinead sits up, puzzled, straightening her dress. Marcus, his back to her, pulls up his trousers, fastens his flies and belt, and walks about the room for a few seconds, his hands crossed behind his head. Then he slumps down in a chair opposite her.

'The thing is . . .' he begins, and stops. 'Have you seen Aidan?'

Sinead laughs at this strange non sequitur. 'The thing is have I seen Aidan? What – ever? Today? This week? What are you on about?'

There is a pause. Sinead tucks her legs up under her, waiting. Marcus has tipped back his head and is staring at the ceiling. She drums her fingernails on the soles of her feet. What is all this?

'Marcus—'

'The thing is,' he says again quickly, 'the thing is, I wasn't exactly faithful to you in New York.'

I didn't know how to pitch things when we got back to the room. Should I leave him to unpack, shower? Should I pretend we were just here as friends? Or should I just seduce him and get it out of the way?

Marcus stood at the window, one hand resting on his hip, the other behind his neck. I kicked the loose clothes on the floor into a rough heap. Sat down on the bed. Stood up. Sat down again. I was being pulled in the directions of two opposing impulses: to remove all my clothes or to suggest we go for a brisk, edifying walk. *Femme fatale* versus Brown Owl.

I tucked my hands underneath my legs to prevent myself acting on either. Marcus's back was towards me. The backs of his legs, his neck, his arms were brown, his boots muddied.

A shuffling sound. The soles of his boots swivelling on the wooden floor, leaving dusty, whitish compass marks on the boards. His boots creaked slightly, I noticed, as he walked towards me. Leather that had been wet, had expanded and then contracted. The toes had a grey tidemark on them.

'How was Beijing?' I was horrified to hear my voice braying. Brown Owl appeared to be winning.

Marcus crouched in front of me. Rested his fingertips on my knees to steady himself. 'I can't tell you,' he began, his voice low, 'how glad I am that you're here.'

There was a pause.

'You can't tell me?' I said. 'Why not?'

Marcus shrugged. 'I don't know. Just can't.'

'Well, how am I meant to know, then? I mean, just how am I supposed to guess that's how you feel?'

'Other things.'

'What other things?'

Marcus leaned forward on to his knees, brushing against my legs. Outside a band of mist drifted off a limestone peak. A woman called for her child in the street below.

'This, for example.' He put his hand on my waist, thumbs at the front, fingers around the back of my pelvis. Then he leaned forward and pressed his mouth to where my neck met my shoulder. He didn't lean back again, just stayed there, breathing into my hair. 'I've wanted to do that ever since I first saw you.'

'Is that right?'

'You've got an amazing neck.'

'Have I?'

My first kiss missed his mouth, catching him below his

cheekbone. But for the second he had his hand cupped round the back of my head and our lips met just as I was inhaling. We were both shuddering, bodies vibrating with each blood-beat.

I always love the first time you sleep with someone. No matter what happens later, there is always that clarity, that amazement, that steep learning curve – how to deal with someone else's body, how it likes to be touched, how it wants to fit into yours, how it responds to the things you do. There are always surprises, always idiosyncrasies, always things that differentiate it from other, similar acts. I believe you could sleep with a hundred people and still be surprised.

Scale enlarges and distance shrinks. What I can never get over is that change: how, before, you know them at a certain range – in clothes, over the other side of tables, with no further touch than perhaps a brush on the arm or a momentary kiss on the cheek. But then suddenly you are pressing your lips to theirs, their eyes blurringly close, touching their teeth, their palate, their gums with the tip of your tongue. You are looking into the one blind eye of their penis, seeing the lie of their body-hair, the creases of their skin, tasting their sweat, their saliva, their tears, their semen. You are knowing them more closely than even they do.

What I would always remember about my first time with Marcus: that we giggled over which bed to use. That he pressed his cheek to mine. That he was tenderer, gentler than I'd expected. The rasp of his stubble on the skin of my inner thigh. The first, unpeeled, round, silk push of him. That I knew, half-way through, or maybe not half-way but somewhere in the middle or near the end or maybe not near it at all but right after the start, that it was going to be good, very good, in that way that things that are right feel already familiar, that I knew what to do before I knew I was doing it, and that this was just the beginning, that they would get better, and keep on getting better and would be better, perhaps for a long time.

The room stops like a lift.

Sinead stares at Marcus. It is a sentence that will return to her over and over again – for months, for years. It will echo round her head. She'll hear it again during the many, many sleepless nights ahead of her. Right now, though, she is attempting to process it. The sentence seems to have lots of different bits: the thing is; in New York; exactly faithful; I wasn't. That weird negative understatement bothers her: I wasn't exactly faithful. Exactly faithful. What does that mean? Why 'exactly'? Does it mean he wasn't faithful or that he was unfaithful? And what's the difference?

The answer pops up in her head like a price total displayed on a cash register: it means something between the two. It means he kissed someone somewhere. Maybe he was drunk. He kissed someone. That's all, and he thinks he should tell me. But Sinead continues to stare at his face. He drops his eyes and that's when she knows. This isn't just about a random, drunken encounter. This is more. Much more. I wasn't exactly faithful. To you. In New York.

'Are we talking just one,' she is astonished at how calm and even her voice sounds, 'or lots?'

Marcus shakes his head and shrugs simultaneously. 'Lots,' he says.

Sinead has never been surprised like this by anything before. If someone had said to her, what's the most unlikely thing for Marcus to do, she might have come up with this, but probably would have felt it was so unlikely as to be off the scale of things Marcus would do. She looks down at the way her body is arranged – legs curled under her, one hand resting on her feet, the other laid across her front. She hardly recognises it. She can't remember how long ago it was that she sat herself down in this position.

She feels hollow, but something flutters around the space inside her: her lover has metamorphosed into some strange, cruel being. Marcus has gone mad. Or this is some tanned imposter, a destructive double. Or he's possessed by some evil spirit. She looks at him closely. He looks the same. A little tired, maybe. A little deadened around the eyes. But how can this be Marcus, her Marcus?

'Why?' she hears herself ask. '*Why?*'

He slumps further into the chair, as if she's physically assaulting him. Sinead is getting up, standing, spinning away from him across the floor like a gyroscope, hair and dress whirling round her. She reaches the kitchen and doesn't know what to do there, so she turns again and looks at him, her mind returning to the sentence: why didn't he come out and say it properly, instead of that cowardly negated, roundabout way, why didn't he just say it: Sinead, I've been unfaithful to you.

And then she is remembering a time at the beginning of their relationship when she'd been considering ending it. She'd arranged to meet him in a pub and when she arrived, he was sitting with some people he knew, playing a game involving sticking cigarette papers on their foreheads. She had sat on a stool, hands folded in her lap, staring at him in disbelief as he talked too loudly and laughed and made jokes she'd never heard before. It was as if she'd never met him, never had anything to do with him, as if she'd just spent weeks in China with someone else entirely. He was a different person, not the Marcus she knew and was starting to love. This one – whoever he was – was louder, brasher, cockier. She looked around at the rest of the table and slowly began to realise that what he was doing was being like them. He had just morphed himself to fit in with these people. It reminded her of a species of bird she'd read about once that had no predators because it could mimic the calls of whichever birds were around it, surviving by dint of imitation. As soon as they were alone again, walking to catch a bus, he switched back instantly to the person she knew. But she was unable to look at him, unable to let him take her hand, unable to touch him. It appalled her that there was such a lack of solidity, of permanence, in his sense of himself that he could be so easily swayed. He hadn't understood, was hurt and angry, and they'd stayed awake until dawn, arguing. She'd got used to his plasticity, in time, but it never ceased to shock her. And as she stands in the kitchen in her new dress, she finds herself wondering what kind of people he must have been spending time with for him to do this.

'I don't understand,' she says, quiet and still now. 'I don't understand. Why have you done this?'

Across the yards of space between them, she sees him flex his shoulders as if shrugging something off. He scratches his head and says with an odd, worldly bravura that doesn't sit well on him, that looks as though it's a gesture he's borrowed from someone recently: 'It's hard to say.' He shrugs, turning his palms up to the ceiling. 'It was a bit of a strange time. You were so far away and everything here seemed so distant and y—' He glances at her, his mouth open, half-way into forming the next word. But something in her face must have made him falter, because the word vanishes into the air between them like steam. He stares at his hands, mutely, moves his lips as if he's about to say something else, but changes his mind. 'You see, I . . .' he begins uncertainly, sitting forward, then stops. 'These things happen,' he mutters.

She is filled with fury – pure, molten, towering fury. 'Do they?' she shouts. 'Do they really? They just happen. Just like that. One minute you're walking along and the next, before you even know it, my God, you're shagging someone. What – they slipped and fell on your dick? Is that what you're telling me?'

Her mouth is suddenly full of rushing, sweet-tasting saliva. She's going to be sick. She darts to the sink and waits, but nothing happens. The nausea subsides. She realises that she hasn't eaten since lunchtime, and is wondering why, when she remembers that she was going to cook a meal for her and Marcus. Artichoke hearts. They are still sheaved into themselves, hard petal against hard petal, at the bottom of the fridge. Then she feels a hand pressed into her back.

'Sinead, are you—'

She whips round, smashing the side of her fist into

his arm. 'Don't touch me,' she hisses. 'Don't even lay a finger on me.'

She sees him flinch with pain, covering the place where she'd hit him with his other hand, and something pulls at her. How could she hurt him like this? How could she strike him? But then the knowledge that the hand, the body she knows like her own, has touched another woman's is agony.

There is a noise on the stair outside — the measured footfalls of someone walking up the stairs, the tinkle of keys. Aidan. They both look at each other and, despite everything, Sinead is surprised to see panic in his eyes.

'What do we do?' he whispers.

Sinead sidesteps him, runs towards their bedroom. 'Do what you want. You always do anyway.'

I was listening to Marcus's story of why he was four days late. It involved a long queue for tickets, a thirty-eight-hour bus journey, a man with a goat, and a minor traffic accident.

'I heard a squeal of brakes and I woke up to find myself, and all the bus — goat included — flying forward through the air. The bus's front wheels had got stuck in a muddy ditch like this.' He demonstrated with his hands. 'I thwacked my thigh on a bus seat when I landed.' He showed me a blackened, purple patch at the top of his leg, uneven and adrift in the white of his skin like a continent that had been shifted by tectonic plates. I'd seen it earlier, but hadn't asked.

'I was terrified I'd missed you,' he said, and his hand on my arm twitched tighter. 'That you'd have gone before I got here, disappeared into China without trace.'

My head was resting on the joint between his shoulder and his arm, my eye facing the aureole of his nipple. I was listening, not to his voice, but its reverberation through his body, my ear pressed to his ribcage.

I turned over on to my front, the rucked sheet catching at my elbows and hips. Marcus turned with me, his hand coming to rest in the hollow of my back.

I reached for his passport on the bedside table, flicked it open.

This night is the saddest. Or so it seems. What she doesn't know yet is that there will be a long, long string of sad nights, some of a different kind, some worse. What she doesn't yet know is that ending a relationship cannot be done in one conversation over one evening, that such extrication takes days and months and sometimes years.

When she reaches the bedroom, she doesn't know what to do. She stands in the middle of the floor, arms crossed behind her body. She feels confused, divided, unreal, as if her actual everyday life has been stopped somehow and she is being forced to act out this strange scene belonging to someone else. It's as if she's mouthing along to a script she doesn't understand and wants no part in. She wants to return to her other life, to step back into it, but doesn't know how.

She hears Aidan come in, close the door behind him; Marcus's voice saying hello and then a rumbling, inaudible exchange between them. Feet over the floorboards, the slam of Aidan's doors. More feet. Her door opening. Someone stepping into the room.

There is silence between them for a while. Marcus sits at the desk by the window, Sinead on the bed. He runs his thumbnail along the edge of the desk. She cannot stop swallowing, as though she has eaten something she cannot digest. She draws her knees up to her chest, pulls the duvet around her: a shivering chill has settled into her bones. Some corner of her mind tells her that she must talk, find things out, to cross somehow this crevasse that has opened up between them, but she can't think of anything to say.

She clears her throat, tries to focus her thoughts. Lots, he said. There were lots. In New York. 'When did you,' she begins, unsure of how the sentence will end, unsure of what it is she's asking, 'when was the first one?'

'Um.' Marcus thinks. 'Just after I'd arrived,' he almost whispers.

'And did . . . how long did . . . it . . . go on?'

'The . . . the whole time.'

Sinead thinks about all the letters and the postcards that dropped through the door, the e-mails that she'd picked up at the end of her working day, the phone calls that came twice, sometimes three times a week, sometimes in the middle of the night. Were they ever there when he was talking to her? Did he ever call her from their apartments? Did they listen in the background? Did they read the letters she sent back? Did he ever call after——?

'The whole time?' she repeats, as if for herself. 'The whole time you were away?'

'What's the G for?'

He raised his head lazily, running his finger down the knuckles of my backbone. 'Huh?'

'The G.' I flapped the passport at him. A picture of him, sealed under plastic, younger, with that soft-edged look that teenagers try in vain to rid themselves of, flicked past. 'Marcus G. Emerson,' I read.

'Promise not to laugh?'

I smiled. 'No.'

'I can't tell you, then.'

'Go on. It can't be that bad. What is it? Gerald? Geoffrey?'

'Gabriel.'

I laughed. 'Gabriel? Are you serious?'

'Unfortunately, yes. My mother has a bit of a New Testament thing.'

I dropped the passport back on to the table, that picture of him, longer-haired then, winking at me. I pulled myself over the bed towards him and laid myself along the length of his back, my head in the curve of his neck. His heartbeat was slower than mine.

'Do you know what?' he said, and his voice rumbled through the mattress. 'There's this artist who did a whole study into the physiognomy of angels. He did research into flying creatures – birds, bats, you know – and worked out that if angels were to fly, they'd have to have a breastbone one metre thick for their wings to support their body weight. At the end of it, he painted a physiognomically correct version of the Sistine Chapel ceiling, with these weird, stocky, deformed-looking creatures winging their way about the celestial skies.

'Imagine it,' and he turned over. I slid off his back.

Sweat had pooled between us where our bodies touched, transpiring against each other. 'One metre thick.' And he held his hand out from his body to demonstrate. I narrowed my eyes, tried to visualise it, but couldn't make the leap, couldn't imagine him any different.

She is staring at him, and he looks unfamiliar to her, as if she's never met him before, as if she's seeing him for the first time. Her imagination wriggles out from under her control, and begins to flash her a series of single-frame images: him thrusting into a woman on a bed, him with a different woman up against a desk, a woman on top of him, a woman bending over him, his hands on another woman's waist, his head resting in the neck of a faceless female, him on—

It all disappears when, suddenly, it hits her that, a few minutes ago, they were . . . that he was . . . on the sofa . . . they were . . .

'How could you?' she blurts, and her voice cracks, choked by shock and disbelief. 'How could you sleep with me after that? How could you *do* that?' She hears her words rise to a wail and her limbs twist and convulse in bodily horror at the recollection of him on her and in her, as if daubing her, smearing her with traces of those other women. '*How could you?*' she shouts again, looking around her, as if for something to hurl at him. She wants to hurt him, to mark him.

'I . . . I didn't . . .' he stutters, 'I didn't mean to . . . it just—'

'Happened?' she yells over him. 'Is that what you were going to say?'

He darts a look at her then at the door. 'Hush,' he says. 'Aidan will hear.'

'Aidan?' she splutters, struggling off the bed. 'Do you think I give a shit if Aidan hears?' Her feet move under her as she paces around the boards and the walls of the room constructed for the life she used to have veer around her giddily.

'Sinead,' he reaches out for her as she passes him, but she swings away from him and his hand closes around empty air, 'please don't shout,' he begs. 'This has all,' he presses his fists into his eyes, 'come out wrong. Let's just . . . let's just talk about this.'

'Talk?' she says. 'You want to talk? OK. Let's talk. Why don't you tell me what it was like, and whether it was any good, and whether you feel like a big brave man now, and was it better than it is with me, and how you could come back from that and sleep with me before you had the decency to tell me, and . . . and why you didn't tell me.' Strength and words ebb out of her. Silence, after the tumble of her speech, pulses between them. 'Why didn't you tell me?' she whispers.

He rubs his fingers across his forehead, not looking at her but at the walls, his feet, the desk.

'Why, Marcus? Why leave me all that time, thinking that everything was the same?'

'Everything is the same,' he says quickly.

She gives an incredulous laugh, then looks at him, trying to see if he's joking, if he really means what he just said. His eyes, a deep navy blue in this light, look back at her, unwavering.

'Nothing has changed,' he insists. 'Nothing. I promise you. All that didn't mean a thing. It had nothing to do with you and me. Nothing. I love you. You know that. I always will.' He is crushing her hand in his, the ring he gave her a year ago pressing painfully into the flesh of adjacent fingers.

'Marcus,' she flounders, unnerved, 'that's ridiculous, I—'

'No, it's not ridiculous. It's not ridiculous at all. You and I couldn't live without each other. You know that. Nothing could ever come between us, or change how we feel about each other.'

Cross now, she wrests her hand from his grasp. 'Really? Is that what you think? That you can behave exactly as you like and I'll just accept it? That you can go off and screw your way around New York City and I'll just be here when you get back saying, "Oh, Marcus, do what you like because I'll love you no matter what?"'

He is still looking at her with that unblinking, wide-eyed stare, but there is now a hint of desperation in his voice. 'I missed you so much,' he says softly.

'Fuck you,' she spits out. 'How dare you say that to me?'

He stroked the tips of my hair with the fingers of both his hands. I was impressed that he knew straight away how to touch it: some men were overawed by it and never went near it; others tried manfully to run their hands through it, which was impossible, not to mention painful. I had one man who wanted to brush it. I think he thought it would be a romantic gesture. I tried to explain that you couldn't brush my hair, that I never did, that it wouldn't work, that it was too difficult and the results too horrific. He went on and on about it and, close to the end of our affair, I seized a brush and showed him why, dragging the nylon bristles through the ravelled curls, transforming my head into a huge, crackling, electrified tumbleweed.

But Marcus, that first afternoon, just explored its properties, didn't force it when one spiral refused to part from its neighbour, didn't try to run his fingers from root to end. He held it to the light, where I knew that he'd be looking at it sparking brown and gold. He spent ages playing with one ringlet, stretching it out to its fullest length down my back before letting it ping back.

'Wow,' he murmured eventually. He elongated it. I felt the ends whisper on my back.

'Imagine if you could harness the energy in your hair.' He released it and it sprang back to nestle among the rest. 'If there was some way of wiring it up to the National Grid you could power the whole country.'

He pulled it straight again.

'Who were they?' she says, standing in front of him, hands behind her back.

'It doesn't matter.' He reaches out for her. She steps back.

'It does matter. It mattered to you at the time. Tell me.'

'Why?'

'Because I want to know.'

'Sinead, it's not important. Believe me, it doesn't matter. They don't matter.'

'They mattered enough for you to fuck them. Just tell me. Were they people you were working with?'

'No.'

'Do I know any of them?'

He hesitates, looks away.

'Do I?' she persists.

'Sinead—'

'Tell me. Do I know any of them?'

'No. I don't think so.'

'But you're not sure.'

'I . . .' he waves a hand around his head '. . . I thought for a minute you might have met . . . one of them, but then I remembered you . . . you weren't at that particular party.'

'So one of them you knew from London.'

'No.'

'But she was in London.'

'Yes,' he says, impatient. 'She was here briefly a few months ago for . . . something . . . work, maybe, or friends, or something.'

'And you planned to sleep with her when you saw her then?'

'No, I did not.'

'So where did you find the others?'

He puts his hands to his head. 'I really don't think—'

'Where, Marcus? In bars? In clubs? Where do you go if you want to find women?' Something occurs to her. 'I take it they were women?'

He looks at her, outraged. 'Of course they were.'

'Well,' she gives a bitter laugh, 'I just wondered if you had any other bombshells you wanted to drop.'

She does another circuit around the room. Anger leaves her and settles on her within seconds. 'Did you plan to do this before you went?' she asks, bewildered.

'Um . . . I . . .'

'Did you? Were you planning this before you left?'

'I don't think so.'

'You don't think so?'

'No, I wasn't.'

'Then when did you decide?'

'When I was there . . . when I . . . I don't know . . . it wasn't something . . . I mean, it isn't like I decided to do it, not like I made a decision or anything.' He suddenly bows his head, as if overcome, burying his face in his hands. 'Sinead,' he cries, his voice breaking, 'this is awful. Awful. None of this is coming out right. I never meant . . . I didn't think you'd react this way. I——'

She gives a short bark of laughter. 'Why? How did you think I'd react? That I'd welcome you back with open and forgiving arms?'

He stares at her for a second, his face wild and miserable. 'I've no idea,' he whispers hoarsely. 'I don't think I'd . . . thought it through properly.'

'You haven't thought any of this through, have you? That's always been your biggest problem. You know that? You have this incredible inability to understand causality. You can never make the connection that if you do A then B will happen. You have this . . .' she has that feeling of

215

having hit her stride now, as she does at the midway point in her lectures, words and ideas pumping together like blood and oxygen '. . . this pathological blindness to the most basic mechanisms of human nature. You're always so focused on the realisation of your own bloody desires that you can't stop and think about what the results might be. You didn't stop, did you, when you were climbing into bed with some woman in New York, you didn't pause for a moment and think, I wonder what Sinead will say when I tell her about this, I wonder what effect this might have on my five-year relationship?' She stops, breathless, suddenly struck by the weirdness of talking about her own life in this way, and not just some text. 'Did you?'

He doesn't move.

'Did you?' she shouts.

He gives a minute shake of his head.

She strides to the window, stares out unseeing, then strides back. Something is preventing her keeping still. Between the bed and the wardrobe, she stops and turns back. 'Were you always going to tell me?'

'What?'

'Were. You,' she says, with sarcastic slowness. 'Always. Going—'

'Yes!' he exclaims, with an unconvincing vehemence, not meeting her eye.

She feels oddly calm and somehow unsurprised by this new discovery. 'You weren't, were you?'

He doesn't reply.

'That's why you haven't thought it through. Because this was never part of the plan.' In a flare of fury, she kicks the base of the bed. But everything she does somehow feels divorced from her, has a tinge of forced theatricality to it, as if she's just following directions, behaving in the way you're supposed to behave when you find out about infidelity. 'You shit,' she says slowly, 'you utter, utter shit. You were going to just come back and pretend nothing had happened. What made you change your mind, Marcus? Last-minute nerves? A sudden pang of conscience? Or were you scared I might find out anyway and thought the best thing was just to come clean?'

He's still silent.

'Hmm?' she persists, then suddenly pulls away from the subject, abandoning it, tiring of it, knowing she'll never get an answer. 'Just how many are we talking about?' she asks, quiet now.

He sighs unsteadily. 'I don't remember.'

'Come on. You must remember.'

'I don't. I don't want to think about it.'

'It's a bit late for that,' she snaps. 'Come on. Think. More than ten? Less than twenty?'

Marcus hesitates. Scratches the back of his neck. 'I can't remember. A lot.'

She sinks down to the edge of the bed, scuffing the woodgrain in the floorboards with her bare feet. Marcus hasn't moved from his seat at her desk. His back, usually straight, is curved, and he rests his elbows on her desk, his face averted. He looks tired – jet-lagged and pale under his tan. She is overcome with an urge to press her palm to the dip between his shoulder-blades, to curl her fingers around his shoulders. But she can't. She can't ever again.

'Why?' she says, very quietly. 'Why did you do it?'

We peeled ourselves from the sheets, forced out of bed by hunger and the airlessness of the room. When I stood up, my head stuttered and blurred, as if filled with fluid. Our clothes lay together on the bare boards, the arm of his shirt across my crumpled shorts.

'It's not that bad.' I protested, as I ransacked my things for a towel. 'I don't spend my life sitting about discussing the finer points of Chaucerian English, you know. And anyway,' I said, flapping a skirt in the air to shake it of its creases, 'I love my job.'

'But aren't all your friends academics as well?' His voice came from the far side of the room, where he was unpacking his bag.

'No,' I lied, with my back to him. 'Not at all. I know lots of people who . . . who do ordinary, normal jobs in the real world.'

'But don't you wish you lived in London?'

'No,' I lied again. 'I like it there. It's . . . small and . . . and friendly.'

'I don't know how you stand it. Everything closes down at eleven o'clock. You can walk across it in twenty minutes. You never meet anyone who isn't attached to the university. It's just a campus that's built like a town.'

'You can't say that!' I turned round. 'You've never even spent any time there.'

'Maybe I will now,' he said, his voice suddenly serious.

I faltered when I tried to look at him. It was far too early for that kind of talk.

It's a question she can't let alone. 'But why?' she says again. 'I don't understand why you've done this. Are you not happy with me any more?'

'No. I mean yes, of course I am.'

'Was it a way of ending things with me?'

'No! Absolutely not.'

'Were you bored with our sex life?'

'No. No,' he appeals to her, holding out his arms. 'No. Sinead, how can you say that?'

She stays where she is, on the bed, ignoring his gesture. 'Then what? What went so wrong that you . . . that you couldn't talk to me about it?'

He lets his arms fall to his sides. 'I . . . I . . . Nothing,' he says firmly. 'Nothing went wrong.'

'What do you mean?' she demands. 'Something must have gone wrong for you to do this.'

'No, no, it didn't.'

She gives an exasperated click with her tongue, gets up, walks around the bed once, then turns back to him. 'Then *why*? If nothing went wrong and you're still happy with me, why did you do it?'

'I don't know,' he says, with a strange, almost surprised look on his face. 'I really don't know why I did it.'

Outside, it was raining – a heavy, sudden downpour with drops like coins – but the air didn't feel any lighter.

'I love tropical rain,' Marcus said, as we stood at the window together, looking out. 'It's so serious. It makes British weather look really weedy and half-hearted.'

In the street below, umbrellas bobbed along the pavements. The bicycles wore bright plastic ponchos. When we ran to the shower-room, a grey, boxed-in building behind the hotel, we were soaked in seconds.

We showered. Everything seemed slow. Cockroaches scudded over the floor, disappearing into crevices. Marcus turned the thin streams of water down to tepid, and then he washed me, carefully and solicitously, soaping my legs and arms, rubbing shampoo into my hair, scooping up water to rinse off the strings of bubbles that spiralled down the drain. I was suprised again by his gentleness. My nipples creased into themselves as he washed my breasts. As the rain rattled the tin roof, I braced myself against the wall, grainy and cold, one foot holding shut the door.

A thought occurs to her, making her sit up straight, making her wonder why she hadn't thought of it before.

'Have you ever done this before?'

He looks puzzled, seeming not to understand.

'Marcus, we've been together for five years – have you ever, in that time—'

He stands and comes across the room, towards the bed. He seems taller, bigger somehow in this room she's slept in alone for two months.

'Don't,' she orders, holding up her hands, 'don't come anywhere near me.'

But she hears the lack of conviction in her voice, and realises she is cold with the craving for physical contact. He crawls over the bed towards her, pulls her to him and as she registers the familiar breadth and smell and weight of him, she feels the first tears come. They surprise her – rapid and hot, they wrench up from her stomach and spill down her face.

'No,' Marcus is saying, as he holds her head to his chest, 'never, Sinead, never.'

'But how do I know?' she sobs against him. 'How do I know you've not been doing this all the way along? You might have been shagging left, right and centre the whole time.'

'I haven't. I promise you I haven't.

'But how can I believe you?'

'Because I wouldn't do that to you.'

She shoves him away from her so hard he falls back on the bed. 'You just have,' she says.

Washed and dressed in clothes that still smelt of my house in England, I sat opposite him in a café. He hadn't eaten for a whole day, and ordered amazing amounts of food from the menu. Steamed dumplings in bamboo pots kept arriving, their tops pursed together like pale lips. I was feeling a bit peculiar, disjointed: my hunger had vanished and I seemed to be having difficulty in catching up with my life. Every time I glanced around me, and saw buffalo-drawn carts, a whole family on a single bicycle, a man dragging a goat on a string, I'd get a slight shock; I'd look at him, and think for a split second, who are you, and what I am doing here?

He pulled from his pocket a pair of metal chopsticks; with one hand he levered torn strips of dumpling into his mouth, with the other he sketched a diagram of a teacher-training college he'd seen in Beijing.

'The roof isn't fluted,' he was saying, 'like a pagoda, but slanted like this.'

I shifted in my seat, drawing up one leg under the other. It was late afternoon but we'd just emerged from bed. A secret ache pulled at the insides of my thighs. I felt a strange urge for cigarettes I'd given up four years previously.

Things have degenerated into cyclical exhaustion and worn tracks of unsatisfied anger. She is sobbing. Pain is bleeding across her forehead into her temples. The bed is covered in wet tissues. Marcus is lying on his front, his head propped up between his hands. They are both shouting.

'Are you telling me,' he is demanding, 'you've never, not once, in all the years we've been together, thought about sleeping with someone else?'

'No. Of course I'm not saying that. The point is—'

'Who?' he says sharply. 'Who have you wanted to sleep with?'

'Oh, for God's sake, Marcus, listen to me—'

'Tell me. Who?'

'Shut *up*. Just—'

'I want to know. Which men, out of all the ones we know—'

'All I'm saying is—'

'Why won't you tell me?'

'Because you're being stupid and jealous and because it's not important and because—'

'Look,' he says, slamming the sides of his hands into their mattress, 'if we split up—'

'If?' Sinead interjects. '*If?*' And before she's even aware of having made the decision, she says: 'Marcus, I'm walking out of here tomorrow morning.'

There is a silence. The air is filled with the noise of their panting breath. There's no traffic on the road outside. They stare at each other in shock.

'No,' he says, 'you can't. Sinead, you can't.'

She nods, miserable, tears sliding down her face to soak into her clothes and the bed and him. Pain and exhaustion and grief overwhelm her and she curls into herself as if with stomach cramps. She kicks her legs off the bed and lets her bodyweight carry her to the floor. Marcus leaps for the door, putting out his hand to keep it shut. She feels as if she might fall, but he holds her to him and suddenly she is face to face with him, the length of her against him.

'No,' he whispers, 'you can't leave. You mustn't. How can you say that? You mustn't ever leave.'

And she has to close her eyes to keep on nodding because she can't look at him at that proximity. He seizes her head between his hands, desperate, and turns her nodding into shaking, and she lets him, but as soon as his hands fall away, she starts nodding again.

When he leaned back in his chair to catch the eye of the waiter, I saw his loose-limbed easiness, the calm well-being that permeated his whole form. It gave me a kind of anxiety. I wanted to ask him: what would you have done if I hadn't come, or if I'd gone by the time you got here? I wanted to say: why did you ask me to come? And: what do you see for us, where will it all go?

But I didn't. When he said, 'Shall we go?' I nodded and started gathering up my things.

And then she is tired and his body close to hers is painful and familiar. She moves away, towards the window. Dawn is greying the light behind the blind. Consciousness of the streets, the people and the city beyond those glass panes filters back to her. The blue walls look black still, but morning is only a few hours away. She has to work tomorrow. She has to give a lecture in four hours.

'I have to sleep,' she says, and her voice sounds flat and deadened.

Behind her, Marcus steps towards her, but she draws away. The sudden movement from the bed has made the blood curdle in her head and she presses her hand to the wall for balance.

'I'm going to bed now,' she says.

'OK,' he says, and sits down on the bed, bringing up his foot as if to start untying his shoelaces.

'Marcus!' she says sharply. 'What are you doing?'

His head jerks up. 'Taking my shoes off.'

She stares at him, incredulous. 'You're not sleeping in here.'

Guilt and confusion criss-cross his face like car lights across a room at night. He gets up slowly and shuffles to the door. Stops. Turns. 'Sinead . . .'

She is getting undressed. She doesn't care. She just wants to be in bed, under the covers, her face pressed into the pillow. She lifts the dress over her head, lets it fall to the floor, unsnaps her bra, slides it off each arm. Eases the pants down her legs and kicks them into the corner. Climbs into bed.

He is still in the doorway. He hasn't finished his sentence. She doesn't care. He has watched her. She doesn't care. She pulls the covers up over her head. He leaves, closing the door behind him.

Sinead cries again almost immediately. She doesn't sleep, but pleats the cotton of the duvet into itself, winds her fingers into her hair, worries at a dent in the plaster with a pair of tweezers until, as the dawn light bleaches the room, there is a cone of dust on the mattress next to her.

We climbed a hill with a spherical hole through its centre. Marcus wanted to reach the top before sunset. The heat of the day had passed, scorching stones until they cracked open; but here, on a path next to a twisting, orange-bedded stream, under the dense vegetation, the air was dank and cool. There was the heavy smell of things rotting and regenerating. Monkeys chattered and shrieked overhead. A woman with a pole balanced on her shoulders and two round-eyed toddlers in buckets, fingers curled over the rims, jounced past us. *Ni hao, ni hao, ni hao*, we said.

At the top, Marcus pulled a paper bag full of lychees from his backpack and passed them to me, one by one, juggling their pitted, pinkish skin between his palms. I sat with my back against a tree. The sun swung across the hole in the hill. A virulently green beetle landed on my arm, its antennae extended and reeling in the air. I shook my wrist and it fell to the ground, legs scrabbling frantically. I flipped it over with a twig and it flew off, drunk with relief, wings invisible with movement.

The lychees had tough skin that could be pierced with a thumbnail, then peeled off like the shell of a boiled egg. Underneath was grey-white flesh, viscous, wet, the texture of eyeballs. In your mouth, they felt huge, almost choking, until your tongue split the sweet slipperiness and found the smooth, mahogany-coloured stone.

'Sinead,' Marcus said, his head in the crook between my thigh and stomach, 'if I ask you something do you promise to tell me the truth?'

I held a coil of lychee skin between my fingers. Its inside was already dry in the heat. When he'd arrived he'd had three-day-old stubble. He'd shaved after the shower and his face looked younger and softer now. His head was heavy. My innards shifted and resettled under the weight of it.

'That depends on what it is.'

Marcus opened his eyes, but focused on the tree branches and not me. 'What was someone like you doing with someone like Antony?'

I laughed and looked at how the paddy-fields below us were pulling down fragments of the silver-blue sky. 'I don't know,' I said. 'Why do you ask?'

'I was just wondering how he managed it. What's his secret?'

I laughed again. 'He's not that bad,' I said.

'No. Believe me, he is. He's an idiot. And smug into the bargain. After we'd all met that day in the supermarket, he used to talk about you to me all the time.'

I looked down at him. 'Did he?'

'Yeah. Every time I bumped into him at the department, it was Sinead and me this, Sinead and me that.' He closes his eyes and smiles. 'I wish he could see us now.'

'Now who's being smug?' I broke a twig into pieces with one hand. 'He's not that bad,' I said again. 'And you have to admit he's nice-looking.' Marcus grunted. 'But I suppose, if I'm honest, I'd say that there's not a great deal of choice in a place like that.'

Marcus smiled again. 'I thought so.'

When the bedside clock has unwound to seven thirty, Sinead gets up. She pulls out from under the bed a bag. She keeps her thoughts very practical: pants. I'll need pants. Bras. She lines the bottom of the bag with underwear. Trousers. Socks. Address book. Where is address book? In desk drawer. Pen? Also in drawer. Comb. By bed. Alarm clock. Next to comb. Toothbrush. In bathroom. Will get later. Also get cleanser, moisturiser, shampoo, pill packet—

She stops, hurries her thoughts along. OK, won't be needing pill packet, what else, what else? Tops! My God, can't go with only trousers. Red blouse. Green T-shirt and blue shirt. Blue sweater – oh, no, is in wash. Tears are falling now on to the blue shirt at the top of the bag. She scrubs at her face angrily. Panics. Starts dragging out the clothes she'll have to leave for now and come back for, but when, and how, and how can she leave all this and where is she going? Um, um, take that vest top and need my diary and – and – and—

I'm leaving.
I'm leaving.

Marcus is already in the kitchen by the time she comes out of the bedroom. She walks down the length of the room on her bare feet. He doesn't hear her and she can observe him as he rinses a glass at the sink, his neck curved, his shoulders hunched over, until he lifts the glass to the draining rack and his body uncurls, opens out, his back straightening. She wants to say: do you know how much I missed you, do you know how I longed for you all that time, do you know that I ticked off the weeks until your return like a traveller counting down the strung-out telegraph poles to home?

But she doesn't. She drops the bag to the floor. He jumps and looks up.

'OK. My turn,' I said. 'When did you decide you liked me?'

He crumbled a shard of lychee peeling between his fingers. 'The first moment I met you. When you opened your front door.'

'Really?' I was impressed.

'Sinead, I—' He sees the bag at her feet, and stops. She waits. He says nothing, so she goes into the bathroom and starts collecting her things. Toothbrush. In a mug with Aidan's and—

Toothpaste? No. Wherever she goes will have toothpaste. Face cream. By the bath. Razor – no, will get later. Later? Another time. Whenever. Makeup remover. Open cabinet, avoiding reflection, which looks puffed and swollen and old: cotton wool, vitamin pills, hair serum, conditioner. These things she piles into her arms. Her pill packet she hurls, with a flick of her wrist, to the top of the cabinet.

Back in the kitchen, Marcus is sitting at the table. She walks across the room and empties what she is holding into the open, waiting mouth of the bag. Zips it up. Ready to go.

'I made you breakfast,' he says.

'Why didn't you come and find me sooner?'

'Because . . .' Marcus blinked into the sun, thinking '. . . because I didn't think you were interested. I mean, I thought you might be, but I wasn't sure. You're quite hard to read, you know.'

'So it wasn't the fact that I happened to be with someone else?'

'Oh, God, no.' He grinned. 'I wouldn't let a little thing like that stand in my way. Especially if it was only Antony.'

Sinead sits opposite him at the table. She doesn't look at him but looks down. Two slices of toast are on a plate in front of her. A yellow slab of butter. A jar of marmalade, twists of stippled peel suspended in orange jelly. A thin, blunt-bladed knife with a bone handle. Water in a glass. Is it the same one he was washing a minute ago? No, there it is, still drying on the rack. It's the same type – a thick bottom like a lens, and octagonal sides. She's always liked the solid, geometric-ness of them. They bought them together in—

'I know you're not really going,' she hears him say.

She is surprised. And doesn't know what to say. So she says nothing. He scrapes the blade of his knife over the surface of the toast. *Skkklllrrrufff*. Reaches the end of it into the marmalade pot.

At that moment, Aidan appears out of his room. Marcus lets his knife fall into the pot and turns quickly, almost nervously. 'Aidan! Hi!'

Aidan grunts. Sinead doesn't look up, but sees his feet pace towards the kitchen, hesitate, then move towards her. He is bending over her, very close, close enough for her to catch a wave of him – soap, washing-powder, leather from the jacket he's holding. She turns to him involuntarily and sees that he is looking right into her face. His hand is outstretched for the car keys on the table next to her. His fingers curl round them, then he is dropping them into his pocket, struggling into his jacket, crossing to the door, through it, and gone.

Sinead stands, pulls a cardigan around her, pushes her feet into her shoes, and goes over to her bag. She can't find a way to hold it that's comfortable: gripped in her hand it knocks against her leg; over her shoulder it pulls too much on her neck. Stupid design for a bag. Where did she get it anyway? She settles for it hooked over her forearm and makes for the door.

'Why did you agree to come?'

'I don't know,' I said.

'Not good enough,' he retorted. 'Try again.'

'Um,' I writhed under his head, shifting my legs, readjusting the curve of my body, 'I . . . er . . . Well,' I said, suddenly cross, 'you just disappeared. One minute

I couldn't even go shopping without you appearing to tell me what and what not to buy and then suddenly you fell off the end of the earth. And . . . I . . . well . . . I don't know.'

Marcus rolled up on to his knees and kissed me, his tongue cool, sweetened with lychee juice.

Marcus reaches the door before she does. 'Sinead, don't go,' he pleads, in a low, panicked voice. 'Please don't go. I'm so . . . so sorry. What I did was so fucking stupid. *Stupid*.' He bites down on his fingers. His face is wild, afraid. 'I don't know what came over me. Please. I can't . . . I can't bear the thought of losing you. Please don't go. Please.'

'I'm going,' she says simply.

'But just for a few days. OK? Then we'll talk. You can't just leave. Not like this. We need to talk about this more.' He clutches her arm.

'No.' She shakes him off. 'I'm going.'

'Well, where? Where are you going?'

'I don't know yet.'

'Sinead,' he says, 'for God's sake. You can't just walk out on me like this. You can't. OK, I did a stupid thing – a really stupid thing – but you can't just leave. After five years, for Chrissake, you can't just drop me like this. Please.'

She pulls open the door and she can hardly see the staircase in front of her, which leads down into the depths of the building, and before she heads off down it she turns and slides her arm around Marcus's neck and presses her mouth to his because now she is leaving and not coming back and because it will be the last time, and it feels strange because she is crying and they are both shaking and her face is soaked and slippery and it doesn't feel like it should and she pulls away in case it starts to and before his arms can imprison her and pull her to him as she knows they will.

Suddenly she is alone and walking down the stairs and she can hear him calling her name, over and over, and the strap of the bag is cutting into her shoulder and she concentrates on this – and how she wishes she couldn't hear him shout – and putting one foot down below the other until she is out in the street.

'Why don't you come and live with me in London?'

I was appalled. It was said in exactly the same, conversationally curious voice as his other enquiries. I looked at him and this time his blue eyes were directed right to the retinas of mine.

'What?' I said, nervous. Maybe I'd misheard him. He couldn't have just asked me to move in with him. Could he?

'I've got this space,' he said. 'My parents are going to lend me the money. To do it up. It's my first ever project.'

'Space?' I repeated stupidly.

'Yeah, you know, a warehouse. It's an old Victorian garment factory. Top floor.'

'Victorian?'

'Well, thereabouts. Early Victorian, I think. Big.' He holds wide his arms, then drops them. 'It's in a bit of a state right now. It's a bit like camping, living there. There's no bathroom, or kitchen, or anything. But it could be beautiful – will be beautiful. It's near—'

'Look,' I shouted, pushing him away and staggering to my feet, 'you can't just . . . just go around doing this all the time.'

'Doing what?'

'You know what I mean.' I was standing with my hands on my hips. I almost started wagging my finger at him. 'This . . . this . . . upping the ante all the time. Saying things . . . like that.'

'But I'm in love with you.'

'There!' I shrieked, putting my hands over my ears. 'That's precisely the kind of thing I mean! You can't say that!'

'Why not?'

'Because – because we've spent exactly one afternoon together . . . and . . . and you hardly know me.'

'I don't care. I do love you. You know that.'

'No, I don't,' I blurted childishly.

'Yes, you do. I would hardly have asked you to come out to China otherwise, would I? You knew that when I called you from the Friendship Store.'

I was silent, ruminating.

'And you know what else?' he said.

'What?'

'You wouldn't have come unless you loved me.'

That was too much. Temper fizzed in my sternum, kindled by incredulity and outrage. I snatched up the bag of lychees and began pelting him with the hard, pink orbs.

'You arrogant swine,' I shouted. 'I've never met anybody so . . . fucking cocksure in all my life.'

The lychees were bouncing off his face and head. He

lunged at me, catching me round the waist. I battered his back and shoulders with my fists. 'Get off me! Let go!'

Straightening up, he grasped my flailing wrists in his hands and, with one of his feet, hooked out my feet from under me. Suddenly the sky was wheeling above my head and the ground came up to meet me. I didn't land hard on my back – he was holding on to me, breaking my fall – but as soon as I reached the ground, he had me pinned down. Astonished and infuriated, I wrestled and fought under his grip, but he remained effortlessly above me, laughing.

'Temper, temper,' he said. 'I misspent lots of my youth in judo classes. You might want to remember that. For future reference.'

I tussled and snarled, twisting my head round, trying to bite his wrist. 'I'd never live with you!' I spat. 'Never!'

'Really?'

'And I don't love you – I hate you!'

'Is that right? Well, I love you.'

'Fuck you! Let – me – go.'

'No. Not until you promise to move in with me.'

'I'd never live in your poxy, stinking warehouse – especially not with you.'

'Not even if I paid you?'

I laughed. I couldn't help it. Sweat was soaking into my hair and into the T-shirt, which was clinging to my ribs. I stopped struggling, exhaustion simmering down my fury. 'How much?'

'I don't know. What's the going rate for a concubine these days?'

'How about a tenner an hour and extra for sex?'

'You drive a hard bargain, Sinead Wilson.' He sat back on his heels, pretending to think. 'But your rates seem reasonable.' He nodded. 'It's a deal.'

'OK.'

'You promise?'

'I promise,' I said meekly.

He released his hold from around my wrists. Sensation surged back into my hands. I got up and began brushing grit, twigs and small stones from my back. Marcus picked bits of leaves from my hair.

'You know what?' I said, slowly and quietly.

'What?'

I raised my hand to his face and held it before his eyes. The second finger was crossed over the first.

'Looks like you'll be very lonely in your Victorian warehouse.'

He snatched at my arm, but I was too quick for him, darting from his reach and setting off down the winding path, my boots pounding the stone steps. I heard him thundering after me. Laughter tore up from my throat and my heart sent spurts of blood shooting round my system.

Further down the path, he'd catch up with me and I'd shove him into the stream. He'd be so wet he'd have to take off his clothes and then we'd both disappear for a while into the thick undergrowth where no one could see us.

But for now we were chasing at speed down a twisting path on a hill in south-west China, the light of the day draining out of the sky above us.

Sinead is waiting on the platform for the train that will take her to Michael's house. She hasn't called him to say she's coming: she didn't know how to explain it, how to phrase it in words.

Minutes flick by on the station clock above her head. Blackened pigeons roo-coo in the metal beams of the roof arch. A man opposite her stares with brute curiosity as she cries, tears soaking her coat front and gloves.

It is very simple. Yesterday you had a boyfriend; today you don't. Yesterday you had a flat where you lived; today you're homeless.

She would have been going to Phoebe's launch tonight. She imagines that, in some parallel universe, the person she was yesterday afternoon still exists, that somehow her identity has bifurcated and somehow somewhere she – or someone who looks and sounds like her – is holding hands with Marcus as they walk through the streets to Phoebe's gallery. She can see this Sinead: she is dressed in a tight-seamed skirt, black-tongued boots and a coat with ostrich feathers curled into the neck. She is holding a bottle of wine under her arm. She and Marcus are talking about Phoebe's funny friends, about Phoebe's gallery; they are saying that they won't stay long, that they'll go for a bit then they'll walk back, get a mini-cab, maybe, from a small, lighted room at the side of a road, and when they get back home they'll unwrap each other like gifts.

part | three

We live our lives, for ever taking leave

RAINER MARIA RILKE

Lily pushes the ends of her fingers, nail deep, into a slit between the planks of the table top. The wood is crusted with the delicate fractals of frost, but somehow doesn't feel as cold as it should.

Sinead has stopped. Her breath leaves her body in grey-white streams. She is shaking, either from the cold or from the effort of not crying, Lily can't tell which. She sits turned away from her, legs straddling the bench. Behind her, the Thames slips through the city, a black ribbon splintered with light. Ink-dark clouds race over their heads.

It seems peculiar to be sitting on the South Bank at a picnic table on a winter night. They are surrounded by other, identical tables, all deserted and whitened by frost. A strange muffled silence stretches between the river and the high concrete wall of the Royal Festival Hall. When people pass, giving them no more than a quick glance, their footsteps make no sound.

When they'd sat down together like this, Lily's head had been filled with the protocols of other meetings – you buy a coffee, a drink, discuss where to sit, engage in chat about how you are, what you've been up to. But with this there was nothing — no drink on the table between them, no preamble. There was only one purpose, and Sinead launched straight in.

Lily clears her throat. Sinead looks up, as if she'd forgotten she was there.

'So you left,' Lily says. She finds she cannot look into her eyes. Sinead must feel the same because as she talked she stared dead ahead of her. When their eyes do meet, it feels too acute, almost dangerous.

'Yes.'

'The next day?'

'The next morning.'

Lily rubs her chilled fingertips against her sleeve. 'And you haven't been back?'

Sinead shrugs. 'I came back to get my stuff.'

Lily nods, remembering. 'But after five years,' she struggles to control her incredulity, 'and that's it? One conversation and then you went?'

Sinead presses her teeth into her lip. 'There was . . . I didn't exactly have much choice.'

Lily senses their conversation is over. Part of her has a weird impulse to reciprocate, to tell Sinead something — a secret, a story, anything. To stop herself, she stands up, 'I must go.'

'Lily,' Sinead says her name quickly, in a new, thin voice.

'Yes?'

'Would you mind . . .' she begins unsteadily, her teeth gritted, as if the words are being dragged from her against her will. 'Can I ask you a question?'

'Sure.'

Sinead breathes in. 'When did you meet Marcus? I mean, when did things between you and him start?'

Lily feels in her pockets for her gloves, somehow knowing that whatever she says won't be the right answer. 'It was at a party. At a gallery.'

Sinead stares her straight in the eye. 'Phoebe's exhibition launch,' she murmurs.

Lily nods, shifting from one foot to the other. 'Well, I must be off,' she says awkwardly. 'Thanks.'

As soon as the word leaves her lips, she regrets it, wants to snatch it back from the air. Sinead gives a short laugh. 'For what?' she says. 'For Marcus?'

'No. I meant—'

'You're welcome to him,' she snaps.

Lily scratches her head. 'Goodbye, then.'

Sinead doesn't reply.

She climbs the worn metal steps of Hungerford Bridge two at a time, resting a hand on her knee for balance. At the top she stops, reaches into her pockets and drops what change she has into the battered polystyrene cup of a boy wrapped in a sleeping-bag. 'Thanks,' he calls after her, then returns to his mantra: 'Spare some change, please, spare some change.'

Half-way across she stops, leans on the metal barrier, and looks back to the Royal Festival Hall. The glass front of the building glows with yellow-orange light and people stream out of its doors. Sinead is still sitting at the wooden table, hunched against the cold. As Lily watches, she sees her stand, step clear of the bench, sling her bag on to her shoulder, and walk away towards Waterloo.

These things happen.

Sinead's words are only now beginning to sink in. As they sat together, all Lily could think was, there she is, right in front of her, talking, telling her. But it's only now, as distance stretches between them again, that Lily can start to turn over in her head what she'd said.

She looks down into the water. Boats glide, lit up and vibrating with music, under the bridge. She remembers, years ago, a story in a newspaper about two students – law students, were they? – who got into a fight on this bridge and were thrown over, their bodies washed up by the Thames Barrier days later. She wonders if Sinead had been watching her.

By the time she gets back, Marcus is asleep, the flat dark. She pushes at his door and peers into the gloom. He is lying on his back, one arm flung above his head.

Exactly. I wasn't exactly.

She kneels on the mattress. Marcus sighs and turns his head, his neck flashing white in the dark. But his eyes are still closed. Lily, scanning the room quickly, stretches out beside him, fully clothed.

Her hand moves out to touch his face, her fingertips meeting the ceraceous, heated skin of his cheek. She leans over him, watching his eyes flicker beneath the lids. Her hand moves up towards the fragile, membranous pale of his temple where the bone of the head is at its thinnest. She pictures his skull, grey-white, minutely pitted, fused along meandering lines. Just beneath her fingers cells swell, pulsate and quiver.

Lily has never had a secret before. Not a big one. At breakfast the next morning she feels it curled inside her, hot and breathing. Marcus has an architectural magazine propped up against the teapot, folded vertically, the pages furled. His eyes zoom from one side of the column of words to the next. Then he is talking, saying something to her about a job he's working on, a film he wants to see, a person he spoke to yesterday. With one hand, he stirs milk into his cereal with a spoon. The other rests on the table top, the nails blunt and clipped. Lily pours tea into her mug but lets the heat ebb out of it.

She breathes in through her mouth, feeling the air rushing past her teeth, and holds it. There are sentences crammed into her throat, waiting. Marcus has stopped speaking. He is transfixed by an invisible point midway between the sofa and the fridge, his jaw held in a crooked, concentrated set, mid-chew, his spoon still, resting on the side of his bowl. He is thinking about Sinead. Lily sees this and the secret twitches and vibrates inside her, the sentences twisting helix-like into confusion. She exhales, allowing the air to pass out through her nostrils. It makes a louder rushing sound than she intended and Marcus is roused from his reverie. He blinks, glances towards her, then down at his breakfast. His spoon hand resumes.

'I'm off now.' She walks towards the door. She hasn't eaten any breakfast. There is a kind of ascetic pleasure in her light-headedness, her hollow abdomen.

Aidan stands in the middle of the skeletal structure of his new, semi-erected bed. Metal struts lie scattered like jack straws all over the floor. In his left hand he holds an Allen key – ridiculously small, he feels, for the magnitude of this operation. In his right is an unfolded sheet of instructions. So-called instructions. He doesn't have the right kind of brain for this sort of thing, or doesn't speak the right language. He's not the right species with the right set of adapted physical features. If survival of the fittest depended on furniture construction from flat-packs, the Aidan Nashs of this world would have died out long ago. He only has to glance at the instruction sheet – large, white, with complex, incomprehensible diagrams of unidentified parts of furniture fitting effortlessly into other equally unidentifiable parts – and his mind just melts into a horrible, stultifying mix of boredom and frustration.

'Jodie,' he calls.

There is no answer. He can hear her and Rory, who appears to have a temporary reprieve, unpacking crockery in the kitchen, the click of china against china that takes him back to his teenage years, in his bedroom, listening out for when dinner would be ready.

'Jodie!'

His sister appears round the door, her arms folded. 'Hey, flat-pack king, how's it going?'

'I am not the flat-pack king. If flat-packing were a feudal system, I'd be the lowliest serf in history. I wouldn't even be a swineherd,' he mutters, looking around for something called 'axel B'. 'I'd be the swineherd's . . . au pair.'

Jodie laughs. 'Why are you putting the table up in the bedroom, Aide?'

'Very funny.' He is forced to take small, mincing steps through the heap of metal struts and packaging material towards her. 'Hilarious, in fact. Now, can you help me find axel B? It looks like this.' He stabs the instruction sheet with his finger. 'Do you see anything like that here?' He waves wildly at the heap of metal and wooden objects. 'Anything at all? No. Do you know why? Because you don't actually need it. Why would any bed need anything that resembles a small egg whisk? It's all a conspiracy to make you think it's worth spending an extortionate amount of money on a heap of junk.'

'Stop being silly,' she snatches the paper out of his hand, 'and give it to me. Honestly, sometimes I really think—'

The doorbell sounds, shrill and unfamiliar. They look up, surprised.

'Shall I get it?' Rory calls from the kitchen.

'No, I'll go.' Aidan dashes from the room. 'It'll be Sinead.'

He hardly has any time even to lay eyes on her before

she is over the threshold and pressing her glass-cold cheek to his. Then she is off down the hallway, hanging up her coat with the others on the pegs, and into the front room.

'God, Aidan, it's such a nice street,' she is saying, 'really close to the tube. And that amazing ivy all over the front of the house.' She turns to him and smiles. The light in the empty room, filtered through the ivy leaves, seems to oscillate around her, green and cool as river water. 'Can I have a guided tour?'

She is silent in every room: the hall, the kitchen, the lounge. She walks the perimeters, looking up, looking down, looking from side to side – everywhere but at him. Anxiety begins to pulse at his temples. On the stairs, she presses her palm to the wallpaper of dark, twisted, sinuous fronds and branches growing up the stairwell, then moves on. At the top, she turns.

'Aidan, it's beautiful. Really beautiful.' Her voice is serious, modulated, her eyes rapt.

His heart opens like a book and he climbs the last two steps to reach her. 'You think?' He has to be looking at the stretch of the banister, back down to the front door, as if checking it for straightness.

'Yes. Absolutely beautiful.' She enunciates each syllable. He can almost taste them on the air between them.

'Come and see the bedroom, and meet Jodie.'

His sister appears around the door. Sometimes their twinness strikes him as an odd impossibility: he looks at her and cannot imagine their bodies pocketed together in the same womb. And sometimes – often when he is alone – he feels an absence in the air around him, a chill down one side of his body that makes him shiver. Their mother told them that, in the final days, Jodie's foot had been pressed against Aidan's right ear, folded like an envelope against his head; and that when he was born it stuck straight out. They had to bind it back with 'the gentlest Sellotape'. He touches it now, his right ear, as Jodie leans forward and takes Sinead's hand in hers. He wants these two to be friends so much he almost can't bear them to meet.

'Aidan's making a right mess of putting his bed together,' Jodie is saying. Rory hovers just behind her, doing that united-front thing that couples always do when they're introduced to someone. 'Are you any good with flat-packs?'

'Let's have a look.'

Aidan stands in the doorway as Sinead inverts a long, wooden panel and stands it on its end.

'No,' she says to Jodie, 'wait. This must be part of that.'

Jodie stops, and the two of them bend over the instructions.

'You're right.' They look about them, hands on hips. 'If that fits in there, then that means—'

'That this one goes here.'

They laugh at their own ingenuity. Rory, by the window, looks over at Aidan and shrugs. 'I'm going out to get some wine,' he says.

All the surrounding rooms are still and empty; this room, the kitchen, vibrates with food and talk and people and candles. My flat, Aidan thinks, and leans back in his chair. Sinead has soaked a napkin in melted candle wax and is poking the flame with its edges, the light flaring up to pool on the ceiling.

'That's not the point, though, is it?' Rory says.

'It is!' Jodie exclaims.

'It's exactly the point,' Sinead chimes in, hooking her feet around the chair legs so that she seems to levitate out of her seat.

A week ago, in a restaurant, Sinead had told him that her favourite food at the moment was rocket. 'A highly incongruous name, don't you think?' she'd said, as she held up a fragile, limp, serrated leaf. He'd bought it for her tonight, but most of it lies untouched on her plate. Her clavicle is more pronounced than last week, he notices. Unless you knew, he thinks, she does a pretty good job of pretending. Unless you knew, you'd never be able to guess that underneath all that – the smile, the hair, the chat, the careful makeup, the exact clothes – was a broken heart. He imagines it as a fractured china cup in a paper bag, with sharp, snagged edges that could rip open its casing with one slight move.

'But the problem with those kind of trousers,' Jodie says, 'is that everyone can tell what kind of pants you're wearing. I think that's more information than most of my colleagues need.'

Sinead laughs, 'Yeah, but have you seen those high-cut maxi-briefs?' She shakes her head. 'Not pretty.'

Women are amazing. Within two hours of meeting, they're discussing underwear. Aidan stacks up plates and carries them to the as yet unused draining-board. Rory lifts his wineglass from the debris on the table and wanders into the front room. Aidan turns the tap, feeling the pleasure of doing something for the first time that you know you'll be doing over and over again. Water drums into the aluminium sink. A reverberating bass suddenly sounds from the other room and he realises Rory must have got the stereo up and running. There is a slow run of notes, a shift in tempo, then a woman's voice – high and pure – floats out over the top.

His body acts faster than his mind. He is letting the plate he is washing slide back into the water and turning towards her while his thought processes are still catching up: why does this music give him a strange feeling and where has he heard it before and who does it remind him of and someone, who is it, plays this track over and over.

The effect on Sinead is faster and more dramatic. She crumples into herself, her face sliding into horror and fear. She starts up, stumbles across the kitchen, clamping her hands over her mouth and nose as a kind of coughing sob tears out of her. 'Oh, Christ,' they hear her say, and she is scrabbling at the clasp of the windowed doors and then is out into the garden, swallowed up by the gloom.

'Shit,' says Jodie.

'Get Rory to turn that off,' Aidan says, as he pushes through the doors after her.

The garden is cold and not yet familiar enough for him to navigate with confidence in the dark. He is striding through the dew-soaked grass when the black shape of a tree looms up in front of him. He stops, rests his hand against knotted bark. Listens. Distant traffic. The spiralling threads of the music still going inexorably on. Stifled sobbing coming from – where? He dips his head, leans closer to the tree. The far wall. Near the crappy ornamental fountain. He edges closer.

'Sinead?' he half whispers.

He comes upon her more quickly than he thought. She has both hands over her mouth and is bending over as if in physical pain. The sound she is making is not inhuman, but it's like nothing he's heard before – high, ululating, childlike. He hesitates, wondering what kind of sound it would be if she took her hands away and let rip, how loud it would be, how many gardens it would travel. He puts a hand on her shoulder. 'Sinead.' He can't think of what he wants to say. 'Please,' is what comes out. 'Please don't. Please.'

She straightens up, still with her head averted, still with her hands over her mouth. Then he has his arms around her, tight, and her body is shuddering against his.

'I'm sorry, I'm sorry, I'm so sorry,' she is saying between sobs, and he is telling her to hush, his chin against her hair, and her fingers gripping the wool of his jumper, her face crushed into his chest.

'Sssh,' he says, 'it's all right now, it's all right.'

The music is abruptly silenced and they are surrounded by dark and stillness and quiet. Her sobbing is slower now, less high-pitched and frantic. He feels her shift in his arms and he wonders if she wants him to let her go, if she wants to step away, and he loosens his hold on her, but she is just moving her face, letting her head fall into the curve of his neck. Aidan puts his arms around her again.

'It's all right,' he murmurs. 'You're going to be all right.'

It's never usually possible to pinpoint when a friendship

begins, the moment when a casual acquaintance moves up a gear. It's usually a gradual, incremental process that takes place over many evenings, or many drinks or many chats on the phone; a slow attrition of differences or a slow discovery of similarities. But with Sinead it's easy. Aidan can narrow it down to the day, the hour, the minute: when she phoned him on the morning she'd left Marcus. He'd been in the office, working at something on screen and had picked up his phone, unthinking, to hear her voice: 'You knew, didn't you?' He had sat up straight, knocking his mouse to the floor. 'All that time, you knew. Sinead—' he'd begun, scrabbling to retrieve his mouse, already knowing he could never lie to her.

'God,' she says, pulling away. 'I'm so sorry, Aidan. It's ridiculous.' She half laughs, wiping at her face, 'I can't go two hours these days without this happening.'

'That's OK,' he says. The sudden distance between them, filled with chilled autumn air, makes it seem more difficult to comfort her.

'I'm really sorry,' she mutters, her breathing still unsteady, as she turns to go back up the garden. 'It's stupid. It really is.'

He follows her. Her tears have soaked into his neck. Later that night, when he undresses, he'll find mascara-black trails where they ran down his body.

Aidan was quite good with jet-lag. He'd had to get used to it in a job that could send him half-way round the world without a day's notice. So when he arrived in New York he'd been surprised to feel it – a slight nausea, a thickening of the head, leaden limbs – while he was sitting on the bus taking him to Manhattan Island, bag on knee, passport still clutched in his hand.

By the time he reached his hotel, it was worse. He stumbled into his room, tripping on the rug, and closed the door. He'd intended to unpack his laptop, lay out his notes in preparation for the next day's meeting. But he reckoned later that he must have fallen asleep before he actually hit the mattress because his last recollection was crawling over what seemed like metres and metres of crinkly, haemorrhage-red counterpane.

When he woke, sensations filtered through to his consciousness like images on to photographic paper. The light outside was a liquid indigo. He was lying on his back, diagonally across the bed. Incredible thirst. Cold from the air-con. Light too bright. Tongue dry and swollen. Traffic and sirens from the street below.

He turned on to his side, his vision swimming with nausea and exhaustion. He sat up, and tentatively shook his head. Was he drunk? Hung-over? Ill, perhaps? He hadn't yet worked out where he was and what he was doing here. But this was nothing too unusual: he hadn't 'lived' anywhere for the past three years, spending months in Japan, then New York, then LA, then Berlin, then London and then back again. Hotel rooms. Temporary apartments. But that had all changed. He was now going to be based permanently in London. He was buying a flat. His own flat.

Aidan flopped back on to the pillow. It was all coming back to him now: he had accepted a contract with the UK-based branch of an American firm. He was staying at

Marcus's place. With Sinead. While he waited for everything to be sorted with his flat. While Marcus was working in New York. Which was here, in fact. Where Aidan was right now. A hotel in New York. To finalise the designs on an animated music video.

A red light was flashing on the phone next to his head. He turned, stabbed at it with his index finger, and listened blearily to a recorded electronic voice. A message from Marcus to meet him at eight at the corner of Broadway and 57th. He brought his left arm up in front of his face and stared at his watch as if he'd never seen it before. Its round face, reinforced with black plastic, a neat circle of tiny numbers. The lurid, pointing hands, split like protractors. He'd heard about a woman who, in the days when they used uranium for glow-in-the-dark watches, used to lick the tip of her brush before painting the luminous clock face. Ingested all that carcinogenic poison over years and years. Died of leukaemia in the end.

Aidan squeezed his eyes shut then popped them open again and, with effort, squinted at his watch. Small hand – seven. Large hand – three. Or between three and four. Which meant? Seven twenty. Shit.

He leaped off the bed and waited until he regained his balance. His clothes felt stale and stiff, but there was no time to change. He slapped his pockets: wallet, hotel keys and the crinkle of paper in his breast pocket. Aidan pushed his fingers into it and felt hard, sealed edges. Envelope. He remembered: Sinead's letter for Marcus that she'd given him this morning. He'd seen her fold the tightly written pages into three, slide it into an envelope, lick its edges and press them down. Yesterday morning. Whenever.

The bones in his legs felt jointless and malleable as he walked down Central Park West. Joggers and rollerbladers lashed past him. He wondered about hailing a cab, but decided the air would do him good. To his left, the trees of the park rustled and swayed; two men were throwing a baseball between them, the orange sphere ricochetting through the darkening air. His neck and shoulders were crunched up, his forehead stretched with the beginnings of a headache, and as he walked he tried rolling his arms inside their sockets to relieve the pulling on his neck.

At the intersection of Broadway and 57th was a Duane Reade chemist's shop. The apartment Marcus was renting until the job finished was further west towards the Hudson River. After checking up the street to see if he was coming, Aidan ducked into the shop to buy some painkillers. He hadn't seen Marcus for six months, having moved into the flat after he'd already left for New York, and didn't want to be dragged down by a headache.

He stumbled up and down the aisles. Nail varnish. Moisturisers. Shampoos. Toothbrushes. Chocolate. Potato chips. A song came on the store's intercom, a hit from about fifteen years ago; a song that at one point he and Marcus used to listen to when they were at school, on Marcus's Walkman with two headsets. He hoped that Marcus would arrive before it ended, so that he could drag him into this strip-lit shop to listen. Razors. Vitamins. Suntan lotion. His body clock thought it was one in the morning. Toiletry bags. Hair accessories. Leg waxers. Sanitary towels. Slimming powders. Deodorants. Pharmaceuticals. At last.

He stood by the display of coloured, striped, logoed boxes, mesmerised. Throat sweets. Hayfever sprays. Antiseptic cream. Painkillers. There were twenty or so varieties. Did he want Tylenol, Motrin, Advil, Excedrin or Anacin? Soluble or insoluble? Aidan rubbed his palm over his face, smelling sweat and fatigue, stale air and travel. Coated or non? Capsules or pills? Caffeinated or not? Bottled or foil-wrapped?

Then there was a hand pulling at his shoulder and Marcus's voice, oddly American in intonation: 'Hey, Aide, how are you doing?'

He was grinning, tanned and dressed in his architect uniform, sunglasses hanging, folded, from his grey shirt pocket. A jumper was tied by its arms round his waist. Aidan moved forward with a slight lurching movement, pleased to see him yet confused, unable to remember how he and Marcus usually greeted each other, whether they hugged or shook hands or nodded or did nothing.

'You look rough,' Marcus said, as he closed his fingers briefly around Aidan's. 'When did you get in?'

'Couple of hours ago.'

'New jacket?'

'Yeah. You like it?'

'No.'

They smiled at each other, their right arms falling to their sides in unison.

'So, have you had to touch base yet?' Marcus said.

'*Touch base?*' Aidan repeated, one eyebrow raised (an

ability of his that Marcus had always envied). 'Where are you from? California?'

'Yeah, very funny. Listen, what do you fancy doing tonight?'

'I'm not sure. I'm feeling a bit wrecked to tell you the truth, so—'

'Oh, don't be such a wuss. We have to go out. You're only here for . . . how long is it?'

'Five days.'

'Exactly. So I think we should head down to SoHo and—'

Marcus broke off. Two American-Chinese women were coming down the aisle towards them, chatting, wire baskets bumping against their legs. Aidan didn't really look at them, but noticed at this point that one had cropped, spiked hair, and the other a long, silky ponytail and an impossibly short suede dress. Aidan stepped aside to let them past, still waiting for Marcus to finish his sentence. But Marcus was holding his ground, hands on hips. He was widening his eyes and grimacing, and for a second Aidan didn't know what he was doing, pulling a strange face like that, and was wondering if there was anything wrong, when he saw that he was grinning at the two women, who were staring at them, then looking at each other, then laughing and looking back at them. 'Hi,' the short-haired one said as they passed.

What happened next happened fast: the women walked on, one glancing over her shoulder, towards the end of the aisle. Marcus touched Aidan's sleeve, said, 'Hang on,' and went after them. 'Hi. Hi. Hello,' he heard him saying to them, stepping between them, 'how are you?'

They giggled. The long-haired one hoisted her basket on to the other arm. 'Are you British?' he heard her say.

And Aidan just watched. Either jet-lag or surprise or disbelief or all three kept his mental deductions at bay. When his friend disappeared around the corner with the two women, Aidan found himself actually turning back to the pharmaceutical display and selecting a blue box of Advil. Then he walked into the next aisle and picked up a small bottle of mineral water. As he approached the till, he glanced around for Marcus but, not seeing him, stood in line and waited.

Just as he was handing over his purchases and feeling around for his wallet, something came through the air, whizzing past his ear, to crash-land on the counter in front of him. Aidan jumped back in surprise, then saw what it was. A box of condoms. Three. Trojans. Spermicidally lubricated.

Marcus appeared next to him, delving in his pockets and bringing out a ten-dollar bill. 'Right. OK. We're sorted,' he said, 'Thanks,' he said to the cashier, as she gave him his change, and, handing Aidan his things, pushed the condoms into his back pocket. 'They're heading for a club over in TriBeCa,' he began, in a low voice, as they walked towards the door, 'but not till later. We could meet them there or we could all go for a drink first. What do you think?'

Aidan's brain was picking up the momentum of what was happening. He stopped just outside the door so abruptly that Marcus fell into him.

'What are you doing?' he said.

Marcus blinked. 'What do you mean?'

'What do I mean? I mean what are you playing at?'

He gestured at the women, standing a few yards off on the sidewalk – who, he now noticed, were probably still teenagers – and back at Marcus's pocket where the condoms were. He watched, incredulous, as a weary smile insinuated itself into Marcus's features.

'Aidan, you're not going to come over all pious on me, are you?'

Fury flared in Aidan's chest, adrenaline arrowing through his system, banishing all traces of exhaustion. 'Pious?' he repeated. '*Pious?* This has absolutely fuck all to do with piety. Does the word "Sinead" mean anything to you? Anything at all?'

At the mention of her name, something flickered in Marcus's face. Something recognisable, identifiable. Then it was gone, as quickly as it had come. 'Look,' he said, 'I think we should go for a drink with these two. Are you up for that or not?'

Aidan stared at him, aghast. 'No. I'm not.'

'So what do you want to do?'

'Marcus—' he began, then stopped. 'I just think—' Vocabulary eluded him. 'Do what you want.' He waved his hand at him. 'We – we can't talk about this now.'

Marcus didn't answer, but stood where he was, his face turned towards the girls, one foot balanced, jiggling, on top of the other. 'I can't desert you like that,' he muttered, still not looking at him. Aidan watched him, wary, curious as to which way he would go.

'You're really jet-lagged, are you? You're just going to go to bed?' Marcus said, turning his face back to Aidan. 'So give me a call tomorrow at the office, OK?' Aidan was silent. 'All right,' Marcus said, ignoring the fact that he'd had no reply. 'I'll speak to you then.'

Aidan watched as his friend walked off, flanked by the two women, down Broadway. He went to rub one hand against the other and discovered that he was holding a plastic bag containing the Advil and the water, and remembered his headache. He felt as if he was peering out of a mask of pain, his head throbbing, his eyes smarting in his skull.

Aidan had spent the day arguing over the anthropomorph-isation of a penguin. Corners of his brain still twitched with images of the video footage they'd been watching on a big conference screen: penguins sliding down glaciers, penguins sleek-swimming in barely liquid Arctic waters, penguins shuffling over their eggs.

Walking back to his hotel, he scrolled through his mobile messages. He'd diverted five calls from Marcus, telling himself he was too busy, that it was rude to answer his phone when in a meeting, that he'd call him back later.

As he was walking across his hotel lobby – a monstrosity of curtain-glass walls, plastic ivy plants and explosions of fairy lights – towards the lifts, he saw him, sprawled across a seat in the bar, one leg hooked over the side of the chair, reading a folded-up paper. Aidan hesitated, looked at the lift doors, the illuminated descending arrows, then back at his friend. He walked over to him. 'Hello,' he said, when he got within two feet of him.

Marcus leaped up, standing to attention as if Aidan were a teacher and Marcus a pupil wishing to ingratiate himself: 'Hi!'

Aidan readjusted his bag, where the strap was cutting into his shoulder. He felt as if the weight of it was driving him into the deep pile of the carpet, that if he stayed standing there any longer he might never move again.

'So,' Marcus said, rolling the paper into a funnel in his hands, 'how are you?'

'OK.'

'Have you finished for the day?'

'Yeah.'

'Do you want to go and get something to eat?'

Aidan shifted his feet. Static from the carpet sparked under his shoe soles. 'OK.'

The taxi driver had a radio pumping out heavy gangsta rap so, as they sped past Central Park, they were able to sit without their silence becoming embarrassing. Even when they got out of the taxi, slamming their separate doors and fussing over who was paying, they didn't talk much. The sidewalks were so crowded that all the sidestepping and weaving made conversation difficult. Then they were queuing in a line for a Chinese restaurant, which was huge, on three floors. The waiters wore headphones and could radio each other. 'Sending two up to you now,' the tall, ponytailed waiter muttered into his mouthpiece, gesticulating to Aidan and Marcus as they reached the front of the queue, 'a couple of guys.'

The stairs were polished, smoked glass, edged with steel. When Aidan sat down at their small, white-clothed table, it felt like hours since they'd set out. A man behind them was arguing with his wife about crackers, and Marcus was saying something about king prawns and soup. They fiddled with the different menus, folding them and unfolding them, gave their order to a woman with dark lipstick, unsheathed chopsticks, upturned their bowls, poured tea into their tiny china cups, said that, yes, this place was good, very nice, and how long had it been open. Aidan noticed that every time he turned his head there was a rushing sound, like someone crumpling paper.

'Well,' Marcus said, and Aidan suddenly saw that he was nervous, one hand plucking at his shirt cuff, the other picking at its nails. There was a pause. Aidan filled his mouth with beer, let it effervesce on his tongue, then swallowed.

'It's . . . it's good to see you,' Marcus tried again.

Aidan nodded.

'The other day,' Marcus began, forcing a lightness of tone into his voice, 'someone told me that the funny thing about being a Brit in New York is that you never know—'

'Marcus. Cut the crap.' Aidan needlessly readjusted his beer bottle to the other side of his plate. 'Just tell me what's going on.'

Marcus hesitated. Aidan could see he was trying to decide whether or not to pretend that he didn't know what Aidan meant. Aidan studied the features of this man he'd known since he was eleven, and it was as if he barely recognised him. Did he really know him? Did he really know him any better than he knew the man behind him? Or the waitress? Or the people he'd spent the day working with? He had the strange sensation that they'd only just met and that they should be talking about where they grew up, what music they liked, where they'd been travelling, what jobs they did, not some ridiculous personality crisis that Marcus seemed to be going through.

'What do you mean?'

He'd decided to pretend. Aidan sighed and looked away. The waitress was swaying between the tables towards them with steaming plates. Aidan looked down as she placed a plate of thin, frazzled noodles in front of him. The image of a penguin fluttered, inappropriate and unbidden, in a corner of his mind. He picked up a strand between his chopsticks, and blew on it.

'I mean last night,' he said. 'Those girls.' He pushed the noodle into his mouth. It tasted of soy sauce and peanut oil, and coated his tongue with grease. 'I mean your new game of hitting on random women in drugstores.'

'What's got into you?' Marcus said, flushed. 'Why are you being so judgemental? It's not as if you've never . . . I mean, how come there's one rule for me and another for you?'

'I don't have a long-term girlfriend, Marcus,' Aidan pointed out calmly. 'Slight but crucial difference.'

'So that's what this is about.' Marcus rubbed his hand over his brow. 'Look. All I'm doing is . . . getting out there. That's all.'

Aidan tapped the ends of his chopsticks against his incisors, as if considering this statement.

'It's a whole realm of human experience,' Marcus continued when he saw that Aidan wasn't going to speak, 'that everybody should have. I'm in New York City, for God's sake. Do you really think I should be staying at home every night?'

Aidan was silent, didn't move, didn't blink, but held Marcus's gaze.

'And it's not as if . . . I mean, I love Sinead,' Marcus said, filling the silence. 'She is the only one for me, I know that and I've always known that, right from the moment I first saw her. Without her, I'm nothing. Nothing. None of this has anything to do with her.' He sat back in his chair, expecting Aidan's comment.

Aidan took a mouthful of beer, set down the bottle and surveyed his friend. He kept his face blank, impassive for a moment, then inflected his brow, indicating that Marcus should go on. Which he did.

'I've never done this. Ever since I was nineteen, twenty, I've been from one big, monogamous relationship to another, pretty much back to back. Never had the chance to . . . It's something I just wanted to get out of the way, I suppose. So the thought of it wouldn't . . . distract me any more. Everybody should have done it at some time or another – you know, given in to their desires.'

He stopped. Aidan felt him readjusting his feet under the table; the tablecloth tugged at the table corner; a toe of his shoe nudged Aidan's shin.

'And I really think you need to have a period of . . . of exploration before you . . .' He scuffed his feet again, uncrossing and recrossing his ankles. 'I mean, we're going to get married, Aide. We talked about it before I left. And I know this isn't perhaps the most . . . I don't know . . .' he appeared to search for the word in the air '. . . *honourable* way to go about things. But just for myself, I felt I needed to . . . you know . . .'

'Shop around?' Aidan suggested.

'Exactly.' Relief flooded Marcus's face. His lips parted in a smile. 'Shop around. That's it. I knew you'd understand. That's it exactly. And now I do know. I really do. All this is kind of good and nice and easy.' He paused. 'It's amazingly easy. But she's what I want. I think I know that now.'

'You think?'

'I know. I think I know. I mean, I know I know. I've always known, really.' He picked up his chopsticks and started pushing food into his mouth. He seemed happier now, relaxed, pouring tea, gulping down his beer. He looked back at Aidan. 'Well, are you going to say something, or are you going to just sit there staring at me all night like a moron?'

Aidan placed his chopsticks on the side of his plate. His food had cooled and coagulated while Marcus was talking; a tangled mess of cold, MSG-coated threads. 'There's nothing to say.'

Marcus frowned, puzzled.

'What do you want me to say? Congratulations? Well done? You've sown your wild oats. Bully for you.'

There was a long silence. Marcus chewed, his jaw working, his eyes scanning Aidan's face. A waitress hovered on the periphery of Aidan's vision.

'I get it.' Marcus started nodding, smirking slightly.

'Get what?'

'Nothing.'

'What?'

'Nothing,' Marcus said again, grinning now.

Aidan glared at him. 'Marcus—'

'You're jealous.'

A tiny muscle under Aidan's eye started up an invisible, convulsive twitching, as if connected to a distant electrical current. 'Jealous?'

'Yeah.'

'Of you and Sinead? That's—'

'No,' Marcus cut across him, shaking his head. 'No, no. Of this. Of what I've been up to. The time I've been having.'

Aidan gave a bark of laughter. 'You think I'm jealous of you? You think—' He gulped with incredulity. 'Yeah, you're right. I am jealous. I'd love to have sex with teenagers I find on the street. It must be great. Really fantastic. And I'm sure Sinead will agree.'

'Will you stop banging on about Sinead?' Marcus snapped, aggressive, his chin jutted out, his fists curled. 'This has nothing to do with her – I told you.' He stared at Aidan for longer than was comfortable. 'What is all this sudden concern for my girlfriend, anyway?' he said, in a new, steely voice.

'*Concern?* Well, how do you think she's going to react?' Aidan retorted, pushing back his chair. 'What do you think she's going to say? Have you thought about that?'

Marcus threw down his chopstick, rolling his eyes up to the ceiling. 'Jesus Christ, she's not going to say anything, of course.'

Aidan stared at his friend across the table. This time Marcus held his gaze, exasperation and impatience creasing his features. Aidan suddenly remembered a day when they were teenagers, when they were walking through the park in the town where they'd grown up: it was early summer and they were too young for that to mean exams. Marcus was wearing his school tie around his head like a sweatband, both of them had their shirts untucked, and they were flinging a frisbee between them as they walked, fifteen metres apart, still carrying on a conversation. It was one of those rare, isolated moments in adolescence when everything is pure and keen, when you glimpse an adulthood ahead of you that seems unfettered and gifted and worth the wait. The disc of the frisbee spun between them, fast and flawless as an electron.

'You don't think she'll work it out?' he said eventually.

'How would she?' Marcus shrugged.

'She's not stupid.'

'No. But,' and he smiled, 'we haven't seen each other for so long that she's not exactly going to stop to sniff my underwear, is she?'

'*Shut up.*' Aidan spat out. 'Just shut the fuck up. I don't want to hear any more of this shit. You're – you're –' articulacy deserted him, '– you're . . . What the fuck has happened to you?'

'Liberation.' Marcus smiled, folding his napkin on the table with a flourish. 'Liberation is what's happened to me, my friend. The truth of the matter is that everyone would do this. If they could. Very, very few people would hesitate, given the right circumstances. Nobody could resist. And here, in New York, it's completely foolproof. I'm thousands of miles away. The whole Atlantic Ocean lies between us. No one I've slept with knows her. She'll never find out. There's no one to tell her. No one she knows knows.'

'The perfect murder.'

Marcus frowned. 'Hardly.'

There was another pause. Marcus stabbed at a spring roll, mashing it into a pool of soy sauce.

'There is one person,' Aidan said.

Marcus looked at him sharply. 'Who?'

'Have you had some kind of lobotomy?'

'Who?' he demanded.

'Me. Remember? I live with her. In your flat. You remember your flat? Nice place? Big? Architect-designed?'

The anxiety evaporated from Marcus's eyes. 'Yeah, right,' he said, looking around as if for the waitress. Then, as if something had suddenly occurred to him, his head twisted back to Aidan and their eyes locked. And it was as if Aidan could feel their friendship slipping and skidding out from underneath them like feet on black ice.

He stood, letting his napkin drop from his hands on to the table. He suddenly felt incredibly tired, felt the weighted pull of jet lag on his limbs. Marcus stood too. Aidan flung down a couple of notes and lifted his chair to push it back under the table.

'Are you threatening me?' Marcus came fast around the side of the table, almost squaring up to him, shoving his face into his. 'I can't believe this. You're supposed to be my best mate.'

Aidan looked him full in the face. Again, that sensation of unfamiliarity, of disparity, that they were strangers.

'You're not going to tell her, are you?' Fear bubbled beneath Marcus's clenched-fist aggression. 'Are you?'

'Do you realise the position you're putting me in?' Aidan said.

'Position?' Marcus said quickly. 'What do you mean? You don't have a position. There is no position.'

'I live with her,' Aidan said. 'In the same flat. I'll be going back and seeing her every morning and every evening in . . . in three days' time. She'll be asking me how you are, what we did, what you're up to, how you're looking. Don't you see?'

'What? See what?'

'You're making me lie to her. Collude. You're forcing me to be your accomplice.'

'And that's beneath you, is it, Mr Morality?'

Aidan turned, yanking his arm away from Marcus's grip and walked across the yards and yards of dimly lit carpet and down the stairs and out into the pollution-heavy night. Outside the restaurant he passed a man carrying an albino child in a hooded blue anorak on his shoulders, his hands gripped around her socked ankles. The child's skin gleamed like pearls in the streetlights. She had fine white hair that hung out of her hood and a knowing, searching, oddly prescient gaze. She stared at Aidan from the fringes of her colourless eyelashes until he felt ashamed and looked away.

For the next four days, Aidan worked. He watched more videos of arctic wastelands, of creaking blue ice floes, of the small black birds skimming down through the surface of the petrifying waters. Small simulacrum penguins began to emerge in the margins of his notes, at first static, two-dimensional sketches, then proper creatures with depth, dimension and perspective. These were scanned into his laptop. They disappeared from his screen for a day to the software designers, and his creations returned to him, duplicated twelve times, each clone in a different pose. By the end of the last day, a penguin was mouthing something at him silently from the other side of his screen.

At night he ate alone, slept, worked some more, then walked the streets, past illuminated bars, past stilled fountains, through streets overhung with skyscrapers, and past the bright windows of late-night nail bars, where Korean girls bent over the hands of vacant-faced women, filing, clipping, cleaning and painting nails in luscious, glittering colours.

It was only when he got to the airport that, searching in the pockets of his bag for his passport or his ticket or maybe some chewing-gum, his fingers came into contact with the crackle of paper. Gripping it between index and middle finger, he drew out Sinead's letter to Marcus: sealed; a cream envelope with a raised grain; his name on the front with a firm, deft underline. The recognition gave him a shock like the contact of his skin with cold water. He turned it over in his hands and, to his shame, held it up to the light. The double folds of paper created unreadable palimpsests of slanted writing. It struck him as strange that a letter could be creased and worn yet unopened.

Sinead has left. Rory is driving her to the tube station. She kissed them all lightly, one by one. 'I'm sorry about the histrionics,' she said, hovering in the doorway, half in and half out of the light.

'Yeah, we're really angry,' Jodie said.

Sinead had smiled, raised her hand in a small wave, then was gone.

The table is littered with after-dinner debris: wine corks, ruined candles, bits of food, ash, circle-stains of wine and balls of wax sculpted with fingerprints. Jodie puts a cigarette between her lips and presses down on the Zippo lighter Aidan bought her in the States.

'So,' she says.

Aidan is moving plates around futilely, from table to draining-board to sink. 'What?'

'Are you going to tell her?'

He half turns. 'Tell who what?'

Jodie draws on her filter tip, the smoke making a slight kissing sound as it explodes into her mouth, and fixes him with an assessing stare. 'Tell Sinead you're in love with her.'

He turns his face back to the blue tiles in front of him, rests the heels of his palms on the Formica. The tiling distorts his features like a hall of mirrors – lengthening his nose and upper lip and making his eyes disappear into small raisin-sized hollows under a huge dome of forehead. He looks down, sees his thumb picking at the side of his finger's cuticle. He leafs through possibilities: pretend, laugh it off, lie. But this is Jodie. It would never work. Desperation and denial grapple within him. He doesn't want to talk about this, doesn't want to vocalise it because until he does he can convince himself that it's all an illusion, a trick his heart is playing on him, that it will pass, that it's not something he or anyone else need take seriously. He can keep it sealed up inside himself and no one need ever know. He doesn't want to besmirch this secret by opening it to oxygen, to sunlight, to scrutiny. He wants to keep it folded up somewhere deep and dark so that no one need ever know. But this thing – whatever it is – has taken root without him really noticing, and is spreading its lithe, choking branches to every corner of his being.

'Don't,' he says quietly. He moves a plate from the draining-board into the sink and picks up a glass. Behind him, he hears her suck again on her cigarette. Wait. Exhale. He turns, glass in hand. She isn't looking at him but out through the doors into the black garden. It's only two steps to the table, where he sits. Places the glass on it. Rests his elbows on the table top. Pushes his hands through his hair. 'I don't know what I'm going to do,' he says.

She balances her cigarette on the bevelled lip of the ashtray and slides her hand into one of his.

'I never meant for this to happen,' he says. 'I really didn't. I never even saw it coming.'

'You rarely do, though, do you? It's not as if anyone can ever plan these things.'

'Yeah, but there are slightly better situations.'

'Are there?'

He looks up, exasperated. 'How many women are there in London?'

'I dunno. Six million?'

'OK, let's say six million. Out of all of them, I had to fall for her.'

Jodie smirks. 'Of all the gin joints in all the towns—'

'Shut up,' he says, but starts to laugh. 'OK. Out of all the women in all the gin joints in all the city, I had to walk into the girlfriend of my best friend. Which is—'

'Ex-girlfriend,' she interrupts. 'Ex-best friend.'

'Whatever. Which isn't, of course, the only problem.'

'What is?'

'Jodie,' he says impatiently, 'you didn't notice anything slightly amiss tonight? Anything at all? Floods of tears? Extreme misery? No?'

'All right, all right,' she says, 'so she's in possession of a broken heart, which—'

'Which is a rather major stumbling block.'

'Hmm. But that's the *only* stumbling block,' she tells him sternly. 'Who cares about that fuckwit? You mustn't even think about letting him stand in your way.'

'Jodie—' he tries to interject, but, insistent, leaning forward, stabbing the air with the burning tip of her cigarette, she talks over him: 'Aide, you don't owe him anything. Ever since you were both children, you have always looked out for him, always helped him, always picked up his pieces, always sorted out his various cock-ups. You're his bloody stunt man. Yes, he's basically an all right guy but he's messed up too badly this time to get away with it. He treated her like something he'd scraped off the bottom of his shoe and you just have to take one look at her to realise what a fool he is. He's a feckless emotional retard. You owe him nothing. *Nada. Niente.* And neither does she. I'll be livid with you if you don't follow your heart because of any kind of vestigial loyalty you might have to him.' Jodie flicks her ash viciously into the ashtray.

'You like her, then?' he says eventually.

She rolls her eyes in exasperation. 'Aide, she's wonderful. She's clever and funny. And gorgeous. In fact,' she says, 'I hate her.' She grips his hand in hers, hard. 'You have to tell her.'

'I can't.'

'You have to. She has a right to know, apart from anything else.'

'Look, you saw her. The woman's in no fit state for anything. How could I tell her? How do you think it would go down? I'd just come across as some opportunistic bastard, and she'd never want to see me ever again. The last thing she needs right now is more emotional shit dumped on her.'

Jodie sighs, fiddles with the lid of her Zippo. 'Maybe,' she says. 'But you will tell her, won't you? At some point? You're not just going to let this lie?'

Aidan grunts and attempts to press a ball of cold, rigid wax into a perfect cuboid shape with the blood-heat of his hands. Jodie comes to stand behind him, hugging him. Aidan feels the thud of his sister's heart along his back.

'Poor Aide,' she murmurs.

'Hardly,' he says, flinging the wax aside. 'Poor Sinead I'd say.'

'I could kill that fuckface Marcus Emerson.'

'No, I could.'

'No. *I* could.'

'No, no, no. I think you'll find that—'

'We both could,' she concedes.

'OK. When?'

Lily and Sarah sit on a row of three tilting metal chairs, holding a newspaper between them. Sarah is reading the job adverts and Lily is half pretending to do the same, but her mind feels swollen, overblown: things sink into it, as if into wet concrete, never to be seen again.

One of her feet swings over the cold floor of the tube station. The sole of her shoe squeaks ever so slightly on the floor at the nadir of each swing. Back, scuff, forth, scuff. It's reached that point now where the movement has created its own momentum, the pendular sweep powered by its own self-perpetuating physics.

Sarah met her from work and they've been to a café with red leather seats and steamed-up windows, where they ate ribbons of pasta from oval plates and eavesdropped on the first-date conversation going on behind them. They were going to go to a film but they've had one of those London nights where nothing comes together, when the city seems to conspire against you: the film they wanted to see was sold out, and by the time they'd found that out they'd missed the other screening of it across town; the bar they liked was full, the rather smug bouncer on the door told them; walking to another it had started to rain, and then hail, sharp pellets of ice bouncing off the pavement, into their hair and down their collars. They'd given up, beaten a retreat to the tube.

Lily glances up at the box suspended from the arched ceiling, where destinations and times of tube trains are displayed in ever-changing combinations of tiny orange lightbulbs. This movement of her head, which pulls on the muscles and tendons down her back, spine, ribcage and pelvis, combined with the distracting, unbalancing effect of a man in a wide, insulation-stuffed coat walking too closely by them, makes the movement of her leg falter, stutter and lose rhythm. Lily stills her foot, crosses her legs, and glances up at the board again. Still blank. '1,' it announces proudly, 'High Barnet,' but next to it, where the number of minutes in which the train is due should be, is a dense black blank.

'What about a sushi chef?' Sarah says. 'I could do that.'

Lily leans over to look at the advert. 'Must speak Japanese,' she reads.

Sarah peers more closely. 'Damn,' she exclaims. 'That's discrimination, that is. Just because I can't speak Japanese doesn't mean I can't make sushi.'

'But would you really want to spend hours rolling bits of raw fish into balls?'

Sarah sighs. 'I don't know. It'd be better than cleaning toilets or chambermaiding or flipping burgers.' She crushes the paper shut. 'I have to get a job,' she moans. 'Woman cannot live on art alone.' She opens the pages again. 'OK,' she says, smoothing the adverts flat on her lap. 'What can you do in the evenings that's not too strenous or depressing that earns you loads of cash?'

'Be a hooker?'

'Very funny,' she mutters. 'And you shouldn't joke. It may still come to that.'

Lily smiles, leans her head back on the wall and closes her eyes. And as soon as she does, her mind is swarmed with the thoughts Sarah's presence has been holding at bay. Indecision is not something she's ever really experienced before. It's a strange feeling: cloying, unaccountable, gluing everything together. It frustrates and angers her. All day, no matter what she is doing, an internal debate is running in her head, questions and doubts wrestling and fighting each other. She can't switch it off, even when she wants to sleep. Sometimes she wonders if she's spoken it aloud. She's thought about telling Sarah everything, the whole story, and has been on the brink of doing so several times tonight. But somehow she needs to sort it out in her own head first.

She opens her eyes again. Sarah is talking about the pros and cons of dot.com businesses. A man with the polished, slick box of a briefcase in one hand and a red tartan scarf in the other keeps twisting round to glare at the still-blank board. When he turns away, he lets a short sigh snap his tongue against the back of his teeth. It makes Lily think of the momentary suspended click of an alarm clock reaching its assigned hour before its mechanics connect up to the bleep. A woman in the kind of stack-heeled, thin-soled boots that would make the jigsaw bones of her feet ache and strain is marching up and down the yellow-lined edge of the platform. Six paces – the heels of her boots hitting a cloc-cloc sound off the porcelain tunnel walls – stop, a swizzling turn that makes her skirt swirl around her, then six paces back.

In the days since Sinead told her, nothing she does or thinks or feels is separate any more, but connected to and dragged down by another reason or effect and then another and then another, until everything in her head and everything around her seems to sink into an obscure haze of doubt and uncertainty. She's not used to this, doesn't know how to deal with it, can't organise her thoughts. She's always just known how she felt or what she thought, just as she knew her own name. But now, at whatever point she starts, her thoughts go round and round like beads on a rosary.

If she loves Marcus – does she love Marcus? – then she should tell him what she knows. She should be honest. But then he might be angry. Why? Because he did something wrong. But if she thinks it was wrong then why does she love him – does she love him? – why is she still with him? And if she still loves him knowing what he did, is that wrong of her?

The woman's shoes cloc-cloc one way and, when she turns, her hair swoops around her head. A man she'd met once in a theatre bar told Lily that human hair clogs the walls of these tunnels, that cleaners clear tonnes of it away from the tracks every year. The idea fascinates her – those great clots of soot-brushed, matted hair.

How does she know she's telling the truth? But why would she lie? To get Marcus back. How could he do that to someone he loved? She can't imagine him doing anything like that. It doesn't seem like him, but then maybe he didn't, maybe she's lying.

'For God's sake,' Sarah says loudly, looking up at the

board, 'you'd think they'd give us an announcement to tell us how long we're going to be sitting here.'

She should just ask him. Just come out and say it, say, Marcus, is this what happened, and what made you do it. There must be some explanation. There has to be. She's only heard one side of the story, after all. But if he'd wanted her to know he would have told her. So he doesn't, and maybe it's none of her business anyway.

If she told him she knew he'd want to know how she knew, how she found her, how she recognised her. She'd have to tell him. Couldn't tell him that. Couldn't ever tell him that. Couldn't tell him she sees her still in his flat, behind him, next to him, in front of him. Does he still love her, does she still love him, does he love her, should she leave?

There is something about him that binds her to him, and Lily can't quite see clearly what it is. It's as if many narrow strands of wire, twisted together, link her to him; individually, they're inexplicable and frail, but together they are indissoluable, cannot be hacked through. She doesn't understand it, this strength of feeling. It follows her around like a dog on a lead. If she looked at this objectively, she wouldn't love him, maybe even like him. But somehow this transmutes into a sensation of inseparability, of longing, of need. His unhappiness causes a collapse in her chest, as if it has somehow spread to her like a virus. How could she leave him? But disquiet silts up her veins.

'What about a swimming-pool attendant?' Sarah is saying. 'I could do that.'

Carpe diem, she tells herself, as a disturbance in the atmosphere – minuscule at first, but unmistakable – heralds a far-off train rattling along mercury-smooth rails. Seize the carp, she thinks, a screeching of brakes and wheels filling the tunnel, and almost laughs.

The lights are on, and his coat is slung over a chair.

'Marcus?' Lily calls, hesitating on the threshold. No reply. 'Marcus!' Nothing, and then, a plink-plink-plink sound and a kind of swishing. She extracts her keys from the lock and walks into the flat. Again, that plink-plink sound. 'Marcus?' she says again. 'Are you there?'

On the floor, in a trail through the kitchen, are items of his clothes, as if he undressed on the move, as if in a hurry to get stripped. Shirt, shoes, trousers, socks, underpants, scrumpled and collapsed on the boards. Lily walks by them, examining them like a visitor in an art gallery. She cocks her head, listening out for the sound of running water – the shower or the bath. But nothing. Then she hears a noise like a sigh or a gasp.

Coming round the bathroom door, she sees him: the bath is full, water tipping over the sides. He is face-down, naked, his shoulders and buttocks breaking through the surface. The rest of his body shimmers pale under water. His hair trails from his head like seaweed, his feet rest up against the rim of the bath. There is a black tube jutting up through the water, through which comes the sound of his breath.

'Marcus,' Lily says. She reaches out and touches his shoulder. He rears up out of the water, his face encased in a black mask, his feet slipping, and for a moment he flails, limbs thrashing. A tidal wave flops out over Lily's shoes. He laughs, water streaming from his face and hair.

She looks at him, her head on one side. 'What are you doing?'

He takes the snorkel out of his mouth before answering: 'Testing my new gear.' He replaces it and puts his face back in the water, his hands braced on the sides of the bath. 'I think it's watertight.' His words come out of the snorkel tube distorted, consonants fusing into long vowel stretches. 'The man in the shop said to check it straight away and if it leaked I could take it back.'

'Oh.' She lowers the toilet seat and sits down, arms folded. The bathroom is cold, the windows opaque with condensation, whirls of steam rising from the water. 'Are you going snorkelling, then?'

'No,' and then he says a word that comes out as 'die-wing'.

'What?'

He says the word again.

'Die-wing?' she repeats, mystified.

He resurfaces, removing the tube from his mouth. 'Diving. Scuba diving.' He pulls off the mask and starts fiddling with the strap. There is a red weal in a perfect oval around his face. 'It's something I've always wanted to do. And this guy I work with was booking himself a holiday today. Two weeks in Thailand. So I decided to go with him. The diving course takes a week, so I'll have another week to travel about.'

'It's just the two of you?'

'Well, I asked Aidan if he wanted to come, but . . .' He trails off, frowning at his mask strap.

'But what?'

'He said no,' he says quickly. 'So, yeah, it's just the two of us.' He looks at her. 'You don't mind, do you?'

'Mind? No, not at all. It sounds great.'

'I know. I can't wait.' He snaps the mask back into place on his face and dives under the water again.

Beyond the door, something flickers at the periphery of her vision. Her pulse stutters and she tells herself, it's nothing, it isn't real, she wasn't there, she isn't dead. But when she brings herself to look, just to be sure, she's there, standing by the window, her hand resting on the kitchen counter, looking straight in their direction. How can she still be here?

Lily looks back at the bath. Marcus has submerged the end of the snorkel tube. Saucer-shaped bubbles rise to the surface in a steady stream. Then he moves and the tube rises again like a submarine periscope and she hears him drawing in air. Some water has got trapped in the tube, which rattles when he exhales. She resists the urge to block up the end of the tube with her hand.

Lily stands and walks away, through the door, past the kitchen, giving Sinead a little wave, and into the bedroom. She lets the door slam closed behind her. It's only as she's removing the clothes she's been wearing all day, heavy with smoke from the café and damp from the hailstorm, that the idea comes to her. At first, it's slight, a notion, almost nothing, but as she lifts her shirt over her head, it solidifies, calming her mind with resolve. Quick as a flash, she hurls her clothes to the floor, opens the wardrobe, and starts leafing through the hangers. Where is it, must be here somewhere, where did she put it?

Her fingers close on its material before she sees it. There is a sighing sound almost like music as it falls over her skin. She swings the mirror round until she is caught in its frame. The material seems dark and measureless, sucking all light into its depths. It hangs from her shoulders, coating her hips, thighs, pooling around her legs. It was expensive, she can see in the way the seams meet, in the caress of the fabric, in its effortless, fluid drape. It would have been shorter on Sinead.

Lily opens the door and steps out. The dress moves around her like liquid tar, warmed now by her flesh. Marcus is standing by the table, reading a postcard, wearing just a towel, his hair dark with water, standing up in spikes. She glances around. No sign of Sinead. She must have decided to leave them to it.

'Have you eaten?' he says, without looking up. 'Do you want to go out for something?'

'No. I ate with Sarah.'

'Oh. Maybe I'll phone for a takeaway, then.' He moves towards the pinboard, riffling through the menus stuck to it. 'Don't know what I fancy.' And turning round, says, 'Are you sure you don't want anything?' He blinks slowly. His eyes travel down her body to her feet and up again.

She holds his gaze. 'No thanks.'

'Sure?' he says again, turning back to the menus in his hand. 'Maybe I should have Thai. To get myself in the mood.' He sits down at the table and pulls the telephone towards him. 'You know, I can't believe I'm finally going diving. Apparently, you have to sit an exam. Can you imagine? Going on holiday to do an exam. I never thought . . .'

His head turns back to her. She breathes in, the material tightening around her.

'Is that new?' he says, his hand poised to dial.

'What?'

He points. 'The dress.'

'No.'

'Oh.' His face is distracted, slightly perplexed. 'I don't think I've seen it before.'

'Do you like it?'

'Yes.' He nods. 'It's . . . it's beautiful.' Then, drawing his hand across his eyes, he dials the number. 'Hello? I'd like to order a takeaway.'

Aidan turns from the window and picks up the ringing phone. 'Aidan Nash.'

There is an explosion of laughter. 'God, you sound so *serious*. What are you doing? Solving world peace?'

His heart punches his ribs. He's been thinking about her so intensely he is finding it hard to believe it is actually her on the phone, calling him, not just some projection of his imagination.

'Hi. Sorry. I was . . . er . . . I was miles away.'

He had been thinking about when he and Marcus first met her. How he'd been up helping Marcus with some designs. How they'd taken a break, early afternoon. How they'd met someone in a queue for a sandwich in a delicatessen. Someone Marcus knew. And this guy had known someone else who knew about a party and why didn't they come along. Tonight. East, beyond the park. Just say they were friends of Sinead. There'd be no problem. Sinead? Yeah,

Sinead. Tall girl, curly hair. There'd be no problem, he'd said again.

And about the day she'd called him and said, you knew, didn't you, and the way he'd held the receiver clamped to his ear, trawling his mind for explanations, excuses, but found only questions: where are you staying, do you need anything, where are you, we can't talk about this now, tell me where you are and I'll come and find you.

'. . . never thought you'd be at work so late, but I just wondered if we were still on for tomorrow.' Her words puncture his reverie.

'Tomorrow?' He snatches upon the word. Had they arranged to see each other? What day is tomorrow? What had they planned to do? 'Fine.' He gropes around his desk for his diary, encountering memos, computer discs, pens, staplers, then, mercifully, the hard edges of his diary, under a sheaf of film stills. He grabs it and flips it open. Tomorrow. Saturday. The oblong of the day on the page is completely white. 'That would be great.' In the lineless space he writes the word 'sinead' in red ink. 'What sort of time?'

'About midday?'

'Fine.'

'So what are we doing?'

'Um . . . it's a surprise,' he improvises. He'll think of something.

It's quiet for a Saturday morning. Lily is leaning alone on the counter at the front of the cubicles, surrounded by lingerie, frilled like sea creatures. There are only two customers in, and other people are seeing to them. Christmas music spirals from the ceiling. She can see herself in the reflection of a picture frame opposite, containing an advert for 'natural, stick-on, peel-off implants'. She is practising: I'm leaving you, her mouth is telling her silently. Too melodramatic. I'm going. No. I think I should go? Lily sighs and squints more closely at the image of her mouth. What do you want, it asks her, why—

The phone in front of her rings, making her jump. She flings aside the bra and string set she's holding, lifts the receiver to her ear and before she can even say the department how-may-I-help-you spiel, she hears the fuzzing line of a mobile phone and: 'Lily? It's me.' Marcus.

'Hi,' she says. 'how—'

'Guess where I am,' he says over her.

Lily hates games like these. 'Don't know.'

'Go on. Guess.'

'The flat?'

'No.'

'Your office?'

'No.'

Just tell me, she wants to shriek. 'Istanbul?' she says, exasperated.

'No. Do you give up?'

'Yes.'

'Your shop.'

'What?'

'I'm near your shop. About ten minutes away. Do you want to have lunch?'

Aidan sees her before she sees him. He is waiting in the traffic, engine churning over, while she is standing on the corner they'd decided on. Her mobile phone is clamped to her ear. He can tell she's agitated – walking in tight, controlled circles, her free hand jerking in the air then raking through her hair. Who is she talking to? He leans briefly on the horn as his car eases forward and she looks his way, recognises the car, but doesn't break off her conversation.

As he pulls over to the kerb, she is there, opening the door and climbing in. Tears are streaking down her face and the finger she holds to her lips, warning him not to speak, is shaking.

'No . . . no . . . I don't care . . .' she is saying into the phone in a strangled voice. 'I'm going now. No . . . that's none of your business . . . no . . . I don't want to talk about it any more . . . Goodbye . . . I'm not interested in anything you have to say . . . Goodbye.' She drops the phone into her lap and clenches her hands around her face.

'Was that who I think it was?' The words are barely out of Aidan's mouth when the phone in Sinead's lap trills into life.

'Shit,' she says, and looks down at it. Then she stabs the divert-call button. There is a moment's silence and the phone trills once more. 'Bastard,' she shouts, and slams her hand into the button again. This ritual repeats itself over and over again.

'Give it here a sec,' Aidan says, and she hands it to him. 'You can bar calls from his phone, you know,' he says, as he fiddles with the unfamiliar buttons at a traffic light.

'Can you?'

'It's really easy, look.' Aidan shows her how to enter Marcus's number, press a button and get the message 'Call Barred' appearing in tiny, squared-off letters on the screen.

Sinead stares at it. 'Wow,' she says. 'That's fantastic.'

'Well, he may get wise to it and call from somewhere else, so be careful.'

Sinead is scuffling about in her pockets for a tissue, mopping her face and peering at her reflection in the mirror above her seat. 'He's driving me mad,' she mutters.

'What was it about this time?'

'The usual, to begin with. Whingeing on and on about would I come back, and why not and how he made a mistake, blah blah blah. And so I confronted him about Lily.'

'Lily?' Aidan is thrown. 'I didn't know you knew about Lily.'

She gives a short laugh. 'That's exactly what he said.'

'But how . . . I mean, who told you?'

'No one.'

'Then . . .'

She sighs as if she doesn't want to go over it, doesn't want to think about it. 'I called the flat once and hung up when I heard a woman answer. Then . . .' she sighs again '. . . when Marcus called me I asked him about it – stupidly – and he told me this girl had moved into my . . . the room. And, you know, I could just tell. I could just tell from the way he said her name, that kind of falling intonation he has when he's talking about something he's not particularly proud of . . .'

Aidan, changing gear, nods.

'. . . I could just tell he was fucking her.' She clears her throat. 'Then I met her.'

'*You met her?*' The car swings into the wrong lane. Someone behind hoots and gesticulates in the oblong of his rear-view mirror.

'Yeah.'

'Are you serious? You met Lily? What do you mean? When? Where?'

She is staring fiercely out of the window, her hands gripped around her knees. 'Aide, I'd rather not . . .' she begins unsteadily. 'I'm sorry . . . I don't want to talk about it . . . if that's OK with you.'

'Of course.'

Then she is turning her head; Aidan turns his quickly and their eyes meet for a second.

'So where are we going today, then?' she says shakily, pulling her face into a lopsided, unconvincing smile.

They walk along the black iron railings of Lincoln's Inn

Fields. Lily drags a gloved finger over their even rhythm. Next to her, Marcus is holding a bag of crisps between them and, with her other hand, she puts them into her mouth. It feels strange to have one bare hand and one gloved.

She is having one of those days where everybody looks like somebody else. This morning on the bus she thought she saw her aunt who lives in Devon, a boy she knew from chemistry lessons at school, and a newsagent from Ealing. Each time, she'd been convinced, for a split second, maybe more. Then they'd moved or the bus had swung round into a differently angled light, and their familiarity had shifted and slipped away. Just now, she's walked past someone she could have sworn was a man she'd been in love with at university. But when they got close he looked nothing like him – hair another colour, nose too long, face too wide, an inaccurate version of him.

Marcus is taking her to the John Soane Museum. She's been before, years ago with her mother, but doesn't say. The house is cool, dark and tomb-still. A group of Americans, large in coloured jackets, keep appearing and disappearing from view through the many doorways and windows in the Chinese-box structure of the rooms. A green-suited attendant, sitting on a slender-legged chair, cleans his nails with a piece of card. They walk through a dark carpeted drawing room, through a narrow wooden passageway, past small gardens with sanguine-faced statues, through rooms filled with broken bits of classical buildings, pots, paintings, velvet-covered furniture.

'He placed mirrors in odd places,' Marcus tells her. 'In

alcoves. Panels. False window-frames. To give the impression of distance and space where there wasn't any.'

These mirrors disconcert her: she keeps glimpsing slivers of a woman who looks disturbingly like her before her brain catches up and tells her, it's only you. In some obscure way, these reflections frighten her: she's not expecting them, they don't look the way she thinks she does, the women in the mirrors seem trapped, shocked and cold behind the glass. She'll glance sideways and see herself turning away from herself. 'Are you all right?' Marcus asks her at one point and, in a fragmented portico above their heads, twelve Lilys nod back at him.

In a small, high-ceilinged room, he hooks out of the wallpaper a brass handle and tugs at it. The wall seems to come away in his hand, swinging out into the room on a hinge, unfolding like a book to reveal panels hung with strange, faded, meticulous drawings of Grecian buildings, one after another after another. They make her mistrust the building, these traps set into its architecture. She doesn't want to touch anything in case it gives and she is swallowed up in its hidden mechanisms. She walks carefully down the corridors, not touching the walls, thinking of that children's story where a kitten gets trapped behind the wainscot and captured by a grinning, thin-tailed rat.

At a railing, they stand and look down into the room below, and into the hollow of an Egyptian sarcophagus.

'It's beautiful, isn't it?' says Marcus softly. 'Alabaster. Makes it seem almost worthwhile dying, don't you think, if you get to lie in that?'

'Yes, but . . .' She's not sure why it makes her feel ill

at ease. Why is it here? She imagines John Soane packing it tightly into a crate with deft, acquisitive fingers and lowering it on to a ship. Who was buried in it and what did Soane do with the body?

'But what?'

'Well, it shouldn't really be here.'

'Why? Where should it be?'

'Egypt, of course. I mean, don't you think it seems, I don't know, inappropriate here?'

'I hadn't thought of it like that.'

Then Lily sees, walking below them, around the sarcophagus and across the room, a curly-haired, tall woman. Her hands grip the rail. She can't see her face properly. Is it her? And if it is, is it really her or the other her? She turns her head and looks at Marcus. Did he see it? Can he see it? She wants to blindfold him, shield his eyes from the possibility of her. But he is talking about the hieroglyphics inscribed in the alabaster and, when Lily looks down again, the room is empty.

'It says here,' Sinead says, 'that these frogs hold enough poison in their sacs to, and I quote, "fell an average man".'

Aidan peers into the murky tank at a frog the size of a pencil sharpener, green-black with a lurid blue mark on its back, symmetric as an early Christian cross.

'What is an average man, do you think?' she continues. 'Do they exist?'

Aidan adjusts the focus of his vision and sees, in the reflection in the tank, that two men are staring at Sinead. 'Maybe only in Brazil,' he says.

'Brazil?'

'Where the frogs come from.' He touches her lightly on the shoulder. 'Come on, let's go upstairs.'

They pass through the aquarium room, with groups of people huddled round tanks, set like bright, lit windows into the wall. Aidan glimpses, for a second, in the side of a huge tank containing shoals of flitting angel fish, an image of him and Sinead, walking side by side. His brain snaps shut on it, wanting to hoard and preserve it – her next to him, holding up the leaflet about Kew Gardens to show him something. It occurs to him for the first time that when they are together like this people must just take them for a couple.

The stairs, winding like those in a castle, lead to the biggest palm house with arched white struts like the ribcage of a dinosaur. Large spread-leaved plants strain up and out towards the light. The air is as humid and heavy as Tokyo. He tells Sinead this and she looks at him for a moment then asks him questions: how he liked being there, did he mind the travelling, was Japan beautiful, had he ever been to the mountains there, did he ever get lonely, could he speak Japanese, did he prefer working with Japanese or Americans, would he feel trapped now he was based in London.

They wander out of the narrow, white doors of the palm house, and walk past oblong flower-beds, lakes sprouting fountains, a line of very vocal pink-footed geese, a sound garden (which Sinead pronounces a 'load of new-age shite'), a bank full of prickling, thorned cactuses, a high pagoda, a winding pathway through dense foliage, bouffant rhododendron bushes, and giant lilypads a metre in diameter that make her lean over the barrier and pull them up from the water to see what they look like underneath.

He notices that her hair has curled tighter in the humidity of the palm houses, that she bites her lip when she's thinking, that she touches the leaves of the plants she likes, that she walks faster than most people, that one of her shoe soles is slightly more worn down than the other, that she wears a gold ring on the smallest finger of her right hand, that her ear-lobes have been pierced three times but she doesn't wear any earrings, that she carries four books in her bag, along with several lipsticks, a notebook, a pair of retractable scissors, a picture of her brother aged four, and a cowrie shell.

As the light drains from the sky, they sit on a bench, hands tucked into their coats for warmth, at the edge of the gardens. Sinead brings a polished aluminium flask from her bag and they pass a cup of hot chocolate between them that tastes slightly metallic but burns a path down Aidan's chest. Above their heads, planes come into land at Heathrow, stitching the sky with threads of white. They talk about jobs and Aidan's flat and her lectures and her friends and, eventually, Marcus. She doesn't weep, and tips back her head to look at the planes when she says, 'I think if someone rejects you like that, it means they're not right for you, doesn't it?'

When he doesn't reply, she looks over at him and asks: 'Do you think it was out of character?'

Aidan swirls the dregs of chocolate around the base of the cup. A dark slurry of grains has coagulated there, bleeding into the liquid. He knows that it's been inevitable that they would have this conversation at some point. And he knows she wants him to say yes, that she wants to be vindicated for loving him.

'I think,' he begins carefully, 'I think that he's always been rather . . . focused on his own needs.'

She looks away, starts playing with the laces of her boots, untying them and retying them, her face confused and miserable. He can bear anything but that. It makes him want to comfort her, touch her, take her in his arms – and that he really shouldn't do. He puts down the cup and takes a deep breath. 'OK,' he says, 'two things about Marcus. First, he's very impulsive. Agreed?'

She nods.

'Which can be a good thing,' Aidan continues, 'a very good thing. But it can also be annoying. He always has to satisfy his urges immediately, have you noticed? He can't wait. If he's hungry, he has to eat right there and then, no matter what. He can't think about anything else until he has whatever it is he wants. He was the same when he met you. And I think that has relevance to . . . what happened in New York.'

She isn't looking at him, but he can tell she's listening.

'Second,' he says, 'he has this spooky ability to completely compartmentalise his life. I've had loads of arguments with him about this, over the years, and I'm sure you have too. If there's something upsetting him or making him unhappy, he can just switch it off. Just like that. And get on with his life as if nothing at all has happened. I don't know anybody else who has that capacity. I've always found it very disturbing, that he can just put things in a box and shut the lid. And I think . . .' He trails off, suddenly wondering if she really wants to hear this.

'. . . that's what he did with me,' she finishes for him.

Aidan nods. 'Yes.' He picks up the cup again, swirling it around in his hand. 'I also think that what he did is a bit like the Ancient Mariner shooting the albatross.'

She turns her eyes on him.

'That he just did it. It was an action empty of reason. He did it because he did it. And that he – and you – will never really know why.'

She doesn't speak for a long time, and when she does, it is to tell him how, when she was a little girl, she always used to climb up this one tree, a sycamore tree it was, when she was in trouble. And how her parents used to stand at the bottom, shouting at her to come down, but she never would. One day, after she'd been up there for hours, her father had gone to the garage, ripped the chainsaw into action, climbed the tree and lopped off the top half with one swipe. It looked dreadful for years, she says, that half-tree.

Lily's cheek is pressed to his, her head drooping. She is staring at the ridged, whorled flesh of his ear, inches from her mouth. She could strain forward and touch it, brush her lips against it, take its lobe between her teeth. Whisper something – anything – into that small, black hollow. The message would reach him instantly.

Beneath her, his lungs inflate and deflate, raising her ever so slightly up, then letting her down. The water-weight of her breasts is flattened against the dense, fleshless hard of his chest, his hair leaving menhir swirls on her skin.

What would she say? She flexes her tongue between the cage of her teeth. One of his hands is pressed against her lower back. The other lies limp on the mattress beside them. If she elongates her foot, ballet-style, she could touch the round, hard bone of his ankle. He swallows, the muscles at the side of his head tensing.

I know what you did.

It would be so easy. The words are there, ready to be carried out on the carbon dioxide she's returning to the air. Her heart makes flailing punches at him through the arched tent of her ribcage. His eyes open and flutter, his lashes scything at her neck.

I see her. I see her everywhere.

Lily rolls away, sees his ear and his face pull out into distant focus. The sheet beneath her feels cold, starch-sharp.

'You must be Aidan.'

He looks up. Standing in front of him is a petite, untidy-looking blonde woman in a blue coat.

'Yes,' he says, 'I am.'

'I'm Ingrid.' She offers a red-gloved hand, and when Aidan takes it, the wool feels rough and cold to the touch. 'Sinead told me to look out for you.'

They are in a café off Tottenham Court Road. Aidan is waiting for Sinead, who is late. Ingrid strips off her gloves, unbuttons her coat, drops her bag on the floor next to her chair, goes to the counter and orders a coffee, then sits down.

'It's nice to meet you,' he says. 'Sinead's told me all about—'

'We've met before,' Ingrid interrupts him, rather accusingly.

'Have we?'

'Yes. A long time ago. At a birthday party.'

'You mean—' He stops.

'I do mean.' Ingrid nods. 'That party. The one where she met him. Thingy. Whathisname.'

'Shitface,' supplies Aidan.

She smiles, at last. 'Yes,' she says, with relish. 'Shitface. How is Shitface these days?'

'I wouldn't know.'

She raises her eyebrows. 'I thought you and he were best buddies.'

'We were.'

'I see. It's like that, is it? You've taken her side?'

'Um. Kind of.' Aidan is anxious to change the conversation. 'So you were at that party?'

'I lived in the house. I was Sinead's housemate. Well, one of them.'

'I'm not sure if I remember you.'

'I had long hair then,' she says, her grey eyes moving restlessly over his face, as if collating information in order to assess him at a later date. 'We met again, at Shitface's place, a few years ago. You were with your friend.'

'Was I?'

'Josh? No . . . John,' she says, pointing a finger at him as if daring him to correct her. Her hair is so blonde that it's almost white at the temples, where the hairs starts flecking out from the skin. He wonders if she's Scandinavian by origin. Could be with a name like that. He considers asking her, then rejects the idea.

'You've got a good memory,' he says instead.

'You and him and Shitface were all sitting around the table and Sinead and I came in. We'd been out shopping, I think. Your friend John had made lots of paper animals – what do you call them? origami – out of some newspaper and was talking about some girl he'd just fallen for, and agonising about the fact she wasn't Jewish. Or something.'

Aidan nods slowly.

'We were all giving him advice – probably not very useful advice.'

Aidan clears his throat. 'I remember.' He nods again. 'You did have very long hair. Sinead had bought a juicer thing and kept squeezing oranges for us all.'

The waiter places Ingrid's coffee in front of her and removes Aidan's cup. She keeps her hands flat on the table, her head on one side, considering him.

'So,' he says, uncomfortable under her scrutiny, 'you're an academic.'

'And you're a bit of a mystery,' she returns.

'Am I?' He is taken aback. 'Why?'

'The tall, dark and mysterious friend. Always talked about. Never there. Always away. Has some vaguely glamorous job in film.'

'It really isn't glamorous at all.'

'I bet it's more glamorous than what I do.'

'What do you do?'

'I'm an academic.'

'I know that. I meant what's your subject?'

'History.'

'Where?'

'North London.'

'Do you like it?'

'Yes. D'you like your job?'

'Yes.'

For some reason they smile at each other. Ingrid lets a

heaped spoonful of sugar slide into her cup. Aidan feels as though he's passed some obscure test.

'So how do you think she is?' she asks, stirring her coffee vigorously.

'She . . . Very up and down. But on the whole, I'd say . . . pretty bad. Like someone who's had a section of themselves removed.'

'Do you think they'll get back together?'

'What?' For a moment he can't think who she means. 'Sinead and Marcus?'

Ingrid frowns. 'Who's Marcus?'

'Sorry,' he is distracted by the thought, unable to formulate an answer, 'I mean Shitface. Well . . . I don't know. I doubt it. I mean . . . I don't think she'd have him, would she? Why? Why do you ask? Do you think they will?'

'I don't know.' She shrugs, blows on her coffee. 'I really don't know. I obviously would never speak to her again, but he can be very persuasive.'

'She'd never do it,' he says. 'Surely.'

'I hope you're right. Though I wouldn't bank on it. She still loves him. It takes more than behaving like an oversexed imbecile to change that. And *amore* does occasionally *vincit omnia*.' Ingrid puts down her cup and starts folding a napkin into pleats. 'You've heard the latest, I suppose? His little consort's been stalking her as well?'

'You mean Lily?'

'Whatever,' says Ingrid, dismissively, then looks at him with narrowed eyes. 'Of course,' she says, 'you must know her.'

'Well, I wouldn't exactly say know her. She moved in while I was still living there. That's all.'

'Hmm.' She ruminates on this for a moment, still raking him with her gaze.

'Anyway, what do you mean, stalking?'

'Well, apparently he—' she breaks off, staring through the window. Aidan follows her gaze. In the distance, it is just possible to make out a figure running along the pavement towards them. Sinead. The evening is darkening and something she is holding flutters white against her clothes. 'Here comes Wilson,' Ingrid says, getting up, 'and it looks like she may have some news for us.'

'News?' Aidan says. There is something in Sinead's euphoric expression, and the paper she's holding that makes his pulse quicken with a kind of dread. 'What news?'

'Did you get it?' Ingrid shouts, hands cupped around her mouth. The waiter glances over, peeved.

'Get what?' Aidan asks.

Sinead bounces up the steps of the café, beaming, and wrenches open the door.

'You got it?' shrieks Ingrid.

Sinead nods. Ingrid flings her arms around her, laughing and shouting congratulations, I knew you would, I knew it.

'Got what?' Aidan asks again.

'She got it, she got it!' Ingrid is chanting.

'I just heard,' Sinead is babbling, 'I checked my e-mail before I left, just in case. I didn't really think it would be there, but it was! I can't believe it! I printed it out for you, look.'

Ingrid grabs the paper and scans it quickly. Sinead laughs, watching her, and claps her hands.

Aidan catches her by the elbow. 'Sinead, what is it? What have you got?'

'Oh, Aide,' she wraps her arms around his neck and smacks a kiss on to his cheek, 'the post I applied for. Didn't I tell you? Maybe I didn't. It's in Sydney. Literature and Gender. Teaching and research.'

'Sydney? As in Australia?'

'It's not exactly my field, but—'

'How long for?'

'A year. Two years. Who knows? It all depends on whether or not . . .' She trails away, staring at his obviously blank face. 'Aidan, I'm sorry I didn't tell you. It all happened so fast. The person they had pulled out last weekend and they called me and asked if I'd be interested, and it seemed like just what I needed. I just have to get out of London, what with . . . everything. You know. I'm sorry. You're not angry, are you?'

'Angry? No, no, not at all.'

Ingrid thrusts the paper into his hands and hugs Sinead again. 'I'm so pleased! I'm so proud of you! It'll be fantastic.'

'You will come and stay, won't you?' Sinead is saying. She is clutching both of their hands, her fingers curled into his palm. He is reading the lines of the e-mail, but is unable to get beyond the first lines. Dear Dr Wilson. Dear Dr Wilson. We are delighted to inform you. Delighted. Dr Wilson. We are delighted.

'I've never been to Australia,' she is saying. She turns

to him and as she does so, her hand slides from his grasp. 'Have you?'

Lily has bought herself a new lipstick. In the loos, she swivels it in and out of its metal case, its glistening column of colour rising and retracting. The walls are covered in tiny pale green mosaic tiles. She stares at them, wondering who would have been patient enough to line up these minute squares in such neat, regular rows. Then she leans in to the mirror and applies the lipstick, smoothing the colour to the edges. She rips sheets from a loo roll and dabs at her lips, leaving tissues with dark purple mouths strewn along the shelf. They look too personal, too strange to leave there, so she sweeps them into her bag and zips it up.

She's wearing new, sleek boots with steep, slender heels. Her feet seem narrower and longer, and her ankles ache as she climbs the stairs back to the main room. She's at the opening of an architectural exhibition. Why? She's not sure. Sometimes, when she tries to explain herself to herself, there is a gap, a crevasse before which her comprehension falters.

She sees Marcus at the far end of the room, talking to an Asian man with an exaggerated, spiked hairdo and thick, black-framed glasses. The drawings on the wall confuse her: a swarm of lines, axes, angles, measurements. Some bleed into smudgy, sketchy impressions of buildings that look dark and gloomy to her. But the models, on long tables down the middle of the room amaze her: tiny replicas, like dolls' houses, built in white card, complete with stairs, doors and acetate windows. Leaning over them, she feels the glee of perfection run through her; she can bend over and peer into their white, empty, people-less rooms, run her finger down the roofs and, if she wanted, crush them with one blow of her fist.

The room is littered with people. None of them look at the exhibits. The man who opened the show earlier with a short speech that Lily, standing at the back, couldn't hear is in the centre of a group of people, flushed, drink in hand, the other hand whirling in the air as he relates some complex thing to his listeners.

Marcus is still some distance away, one hand shoved into his back pocket, still talking to the spectacled man. A woman with blonde hair falling straight down her back has joined them. She has her forearm resting on Marcus's shoulder in a way that Lily can't decide is matey or possessive, and is bent at the waist, her head close to Speccy's, saying something into his ear.

Lily feels a weariness in her arms and shoulders. It suddenly seems a long time since this morning, since she left the house. She's going to go to Marcus and tell him she's going home, but there are so many people between them it's going to take an extra push of effort to get to him. Then she realises that because the room is really two rooms knocked into one, she can disappear through one door, walk along the corridor, and reappear next to him through the other.

She slips through the door into the stilled hush of the corridor. Papers and notices on a pinboard rise and stir as she passes. As she reaches the door she hears Marcus's voice, and the mention of her name makes her stop.

'Do you know what Lily said when she saw that building in the *AJ*?'

'No. What?' The blonde woman.

'She said, "It looks like a sauna."'

Marcus gives her a high-pitched, squeaky voice, almost a whine. They all laugh. Lily hears a slapping, as if someone has thwacked their palm against their leg.

'A sauna!' Marcus is repeating his punchline again, and everyone laughs back: hegh hegh hegh hegh, says the speccy man, hee hee hee, says the woman, ha ha ha, says Marcus.

'The lay-woman,' Blonde says, each word savoured in her mouth like a taste.

There is a pause. Lily realises she is on the opposite side of the wall to them, their mirror image. She is just putting up her hand to touch the width and mass of the bricks and mortar separating them, when she hears the speccy man: 'Now don't be unkind. That's not all you use her for, is it, Marcus?'

Again, there is a heartbeat of silence. Then her skull is filled with their laughter: great whooping jerks, high giggles, low coughs, and in among it the broad sound of Marcus's ha ha.

She stands there, stupid in her new shoes, her nails just touching the plaster of the wall enough so that when she turns to go there is the roughened, emery-board sensation of them scraping along the paint, before her hand falls back to her side.

When she arrives in Ealing later, her mother's hall light is on. The pavements have a thin sheen of ice and she has to walk carefully down the path. When Diane opens the door, her face for a second looks troubled and worn before she sees who it is.

'Hi,' Lily says, and her mother takes her by the hand.

'I was just about to get the Christmas decorations down from the loft,' she says, as they walk through the hall. 'You can help me if you like.'

They stand in the sitting-room together. The house feels cold, Lily notices, and the sofa has been moved.

'Are you staying over?' her mother asks, her head on one side.

Lily nods. 'If that's all right.'

She calls in sick, sits in her room, stares out at the swollen grey sky that threatens snow. She goes for a walk on the common with Sarah, who whips twigs against the stacks of wet, disintegrating leaves and shouts, 'Lay-woman, my arse!' at the trees. She cooks dinner for her mother, dusts the house, paints the downstairs toilet, stews apples from the garden in saucepans with cinnamon and raisins. In the room that used to be her father's study, a long time ago, she lets the globe spin under her hand, countries, oceans, mountain ranges, continents, islands, latitude lines skimming past her fingertips.

She clears out the garden shed, mends her mother's bike chain. She covers a chest of drawers in woodworm repellent, a thick, tawny mixture the consistency of treacle. She plays a new game with the globe – letting it spin and then stopping it and seeing where her index finger is. She hoovers.

After a while, she creeps back up the rickety stairs in the middle of the day when she knows he'll be at work. Everything is the same, which somehow amazes her. It's only been a few days, not even a week, since she was here, but already it seems like a different lifetime. Sunlight stretches along the floor and over the furniture; the tap drips in the sink. The plants droop, yellowing and curling.

There is a low, regular murmur coming from some-where. She turns her head, glances about. The phone extension cord runs the length of the space and disappears under Marcus's door. She approaches on the balls of her feet and presses her ear to the wood of the door. 'No. Please,' she hears. 'Just listen. What I did was stupid, so . . . so fucking stupid and I am sorry. I'm so, so sorry. Don't take this job. Please. I couldn't bear it. Just give me another chance. I know I don't deserve it, but please. What can I do to make you come back?'

As a child, the boldest thing she'd ever done was, one day after baby Mark had died, she'd gone to the triangular cupboard under the stairs where they kept their coats. It was dark and smelt of old, pungent wood. She'd taken her stiff woollen coat off the brass peg that was hers and was screwed into the wood at her height, except that was last year and she had grown by now, buttoned it up and walked to the front door. She'd stood in the porch for a moment, then yanked at the front door, which had blurry glass shot through with a wire mesh. She'd first seen Mark through this glass, a hazy bundle with – the surprise – red hair, as she stood in the hall waiting for her mother to bring her new brother in from the car. She walked away down the front path fast, thinking, I'm leaving, I'm leaving, the words turning over in her head like wet clothes in a washing-machine. She got as far as the first road, where she was hesitating because she knew she wasn't supposed to cross it on her own, before Diane caught up with her. Her mother snatched her off the pavement and pressed her to her, saying her name over and over. Don't go, her mother said, in tears, don't ever go. Lily could never get over that her mother had somehow known that she was running away, that she didn't just think Lily was going for a walk.

She takes her hand off the door-handle and tiptoes away. In her room, she looks about: books, shoes, papers, makeup. These she shovels into bags, quickly and quietly. Her clothes she drapes over one arm. She leaves Sinead's dress, just as she found it.

She walks back through the flat. Marcus is crying now, heaving deep sobs down the phoneline. At the door, she turns. ''Bye,' she says, to the empty air. She looks around. Nothing. The windows, at either end, are open-eyed to each other. A mass of cloud passes, slow as a ship. ''Bye,' she says again. A lampshade moves at the other end of the room. Without thinking about it, Lily moves towards the phone point, a white box low on the wall. Her fingers close over the small plastic plug and flick it out of its socket. She straightens up and waits. Marcus's voice blunders on, unchecked, oblivious, into the silence. She steps out over the threshold, closes the door and drops the keys back through. She listens for metal hitting wood, then withdraws her hand from the jaw of the letterbox.

She is surprised at how easy it is to dismantle her life. She leaves a message on the agents' voicemail saying she's not coming back. She writes a letter to the shop. She visits Laurence and his mother, and hugs him goodbye. He squirms in her arms, affronted by this sudden display of emotion. She inserts her card into an auto-teller to find her bank balance. She calls up a number she finds among adverts in a newspaper and buys a flight out of Heathrow. She buys a rucksack and guidebooks. She changes money into foreign currency and finds the notes are too long for her wallet. She and Diane sit hunched on the floor over a world map. Sarah comes round and gives her a length of string: 'You always need string,' she says. Diane buys her travel wash, mosquito repellent and diarrhoea tablets. Lily packs and unpacks her rucksack three times.

On her last morning in London, finding she's done everything she needs to do and having several hours of dead time to kill, she goes swimming, rolling her costume tight into the length of a towel, and taking a bus to the pool. She used to like swimming. Her father would take her when she was a child, sliding the armbands on to her arm before blowing them up, his teeth around the transparent nozzle. 'They're uncomfy to put on when they're blown up, aren't they?' he would say. In the water, her feet would pedal wildly beneath her, excitement making her shiver. Before long, her father no longer brought the armbands. He kept his palm under her abdomen and the water swung underneath her as she moved her legs in measured, symmetrical flexes. 'The water will always support your weight, Lily,' he said then, 'remember that.' When she was tired she was allowed to rest the curves of her feet on his leg. He would crouch in the water and she would stand, waist-deep, feeling like those women on the prows of pirate ships. But later, at school, there were girls with speed-racing bathing suits and taut glossy skin who could do strokes that churned the water into white froth, and she lost interest.

At the pool, she shuts her eyes and jumps through the surface into a wide, long, mercury-ceilinged room that sways with trapezoids of light. Whitened, bleached bodies flail through the slow blue. She pushes up and, breaking into the echoey heat, does backstroke, a tiny replica of herself in the glass ceiling following her up and down the lane. When she gets out, she finds that water has got trapped in her ear.

Half-deaf, she goes home and packs up her last things. When she catches the train to the airport, her mother runs beside it as far as she can, saying something Lily can't hear, her face distorted with fierce grief, her hand, clutching a shopping list, waving or flailing in the air.

As the plane rises and falls through the night, Lily's ears block and unblock, but always in her left ear is the muted, secret roar of water. She shakes her head, pulls at the soft nub of her ear-lobe, tilts her neck and, in the toilet, hops up and down with her head on one side. But nothing. She bundles up her cardigan and sleeps against it, hoping to wake to a clarity in her left hemisphere. When she arrives and stumbles down the metal stairs, she has to lean in close to hear the immigration officer over the shifting swell of chlorinated water.

Later, she's found a hotel, left her bag, and is walking down a hill through the city's heat. People in bright clothing on motorbikes swish past her and wave. Her rubber-soled shoes feel soft against the melting tarmac. She buys a prickly pear from a streetside seller, who cleaves it with a blade, revealing the wet orange flesh for her.

As she walks away, pear held gingerly in her palm, there is a sudden break, a release, then a hot rush: water from a London swimming pool drops to the curve of her breast, where it quickly evaporates in the heat of the afternoon.

After checking the number, Aidan turns in at the gate and walks down the unfamiliar garden path, tiles loosened from the concrete plinking under his shoes. He tries to ignore his heart, which is sending blood around his system at a rate that is far too fast. Stop it, he tells it, stop it now. You're not helping.

He rings the doorbell, his heart openly and brazenly defying him. I'll talk to you later, he is saying to it when a man opens the door.

'You must be Aidan,' he says. 'Hi. I'm Michael. This is Lindsay.' He points to a heavily pregnant woman behind him, who smiles as she buttons up her coat.

'We're off out,' she says. 'Sinead's through there.'

Aidan passes quite close to Michael. There is very little of his sister in him: the line of the nose, perhaps, and the slightly fragile chin, but otherwise nothing.

'See you,' he says, as he closes the door after him.

''Bye,' says Aidan, 'nice to meet you.' He stands for a moment in the hallway. His pulse is so quick and light he wonders if he's about to faint. That would be just great. Perfect. How to win women and influence lives. He hears them whispering to each other on the doorstep and Lindsay exclaim, 'He's delectable! Why don't you have friends like that?' and Michael, laughing, telling her to shush, he'll hear you.

'Sinead?' he calls.

'In here.'

Aidan walks down the corridor and into the first doorway. It is a small basement flat. Sinead is sitting crosslegged like a tailor in the middle of the floor, surrounded by heaps of clothes. She holds up two jumpers.

'What do you think?' she asks.

'About what?'

'Should I take this one or this one?'

Aidan sits on a sofa. 'Can't you take both?'

'No! I'm going to Australia, for heaven's sake. You don't need more than one jumper in Sydney.'

Aidan looks around. They are in a small sitting room. White linen blinds cover the windows. A cat lies curled like a lifebuoy on a patchwork cushion. There is a pile of boxes in the corner labelled things like 'Sinead's books', 'Sinead's crockery', 'Sinead's winter clothes'.

'Are those going too?' He points at the boxes.

'No. Michael's going to store them for me.' She flings down the clothes she's holding, gets up and, bending over at the waist, gives him a brief hug. 'How are you? It's nice to see you.'

'Yeah, I'm . . . pretty good.'

'Do you want tea? Wine? A whisky?'

'Whatever you're having.'

She wanders from the room and a few moments later he hears clashing glasses, a fridge door opening, liquid glugging out of a bottle neck. He gets up, paces the rug. He has to do it. He's going to do it. He's going to do it now. When she gets back from the kitchen. He knows what he's going to say. He has it all laid out in his head. He rehearsed it in the car. Now he's here, though, it's doesn't quite hang together. She seems preoccupied, distracted. And the words he'd selected so carefully in the car now sound hollow and trite. But he has to do it. He has to. She'll be on a plane to Sydney this time tomorrow.

'Is this where you've been sleeping?' he calls, trying to ignore the waver in his voice.

'No. Michael's got a spare room.' She appears in the doorway, a glass in each hand. 'Well, it'll be the baby's room when it arrives. So it's about time I was out of here.'

He takes the wine and sits down in a chair next to a table. A bouquet of red roses is spilling out of its wrapping. They are limp and wilting under the cellophane. She sees him looking at them.

'I should put them in water, shouldn't I?' she murmurs, stroking the velvet of their petals with her thumb. Then she tilts the glass to her mouth, swallows, walks over to her heaps of clothes, picks up a pink T-shirt, and lets it fall. 'Do you think I'm doing the right thing?'

Aidan wets his finger and runs it around the rim of the glass. 'In going to Australia?'

'No . . .' She hesitates. 'I mean . . . I mean . . .'

'Marcus?'

'Yes.'

'I . . .' the glass beneath Aidan's thumb begins to hum and vibrate, making her look up, '. . . I really can't say.'

She nods, her mouth pressed shut.

'Are you . . .' he begins, '. . . do you think you'll take him back?' His heart hurls itself against its cage. He is sure she'll be able to hear it.

She sighs. 'I don't know,' she admits. 'I just don't know. Sometimes I can't envisage a future without him. Sometimes it seems . . . inevitable . . . that he and I will be together again. Like I can't see a way around it. But I don't know, Aidan. What he did was so . . . well, it was so unnecessary and . . . and so painful.'

Aidan says nothing. The glass murmurs and cries in his hand.

'But I just have this feeling that I can't get around him. I was talking to someone about it the other day,' she continues, 'and they said, "Well, you need to weigh up whether you'll be happier with him or without him." And that if I thought I'd be happier with him I should try to get over it and forgive him.' She shakes her head, tugging at one of the ends of her hair.

He puts down the glass, his fingers brushing against the flowers. He stands and crosses the room to the window where he can see slices of the street between the blinds. He is foolish and deluded, coming here thinking he could say those things to her. He must be mad. What kind of a response did he expect? He is ridiculous, but still wants to say to her, it's not inevitable, if you take him back he will only do something worse, can't you see he doesn't value you, and what am I to do when you are gone, what shall I do with this weight in my heart and why did you have to infiltrate me like this.

'I should go,' he says instead, turning back from the window.

'Already?' She is looking up at him, surprised.

In the hallway, he puts his arms around her, he knows for the last time. She won't come back and even if she does it won't be for him. He touches her hair, pressing her forehead to his shoulder, then pulls away, reaching for the door lock, because starting up in him is a pain so deep, so profound that he feels it will never leave him.

''Bye,' she calls after him. ''Bye!'

He doesn't look back, but climbs the spiralling concrete steps to the pavement. He walks past his car, past the end of the street, and on. And he feels as though she is holding on to the end of one of his essential fibres and that every step he takes away from her is, bit by bit, unravelling him.

part | four

To know and love one other human being is the root of all wisdom

EVELYN WAUGH

The earth was red here, sodden clay that sucked and pulled at the soles of her feet as she walked to the side of the road. The colour had ingrained itself everywhere – her hair, her backpack, her trouser bottoms, and the grooves of her palms, where scarlet rivers flowed from her wrist to the base of her fingers.

Yesterday there had been sand, and wind that flung and sprayed the minute particles into her eyes and mouth. Lily had sat at the front of the truck, a scarf swathing her head, sunglasses jammed down on to her face, teeth gritty against each other, her skin grained with the surface of the desert that was rolling past.

The other people were jumping down from the truck, their feet thudding on the soft ground. The driver sat on his heels beside his open door, flexing his shoulders, a cigarette poised between his fingers. Lily peeled off her hat, soaked her scarf with water from her bottle and held it against her face and neck as she wandered off the flattened dirt track into the uneven scrub. The soles of her sandals clacked against her heels. A small, sweet-voiced bird swung overhead on a high thermal draught. She could see so far she was sure she could almost make out the curve of the earth.

She shaded her eyes, her gaze travelling along the vanishing point of the track. In the far distance there was a black, heat-haloed spot or fleck. It shimmered and wavered on the horizon. The light glanced off it, and staring at it brought salty water to sting at her eyes, her lashes forming coloured prisms around her vision. She blinked, pressing her eyes shut then opening them again. Light flooded her retinas, putting everything in negative, the scene before her dancing with hundreds of white spots. The fleck, when she located it, had got larger, and was swirling with dust and speed. A truck.

The water held in the fabric of her scarf had warmed to air temperature. She glanced back to her own truck at the side of the road. The driver was standing up and waving at her to come back, to get on. The other travellers were staring and pointing in the direction of the oncoming vehicle. Lily moved back towards the road, the red earth caking her shoe soles. At the side of the truck, a Belgian man offered the cradle of his entwined hands; she put her foot into them and felt the ground fall away and her rising past the wooden side of the truck. She gripped it, her feet finding the foothold of the wheel, and swung herself into the back of the truck, which was littered with backpacks, people, water-bottles, tents, sacks of food.

The other truck ground towards them. Lily leaned out over the side to watch it. It was moving fast, its wheels kicking up dirt, its glinting radiator grinning like teeth. It was newer and faster than theirs, a gleaming blue, and was close enough now for her to see the faces of the two drivers and a leather doll that was suspended as if on a gibbet from their rear-view mirror. The noise of its engine clapped like thunder around her ears. Twenty yards or so from them it slowed suddenly as they realised the narrowness of the track. Her own driver stood out on the road, watching, his arms folded. The blue truck rumbled on to the opposite side of the track and began easing itself past them. She saw the drivers eyeing the narrow gap between the vehicles and then the people in the back were sliding past her, as if on a slow conveyor belt.

What Lily saw next was an image that would be sealed up inside her for ever like the packed pod of an unborn twin. She would never speak of it to anyone, never refer to it, and would only think about it when she was alone. It had been a long time – months, perhaps over a year, she couldn't remember. Long enough for it to seem like something she'd read or seen in a film, or something that had happened to someone else. But as the truck jolted past her in the desert, it was as if that time had been telescoped shut into itself. Just in front of her, close enough for her to reach out and touch her, was Sinead.

She was standing in profile, looking out over the top of the cabin to the road ahead, one hand gripping a spar of the tarpaulin roof above her. The air around Lily seemed suddenly hot, too hot to breathe in. Her eyes travelled again over the long neck, the thin arms, the coils of hair. It was a sight so familiar that it tipped over into strangeness. It seemed at once the most natural thing to see in the middle of the desert and the most preposterous. Lily stared, put her fingers up to press her cheek. Was she really seeing this, or not? Sinead half-turned, her gaze taking in the other truck, the people she was passing. Her lips curved slightly. If she had turned her neck just an inch more, she would have seen Lily standing there.

Lily watched as she turned back to the road, watched as she saw something, and as she exclaimed, pointed, and reached her hand behind her, like a relay runner stretching back to grasp the baton. Lily knew even before she looked at the man she'd failed to notice before. He withdrew his hand gently from Sinead's and passed it instead around her waist, pulling her towards him, looking out to whatever it was she was pointing at. Just before they slipped out of sight, Lily saw that she was saying something to him and that Aidan was turning, laughing, looking Sinead full in the face.

The truck vanished in an eddy of dust and fumes. Lily didn't lean out to watch it go. The air around her settled back to its still, simmering heat. The woman next to her was spreading sun lotion over her arms and relating an elaborate story about a hotel manager. The Belgian man was offering round a packet of dried apricots. Lily took one and bit into its dense orange flesh. Beneath her, the truck quivered into life, the engine straining and pulling against the brakes.

The scenery slid into motion. There was no wind, just a vertical sun, and miles of red, red earth, the trees writhing up from the ground, bone-white, like petrified forks of lightning. Lily shaded her eyes against the glare. Far away into the distance, a large-eared dog-like creature was standing on the crest of a rock, nose high, reading the air for her scent.

You can buy any of these other **Review** titles
from your bookshop or *direct from the publisher*.

FREE P&P AND UK DELIVERY
(Overseas and Ireland £3.50 per book)

Kissing in Manhattan	David Schickler	£6.99
Hens Dancing	Raffaella Barker	£6.99
Summertime	Raffaella Barker	£6.99
The Last Hope of Girls	Susie Boyt	£6.99
Of Cats and Men	Nine de Gramont	£6.99
Two Kinds of Wonderful	Isla Dewar	£6.99
The Pale Gold of Alaska	Éilís Ní Dhuibhne	£6.99
Startling Moon	Liu Hong	£6.99
After You'd Gone	Maggie O'Farrell	£6.99
The Brutal Language of Love	Alicia Erian	£6.99
Cranberry Queen	Kathleen de Marco	£6.99
Living with Saints	Mary O'Connell	£6.99
Baggage	Emily Barr	£6.99
Fruit of the Lemon	Andrea Levy	£6.99
Dumping Hilary	Paul Reizin	£6.99
Infidelity for First-Time Fathers	Mark Barrowcliffe	£6.99

TO ORDER SIMPLY CALL THIS NUMBER

01235 400 414

or visit our website: www.madaboutbooks.co.uk

Prices and availability subject to change without notice.